W9-CBV-937

"You're right not to trust me."

He paused, as if some terrible struggle were going on in his mind.

She was aware of her beating heart, of the room growing warmer. He grazed her palm with his thumb, tenderly, with affection, and the sensation of it sent a shiver clear up her spine.

Then without warning, as if he'd been dreaming and had all of a sudden come awake, he laughed. His face lit up, his eyes flashed mischief. She tried to draw her hand away as the man withdrew and the rogue appeared.

His fingers tightened over hers. "I've been known to lead women astray." To punctuate the point, he arched one dark brow in a scandalously suggestive manner.

Dora pulled herself together. "Yes, well…" She yanked, and her hand was freed. She shook it to revive her circulation. "This woman is miraculously unaffected!"

* * *

Rocky Mountain Marriage
Harlequin Historical #695—March 2004

Praise for Debra Lee Brown's previous titles

Gold Rush Bride

"Debra Lee Brown's traditional romance
captures the era's excitement and excess in
lively characters meant for each other."
—*Romantic Times*

Ice Maiden

"*Ice Maiden* is an enticing tale
that will warm your heart."
—*Romantic Times*

"This Viking tale of high adventure gallops through time
and into the hearts of the reader."
—*Rendezvous*

The Virgin Spring

"Debra Lee Brown makes her mark with
The Virgin Spring, which should be read
by all lovers of Scottish romances."
—*Affaire de Coeur*

"A remarkable story. The fast pace, filled with treachery,
mystery, and passion, left me breathless."
—*Rendezvous*

ROCKY MOUNTAIN MARRIAGE

DEBRA LEE BROWN

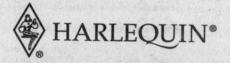

HARLEQUIN®

TORONTO • NEW YORK • LONDON
AMSTERDAM • PARIS • SYDNEY • HAMBURG
STOCKHOLM • ATHENS • TOKYO • MILAN • MADRID
PRAGUE • WARSAW • BUDAPEST • AUCKLAND

If you purchased this book without a cover you should be aware that this book is stolen property. It was reported as "unsold and destroyed" to the publisher, and neither the author nor the publisher has received any payment for this "stripped book."

Special thanks and acknowledgment are given to
Debra Lee Brown for her contribution to the
COLORADO CONFIDENTIAL series.

ISBN 0-373-29295-3

ROCKY MOUNTAIN MARRIAGE

Copyright © 2004 by Harlequin Books S.A.

All rights reserved. Except for use in any review, the reproduction or utilization of this work in whole or in part in any form by any electronic, mechanical or other means, now known or hereafter invented, including xerography, photocopying and recording, or in any information storage or retrieval system, is forbidden without the written permission of the publisher, Harlequin Enterprises Limited, 225 Duncan Mill Road, Don Mills, Ontario, Canada M3B 3K9.

All characters in this book have no existence outside the imagination of the author and have no relation whatsoever to anyone bearing the same name or names. They are not even distantly inspired by any individual known or unknown to the author, and all incidents are pure invention.

This edition published by arrangement with Harlequin Books S.A.

® and TM are trademarks of the publisher. Trademarks indicated with ® are registered in the United States Patent and Trademark Office, the Canadian Trade Marks Office and in other countries.

Visit us at www.eHarlequin.com

Printed in U.S.A.

Please address questions and book requests to:
Harlequin Reader Service
U.S.: 3010 Walden Ave., P.O. Box 1325, Buffalo, NY 14269
Canadian: P.O. Box 609, Fort Erie, Ont. L2A 5X3

For Dad, Dorothy and Uncle Dickie

Chapter One

Colorado, 1884

"It's a *saloon?*"

"Yes, ma'am. The pride of Last Call. Draws customers from Fairplay to Garo." The driver hefted her trunk from the buckboard and set it on the ground under a young oak, in front of the steps leading up to the entrance.

There had to be some mistake. Her father had owned a cattle ranch, not a…a… Dora couldn't breathe. She gawked at the gold-leaf-lettered sign above the swinging doors. The Royal Flush. Established 1876. William Fitzpatrick, proprietor.

"The best damned gambling house in the state, if you ask me." The driver tipped his hat to her, then climbed atop the buckboard to depart.

"W-wait. Please." She plucked her father's letter from the small, leather-bound diary she always carried with her, and read the first shakily written paragraph again.

If you're reading this, Dora, I'm dead. Seeing as

you're my only living kin, I'm leaving you the place.
Lock, stock and barrel, it's all yours.

She gazed out across the high-country pasture surrounding the opulent two-story ranch-house-turned-saloon. A few stray cattle grazed in the meadow below the original homestead. Nowhere were the herds she'd expected, or any evidence that her father had made his fortune in cattle.

Several outbuildings were visible behind the house: a barn, what looked like a bunkhouse, and a few small cabins nestled between naked stands of aspen and oak. It had been a ranch once, by the look of things.

"I guess you'll be running the place now. Good luck to you, ma'am." The driver snapped the reins and the horses sprang to life.

Running the place?

"Wait a moment. Please!" Dora ran after the buckboard. "You're not just going to leave me here?"

"You want to go back to town?" The driver pulled the horses up short. "Before you even get a peek at the place?"

The sun had already dipped well below the snow-capped peaks in the distance. Spring columbine checkered the rolling grassland as far as the eye could see, but winter's chill still frosted the air. Dora pulled her cloak tightly about her as she glanced back at the bustling business her father had never once mentioned in his letters to her.

Horses stood in a line, tied up at the long rail outside the saloon. Buggies and buckboards and other conveyances were parked along the side. A corral flanked the building, where other horses were feeding. Presumably they belonged to customers, *regulars* she believed the term was.

Soft light spilled from the entrance of the saloon and from windows draped in red velvet. Tinny piano music, men's voices and coquettish laughter drifted out to meet her. Fascinated, Dora took a step toward the entrance, then paused to consider her predicament.

"Ma'am?" The driver fished a pocket watch out of his vest. "Got to get these horses back to town. Are you coming or staying?"

Not once in her twenty-five years had she ever been inside a saloon. God would strike her dead, her mother had been fond of saying when she was alive, if Dora so much as set foot in one.

"Last chance, ma'am."

Last chance.

She heard the driver's words, the snap of the reins, and the buckboard rattling back down the two-mile stretch of road to the mining town of Last Call, where her only hope of securing proper accommodations for the night was to be found.

But Dora was already on the steps, her gaze pinned to the swinging doors, her eyes wide with excitement, her stomach fluttering. Lock, stock and barrel, she thought as she tucked her father's letter carefully away between the pages of her diary.

She placed a gloved hand on one of the swinging doors and pushed. A heartbeat later she stepped from her comfortable and orderly existence into a new world. By some miracle, God did not strike her dead after all.

The air was thick with cigar smoke and the foreign aromas of liquor and cheap perfume. Instinct compelled her to cover her mouth. The first thing she laid eyes on was a painting of a woman, a redhead without a stitch on, in a gilded frame above the bar.

"Oh, my."

A stage draped in crimson velvet was positioned at the far end of the room. Mercifully, no one besides the piano player was performing. Men stood drinking, crowded together at the bar and huddled over card tables packed into what was once the parlor of the stately house. Brass spittoons were everywhere, though it was apparent no one paid them any mind.

"Disgusting."

She felt warm all of a sudden—too warm—and realized men had stopped their drinking and gaming to look at her. In an attempt to avoid their stares, her gaze followed a spiral staircase leading upward from the end of the bar to the second floor.

A long balcony of dark pine showcased walls lined in flocked red paper against which lounged scantily clad women and overeager men. The house's original bedrooms were on this floor. Dora didn't want to think about what was going on inside those rooms.

The noise, the smells, the bright colors—all of it taken together was overwhelming. She felt light-headed, not herself at all. The last thing she saw before she fainted was a man. His whiskey-brown eyes drank her in as he flashed her the wickedest smile in three states.

"Ma'am? You all right?"

Someone was patting her hand. She felt a cool compress on her forehead, then flinched at the whiff of smelling salts. Her eyes flew open.

She tried to sit up, but firm hands pushed her back down again. She was lying on the… "Good Lord!" She was lying on the bar, stretched out like a corpse.

People crowded around her, offering assistance.

She recognized the bartender by the linen towel wrapped, apron style, about his waist. He was a wiry, balding man with a thick black moustache and a face that was all concern.

"You fainted dead away when you saw it."

"S-saw what?" Her head was still spinning. She thought he was talking about the man, the devilish-looking one with the smile.

"Wild Bill's favorite whore." The bartender glanced up at the painting, now directly above her on the wall. Dora didn't need a second look. "No one's ever had quite that reaction to her."

"Oh, Jim, stop it! Can't you see the poor thing's confused? Must have taken the wrong road out of town, wandered in here by mistake."

Dora turned to the woman who was patting her hand. She was about Dora's mother's age when she'd died, Dora guessed, but that was where the resemblance ended. Her mother had always dressed plainly, in dark colors, as did Dora, and wore no ornamentation of any kind.

In comparison, this woman looked like a peacock. She had brassy red hair and painted lips to match, and a dress of bright blue silk cut so low Dora thought the woman would pour right out of it each time she leaned over to smooth the compress on Dora's head.

"I'm…sorry." Again she tried to sit up. This time they helped her.

"Oh, don't be sorry, honey," the woman said. "It's easy to lose your way if you're not from around here. You a preacher's wife?"

"A schoolteacher."

"Told you," the bartender said. "Pay up, 'Lila."

To Dora's shock, the woman pulled a bank note

out of her cleavage and slapped it down on the bar. The bartender pocketed it, grinning.

She blinked her eyes, which were tearing from the cigar smoke. The music had stopped, and she realized everyone in the saloon was staring at her. Well, why wouldn't they be? She must look a fright. Her hair had come loose and fell in mousy hanks around her face. She realized with a shock that her skirts were rucked up to her knees, revealing her bloomers. She quickly smoothed them down again.

"Here," the bartender said, and handed her a full shot glass. "Drink this. It'll clear your head."

She accepted it without thinking.

"Go on, honey," the woman said. "It'll make you feel better."

"Oh, no, I couldn't possibly." Fainting dead away in a saloon was one thing. Drinking whiskey in a saloon was quite another.

The crowd parted, and she found herself eye-to-eye with the devil incarnate, the man whose heated gaze and sinful smile were burned permanently into her memory. Growing up she'd heard plenty about men who frequented saloons. Never trust one, her mother had warned her, especially a gambler.

The man standing in front of her had been sitting when she'd first seen him, a perfect fan of cards in one hand, a glass of beer in the other, his feet propped up on a gaming table. Hell would freeze before she'd be taken in by such a character. He was different from the others, and that's what worried her.

His three-piece suit looked as if it had been tailored back East. His hair, a rich brown that matched his eyes, fell nearly to his shoulders. That wasn't uncommon for mountain men, but it was for city dwellers, and he was clean-shaven, which was unusual for both.

"Delilah's right." His voice was soothing, and put her instantly on her guard. "It'll do you good. Drink it."

"I'll do no such thing." She handed the whiskey back to the bartender, who shrugged, then drank it down himself.

The piano player started up again, and the saloon's customers went back to their drinking and card-playing and... She flashed a glance at the barely dressed women leaning from the balcony. One of them waved to her. Dora shuddered.

The man who was decidedly too handsome for his own good smiled again, but this time she didn't let it affect her. "Let's get you back on your feet, Mrs...."

"Miss," she said curtly. Carefully, she swiveled her legs around so they dangled off the bar. "And you are?"

"Charles Wellesley." He offered her his hand. "But most people call me Chance."

"That's quite fitting." She ignored his proffered hand and readied herself to jump down.

"Is it? How so?"

She arched a brow at him. "You *are* a gambler, aren't you?"

A few of the onlookers laughed, but he didn't.

"Can't always judge a book by its cover, Miss..."

She scooted to the side, avoiding him altogether, then slid off the bar to her feet. Taking a moment to gather her thoughts, she risked another look at the base establishment her father had bequeathed her.

The bar was crafted of rich, dark pine, had polished brass fittings and was dressed nearly to the ceiling in bottle racks jammed with liquor. A cash register stood in the center below the painting, a few bills poking out from its half-closed drawer. An old mirror flanking the portrait confirmed her appearance.

She looked as if she'd just been scraped up off the floor, which, she reminded herself, she had. Someone—and she could guess who—had unbuttoned her high-necked blouse, revealing her throat. "Of all the—" She quickly buttoned it up again.

"Miss?" Chance Wellesley said again.

"Pay him no mind," Delilah said, and stepped up to help her fix her hair. "He's a charmer, that's what he is."

He did laugh then, and despite her intention not to look at him again, she did, and was instantly sorry. His gaze swept over her body as if he were appraising a side of beef ready for market. How rude!

"Here's your bible." He slid a hand into his coat pocket and produced her red, leather-bound diary. "You dropped it when you fainted."

"My…bible." His intellect apparently didn't match his looks. She made a derisory sound in the back of her throat and snatched it from his hand. Her father's letter was still tucked carefully away inside it. "Perhaps you're right, Mr. Wellesley. One can't always judge a book by its cover."

"Oh, I don't know." He looked her up and down again. "Take you, for instance. I'd bet my last double eagle you're lost."

"You'd lose that bet, I'm afraid." She was right. He *was* a gambler.

"A woman like you, waltzing into a place like this on purpose? Hard to believe."

"A woman like me? I'm sure I don't know what

you mean.'' She'd had just about enough of him. Back in Colorado Springs where she'd taught school, she knew just how to deal with impudent boys, even overgrown ones.

She looked around for her cloak, but didn't see it, and her reticule, which had been hooked to the inside. All the money she had in the world, which wasn't much, was hidden in its lining. To her relief, the bartender produced them both.

''Thank you,'' she said, and slipped the braided strap of the reticule over her gloved hand. The bartender helped her into her cloak.

''Chance here took it off you, ma'am, after he picked you up and carried you to the bar.''

Just as she'd suspected. She turned to look at her knight apparent one last time before leaving, and felt her cheeks blaze anew when she met his amused stare. ''Well, I'm grateful to you all, I'm sure. But I'll be going now.''

She'd rather walk the two miles back to Last Call in the dark than stay here another second. Tomorrow she'd see a lawyer in town. Perhaps he could straighten everything out for her, and she'd never have to set foot in this place again.

Chance Wellesley tipped his hat to her. ''Have a safe trip to wherever it is you're going, Miss…? You never did tell me your name.''

This time he looked at her as if she were wearing little more than the redhead in the painting above the bar. Never in her life had she met a man so insufferable.

''Fitzpatrick,'' she said, louder than perhaps she should have, but then she was mad. She always did have a temper. One day it would catch up with her,

her mother had been fond of saying. "Eudora Eliza-beth Fitzpatrick."

"Well, what do you know?" the bartender said.

She felt Chance Wellesley's eyes on her as she marched toward the swinging doors, men scattering before her like spooked quail.

"Wild Bill Fitzpatrick has a daughter!"

She had sturdy boots and strong legs. Two miles on a good road under a full moon was next to nothing. Unfortunately, it turned out to be the longest, most unpleasant two miles of Dora's life.

"Will you please stop following me!"

Chance reined his mount alongside her and picked up the pace to match hers. "I'm not following you, particularly. I'm just heading into town."

"Why?"

He'd stormed out the door of the Royal Flush after her, and had tried, but failed, to dissuade her from leaving. He'd gone so far as to suggest there'd be no accommodations for her in town. She knew better. Besides, her mind was made up. She refused to spend another second in that saloon.

"No reason. Just exercising old Silas here."

She glanced at his mount, a tall black-and-white gelding. A paint. As horses went, Silas appeared to be an agreeable animal. Too bad the man riding him was not.

"You left your trunk behind," Chance said. "Bet-ter hope no one steals it."

"The bartender said he'd put it away for me. Be-sides, there's nothing important in it." Which was a lie. The letters her father had written her over the years, letters her mother had kept from her and that she'd only just discovered after Caroline Fitzpatrick's funeral, were secreted away in the lining. "Everything I need I have with me."

Including the small brass key that had been tucked inside the envelope of his last letter to her, the letter informing her of her inheritance. She patted it inside the pocket of her dress as she walked. She had no idea what the key opened. On the stagecoach from Colorado Springs she'd been excited by the mystery. Now she just wanted to get as far away from the Royal Flush as possible.

"You should have said something when you first arrived, about you being Wild Bill's daughter."

"I wish you wouldn't call him that." Though it did seem fitting. Her childhood had been peppered with stories of her father's wicked ways. It had been her mother's way of insuring Dora steered away from men like that. Men like the man riding beside her, who, despite her numerous protests, seemed intent on escorting her back to town.

"Why not? Everyone called him that. Besides, he liked the name."

"Did he? Well, that doesn't surprise me."

"You sound angry."

"I'm not angry. I'm just…" Confused was what she was, though she'd never in a million years admit it to the likes of Chance Wellesley.

She barely remembered her father. Growing up, all she'd known of him was what her mother had told her, and Caroline Fitzpatrick hadn't painted a very pretty picture. Dora had believed every word of it—until she'd found the letters.

"Funny he never told me."

"Told you what?"

"That he had a daughter."

Dora stopped and looked at him. "Why would he? He left when I was five. I haven't seen him since." But he'd seen her.

In his letters, her father had described his visits to Colorado Springs over the years, how he'd watch her from afar on her way to school or leaving church on Sundays. They were full of fatherly observations and practical advice. The last one, the one tucked carefully into her diary and that she'd read over and over on the stagecoach, had said how proud he was the day she'd become a teacher.

"That doesn't sound like Bill."

Now, after reading his letters, she didn't know what to believe. Why hadn't he made himself known to her? And why had her mother told her he didn't want her, that he didn't care? Her mother had obviously lied, but why?

"You talk as if you'd known him well. Did you?"

He sat back in the saddle, toying with what looked like a watch fob that hung from a short chain attached to his belt. "As well as anyone, I guess. I spent a lot of time in that saloon."

"Yes, you would, wouldn't you? Given your profession."

"My profession." He smiled at her in the moonlight, and for a moment she caught herself thinking how handsome he was. "You say it like it's a dirty word."

"Well, you *are* a gambler, and you do work in a saloon."

"A saloon you own."

The reminder shocked her to her senses. She pulled her cloak tightly about her and continued her march toward town. "I plan to sell it, if you must know. That and whatever ranch land goes with it."

"Good luck. You'll find out soon there aren't any buyers."

"Really? I'm not stupid, Mr. Wellesley, despite what you may think of me on first impression. My father's business appeared quite robust."

The rich sound of his laughter in the dark sent a shiver straight through her.

"You have no idea what I think of you, Miss Fitz-patrick, and if you did, I suspect you'd slap me."

Of all the nerve! Dora quickened her pace.

"And robust it may be, though I've never heard a saloon described quite that way before."

"I'm certain you know what I mean." The image of a scantily clad employee waiting with a drunken cowboy in the long line outside one of the upstairs bedrooms popped unbidden into her mind.

He laughed. "I know exactly what you mean."

"Hmph." She kept walking, curtailing any further conversation with him. Though she didn't know what to believe anymore—her mother's warnings or her father's adulation—one thing was clear to her.

Chance Wellesley was trouble.

He trotted along beside her, whistling bawdy tunes, while at the same time making certain she moved safely off the road when carriages rumbled by. She thought that bit of chivalry amusing, given his character.

Why was he so interested in her? What would pro-voke a gambler she'd never laid eyes on before to-night to give up an evening of card-playing to see a schoolteacher on her way? She didn't know and she didn't care. She just wanted to get away from him.

When at last they reached town, she headed straight down the muddy main street toward Last Call's only hotel, the one she'd spied that afternoon when she'd first arrived.

"There's something you ought to know about your, uh, inheritance." He didn't say saloon, and for that she was grateful. To think she actually owned the place!

"What's that?" she said curtly, refusing to look at him again.

"Your father owed a lot of money to a lot of people, some of them not so nice. The Flush is likely mortgaged to the hilt. The ranch land, too."

"How would you know?"

"Let's just call it a hunch."

"I don't believe in hunches, Mr. Wellesley." The bank was just ahead, across the street next to a law office. She'd make visits to both establishments first thing tomorrow morning.

"No?"

"No." She shot him a hard look to make the point, then stopped in front of the hotel, relieved that the Vacancy sign she'd seen earlier that afternoon was still displayed in the window. "Well, here we are."

Chance dismounted and tied Silas to a hitching post jammed with other horses. Cowboys and miners and men of every description roamed the street. She'd never seen a town so small so busy, and at this time of night.

"You see?" she said, turning toward him. "I was perfectly capable of getting here on my own."

"Maybe so. But you might be needing a ride back to the, uh, ranch, after all." He nodded toward the hotel.

She followed his gaze, then gasped, thunderstruck, as a hotel clerk snatched the Vacancy sign from the window.

"Told you they'd be full up. One of the big mines outside Fairplay struck a lode last month. Paid off today. The town's crawling with miners who've got money to burn. Can't say I didn't warn you."

She ignored him, marched up the steps to the hotel and threw herself on the mercy of the clerk. He had to find her a room. He just had to! Five minutes of pleading later, she was back on the street, fuming.

Chance leaned casually against the hitching post, his hat pushed back on his head, that irritating grin of his aimed right at her.

"I will not spend the night in that saloon."

"You sure?"

"And I will not ride double with you on that horse." It was out of the question. She never intended to be that close to him ever again.

"It's either that or walk back. Silas doesn't take to people, especially women. In fact, he's downright ornery. Likely he'd buck you off if you tried to ride him solo."

She eyed the horse. "He doesn't look too terribly ominous. I'm sure I'll manage."

"So you *will* come back to the Flush with me."

It appeared she had no choice, unless she wanted to sleep in the street. If she had to stay the night in a saloon, at least it would be her saloon and not one of the questionable-looking drinking establishments lining Last Call's main street.

She approached the gelding and matter-of-factly untied him from the post. Silas looked at her, seem-

ingly unconcerned. "I'm not *with* you, Mr. Wellesley.
I'm simply borrowing your horse."

"Whoa, wait a minute. I meant what I said about
him not liking women. It's too dangerous for you
to—"

She ignored him and mounted without incident,
then arranged her skirts as modestly as possible under
the circumstances. Silas glanced back at her, waiting.

"Well I'll be a—" He gawked, first at the horse,
then at her.

"A what?" she said, casting him a smug expression. A number of nouns, all of them improper, came
to mind.

He smiled suddenly, his gaze heating with the same
underlying carnality he'd exhibited in the saloon. She
swayed a bit on the horse.

"Come on," he said, and took Silas's reins from
her hand. "I'll lead."

Chapter Two

Chance Wellesley knew a sure bet when he saw one.

He sat in the window seat of the upstairs room he rented at the Royal Flush and, through a pair of opera glasses he'd won off a Denver politician in a poker game, watched Miss Eudora Elizabeth Fitzpatrick scribbling madly into what he'd thought last night was a bible.

"Well I'll be damned. It's a diary!"

He would have given his last plug nickel to know what she was writing in it.

She'd made quite the commotion when they'd returned to the saloon last night. Delilah had tried to set her up in her father's old room, but the intractable Miss Fitzpatrick would have none of it. He laughed, recalling the look of horror on her face when Delilah had suggested it.

In the end, a few of the girls fixed up one of the cabins out back for her, and there she'd passed the night. He'd been up since dawn, waiting to see what she'd do next. Everybody knew schoolteachers rose early, and Wild Bill's daughter proved to be no exception.

She sat at the desk under the cabin's single window, her back straight as a washboard, her lips pressed into a tight line, penning God knows what into that little red book of hers. In the morning light she looked different than she had last night. Younger, softer, almost pretty.

He ran a hand over his beard stubble, then took a swig of hot coffee to clear his head. "You're seeing things, Wellesley."

After wiping the lenses of the opera glasses with his handkerchief, he looked at her again. Nope. Nothing different, after all. Just a trick of the morning light. She had the same dishwater-blond hair, pale skin and wore the ugliest gray dress he'd ever seen.

Not that it mattered. She was a woman, and women generally liked him. He didn't have to like her. He'd made a bad start of things last night. Today he'd do better. By sundown she'd be mooning over him, and he'd know everything he needed to know about what her father might have told her before he died.

He'd spent six long months at the Royal Flush, watching and waiting for Wild Bill to make a slip. He'd come too far to quit now. Maybe his daughter knew something the rest of the folks around here didn't.

Maybe she knew where the money was.

Dora capped her fountain pen and sighed. She'd spent a sleepless night on a lumpy mattress huddled under a pile of musty blankets. The potbelly stove had gone out in the middle of the night, and when she'd gotten up to relight it she realized she had no matchsticks. This morning she'd found an old flint on the floor near the coal bin and in no time was toasty warm again.

"Now, one last thing…" She slid her father's final letter to her out of her diary and carefully reread every word.

The small brass key that had accompanied it was still tucked safely away in her pocket. She fished it out and held it up to the sunlight streaming through the window. It had an odd marking on it, one she couldn't decipher. She was certain the key fit something, but what? Nowhere in the letter had her father mentioned it. Why would he send her a key and not tell her what it opened?

She had to admit, the enigma sparked her curiosity and appealed to her intellect. In secret, the past few months she'd been reading mystery novels in her room at night. Her mother, God rest her soul, would have been shocked had she known.

Dora had begun her diary shortly after discovering her father's letters to her. In it she wrote her most private feelings and thoughts, in addition to faithfully recording her observations regarding any unusual events. She'd learned something from those mystery novels, after all.

Her journey to Last Call and the Royal Flush counted as perhaps the most unusual event of her life, and so she'd decided to record everything, including descriptions of the people she met. She'd wasted half a dozen pages this morning on Chance Wellesley alone. Perhaps now she could banish him from her mind.

She returned her thoughts to the letter and read the most cryptic paragraph again.

I know I haven't been much of a father to you,

*Dora, but rest assured, your financial future is secure.
I've left you something at the ranch. Something only
you, seeing as how smart you are, will recognize. It's
the Chance of a lifetime, Dora. Take it.*

She held the key up to the sunlight and studied it
closely. "The chance of a lifetime." Whatever did he
mean? As she pondered her father's parting words,
her eyes refocused on an upstairs window of the
house.

She gasped and dropped the key.

Chance Wellesley dropped his opera glasses. The
insufferable man was spying on her!

He made it to the bottom of the spiral staircase a
second before she burst through the kitchen into the
saloon.

"How dare you!"

"Coffee?" he said, motioning toward the bar,
where the bartender was pouring himself a cup. "I
don't mean to be rude, but you look like you could
use it."

"You were watching me from that window."

There it was again, that trick of the light. She was
pretty when she was mad, despite the ugly dress. Her
eyes were gunmetal gray, he noticed for the first time,
and flashed him a murderous look in response to his
smile.

"Explain yourself."

He shrugged. "I can't. Guilty as charged."

"So you admit you were watching me?"

"I do. Now, how about that coffee? I know I could
use another cup."

She took stock of her surroundings, as if she'd just
now realized she was standing in the saloon. It wasn't

much to see this time of the morning. Delilah and the girls were still asleep, and the bar didn't usually open until ten, not until two on Sundays. Wild Bill had had standards, after all. For regulars like himself it was different, of course.

"Miss Fitzpatrick?" The bartender held out a cup to her. "Could rustle you up some breakfast if you like."

"No, I, um…" She calmed herself down—for the bartender's benefit, not his, he presumed. "Yes, a cup of coffee would be wonderful." She walked up to the bar and he set the cup down in front of her. "Thank you."

"My pleasure. Cream?"

"Yes, please. And sugar, if you have it."

"Comin' right up."

Chance watched her as she fixed her coffee, doing the best she could to ignore him.

"I don't think we were properly introduced last night. You are…?"

"James Parker, ma'am. But you can just call me Jim. We're pretty informal around here."

"Jim, then." She nodded, looking past him along the bar, which hadn't been wiped down from last night, to the pile of dirty glasses in the sink. The floor was littered with cigar butts and sticky with spilled beer.

"Oh, I, uh…" Jim cast her a sheepish look. "I meant to get this mess cleared up last night, but you know how it is."

She wasn't listening to him. Chance followed her gaze to the portrait above the bar. Her pale cheeks flushed the most disarming shade of scarlet he'd ever seen.

"Something wrong?" he asked.

She instantly averted her eyes. "Yes. No. I'm perfectly fine."

He hadn't been up long, and while he was wearing trousers and boots, his shirt was only half buttoned. Her gaze drifted to the opening, lingering on his chest hair. He knew she'd come around. They always did.

Their eyes met, and true to form she blushed hotter and turned her attention back to her coffee. He was beginning to enjoy this.

"Don't like that painting much, do you?"

"No. No, I don't."

"Well, it's your place now. You could always take it down."

"Take it down?" Jim, who was hastily wiping the bar down, froze in midstroke.

"That won't be necessary. I told you. I'm selling the place as soon as possible."

"Selling it?" Jim had worked at the Flush since Wild Bill opened the place. He didn't look happy about the prospect of losing his job.

"Yes. In fact, I'm going into town this morning to see a lawyer."

"But, uh, Miss Fitzpatrick..." Jim ran a hand over his balding head, then toyed nervously with the ends of his moustache. "Your pa wouldn't have wanted you to sell the place. Not right away, at least."

"I've been meaning to ask someone." She drew herself up in what Chance was beginning to think of as her schoolteacher pose, and said, "How did my father die?"

"You mean you don't know?" Jim tossed him one of those *you-tell-her* looks.

"He was shot," Chance said. "Right here in this very room."

She sucked in a breath, and from the stunned look in her eyes he knew her surprise was real and not fabricated.

"W-who did it?"

"Nobody knows." But he was going to find out, if it was the last thing he did. "It was a Saturday night. The saloon was packed. We heard the shot, and he just went down."

"Right here," Jim said, nodding at the floor behind the bar.

"You were here? Both of you?"

"Sitting right over there, playing cards." He cocked his head toward one of the tables.

"I dropped a tray of beer mugs in the doorway there." Jim nodded toward the kitchen. "Glass everywhere." He shook his head. "Damned shame."

"Excuse me?"

"About your pa, I mean, not the glass."

"Oh, of course." She stared past Jim at the dark stain on the well-worn pine flooring behind him, where William Fitzpatrick's blood had soaked the unvarnished wood.

Chance caught himself feeling sorry for her. He downed the rest of his coffee and adjusted his attitude. He had a job to do, and it was time to get some answers. "Your father, uh, write you any letters before he died?"

She snapped to attention, her spine straightening, and cast him a suspicious look. "Why do you ask?"

"No reason." He shrugged convincingly.

Not ten minutes ago he'd watched her read a two-page letter he'd mistaken last night for prayer sheets.

His first erroneous impression of her and that red leather-bound book had cost him time. No matter, he thought as he noticed the diary and the letter sandwiched inside it poking out from the pocket of her dress. He'd get his hands on it soon enough.

Jim leaned toward her in his bartender-like "you can trust me" slouch, which Chance had seen him use with great success in wheedling information out of the most secretive of customers. "Your pa didn't, uh, mention that he'd left you anything special here, did he?"

Chance went statue-still.

"What do you mean? Left me what?"

Jim looked at him, but Chance didn't come to his rescue this time. He was busy viewing Jim Parker with new eyes.

"Well, uh, anything. Important papers, family keepsakes…" Jim ran a sweaty palm over his balding pate. "…valuables, maybe?"

"Valuables? You mean like jewelry or money?" Her frown deepened. She looked around the room again, this time with renewed interest.

"Oh, uh…" Jim looked away. He grabbed a wet towel and began wiping down the bar. Chance had never seen him so agitated. "Was just a rumor I heard, is all."

Chance watched her closely to see if her gaze lingered too long on any one area of the saloon. It didn't. "I suspect Miss Fitzpatrick doesn't much believe in rumors."

"You're right," she said curtly, avoiding his eyes. "I don't. I base all my decisions on facts."

She tried to mask her natural reaction to the painting over the bar when her gaze darted past it, but couldn't. He smiled inwardly. Her prudish sensibilities were predictable, and that would make his job all the easier.

Eventually she dropped her gaze to the letter sticking out of her diary. He could tell by the twitch of her hand against her pocket that she fought the urge to take it out and read it again in front of them.

He had to know what was in that letter.

She caught him staring at it, and abruptly turned away.

"Well," she said to Jim. "I'll be going into town now, Mr. Parker. Is there a buggy or some other kind of conveyance I might borrow?"

"The place is yours, Miss Fitzpatrick. Take whatever, uh...conveyance you like." He nodded in the direction of the kitchen door. "One of the boys out back will set you up."

"I could take you in," Chance said and risked a smile.

She arched a disapproving brow at him as if he'd suggested they run buck-naked together down to the creek and jump in. Hmm. He gave her dowdily clothed figure another once-over and thought the notion wasn't a half bad idea.

Her nostrils flared. "That won't be necessary." She turned away. "Thank you again, Mr.—"

"Jim," the bartender said.

"Jim, then." She dropped a smile on him, and after a cautionary glance in Chance's direction, she turned on her heel and marched out the way she'd come in.

Chance set his empty cup down on the bar and figured he had just enough time to finish dressing, grab his hat and saddle up Silas before she was gone.

"You're not really thinking of selling the place, are you?" Jim called after her.

Wild Bill's daughter didn't answer.

For the second time in as many days Chance Wellesley followed her to town. Dora didn't give him the satisfaction of looking back at him. Not once. Well, maybe once, but that had been a mistake. Her hat had flown off in a gust of wind, and she'd stopped to retrieve it a second before he caught up with her. He'd tipped his hat to her and smiled. She'd promptly ignored him.

As it turned out, her father had owned a number of good horses, a sound buckboard, a surrey and two wagons used for hauling loads of supplies from town. Rowdy, one of two ranch hands whom he'd continued to employ long after he'd quit the cattle business, had, true to the bartender's word, set her up. She'd opted for the buckboard.

Guiding a pair of dappled mares, she pulled off the deeply rutted trail leading from the Royal Flush onto Last Call's main street. It was a fine spring day, and the town looked far more welcoming in the sunshine than it had last night.

Out of the corner of her eye she spied Chance making the turn into town behind her, Silas dutifully trotting along in her wake. Why wouldn't the man leave her alone? She was determined not to encourage him. She'd seen the way he'd looked at her in the saloon, and the suspicious way he'd eyed her diary. She'd simply have to ignore him.

Last Call was a fair size for a mining town. In addition to the establishments she'd already seen, the long boardwalk-lined main street boasted a mercantile, telegraph office, the livery where yesterday afternoon she'd hired transportation out to the ranch, a cattle exchange, grange building and a small, whitewashed church.

No school, at least not here in the center of town. Perhaps it was tucked away on one of the side streets among the residential buildings and boardinghouses. Boardinghouses that were full up, she remembered with irritation. Then again, perhaps Last Call had no school. She noticed a number of children playing in the street, children who should be in school on a Friday morning.

"The sign says Harrington, but his name's Grimmer."

"Excuse me?" She hadn't noticed that Chance had spurred Silas up alongside her.

"Your father's lawyer." He flashed his eyes at the sign as she pulled the buckboard up in front of the law office she'd seen last night.

"How would you know my father's lawyer?" He seemed determined to insinuate himself into her business. The question in her mind was why?

Had her father left her something more than the saloon and ranch, as both his letter and Jim the bartender had implied? He very well might have, and if Chance Wellesley knew about it, he was exactly the kind of unscrupulous character who would attempt to swindle her out of whatever it was. Perhaps it was money. Hmm...

He dismounted and was at her side a moment later, his hand extended to help her down from the buckboard. He flashed her that trademark smile, and it dawned on her that he meant to seduce her out of it, if money was indeed his motive in dogging her every step.

"Oh, Chance! Yoo-hoo," a coquettish voice sounded from behind her.

She turned to look at the passerby, a surprisingly well-dressed woman, and Chance used her momentary lapse in attention—and judgment—to grasp her around the waist. "Oh!"

"Just helping you down, Miss Eudora."

"It's Dora. I mean—" The man completely discombobulated her! "Take your hands off me! I'm perfectly capable of—"

He ignored her protest and lifted her from the conveyance, setting her, light as you please, on the ground. "You've overstepped your bounds, Mr. Wellesley."

The well-dressed woman winked at her as she passed them. "He's been known to do that a time or two, haven't you, Chance?"

He shrugged boyishly, angering her even more.

Dora stormed past them both, climbed the two steps up to the boardwalk, and a few seconds later opened the door to the law office of H. J. Harrington, Esquire.

"Mortimer Grimmer," the friendly-looking man said to her, extending his hand. "How may I be of help?"

"Told you his name was Grimmer." To her annoyance, Chance had followed her into the office.

"Wellesley! What brings you to town?"

Chance grinned. "I'm here to collect the rest of my winnings from Saturday night's game."

Dora was appalled. Not only did he know her father's lawyer, it appeared they played cards together.

"Oh, and I'd like you to meet someone. Miss Eudora Elizabeth Fitzpatrick." She was surprised he remembered her middle name.

"You're Bill's girl?" Mr. Grimmer grabbed her hand and shook it enthusiastically. "Well, I'll be. You don't much look like him."

She barely remembered what her father had looked like, so she didn't know whether he was complimenting her or not. She knew she wasn't much to look at, but the good-natured lawyer was smiling, so she suspected it was a compliment.

"I take after my mother's side."

"Well, well. Please, have a seat." He gestured to a visitor's chair in front of his very tidy desk. Business didn't appear to be too brisk. "You, too, Chance."

"Oh, but..." She wasn't about to talk about her father's affairs with *him* in the room.

Grimmer read her reaction. "Oh, I apologize. I thought you two were together."

"We are," Chance said.

"We most certainly are not." She refused to sit down until he left Mr. Grimmer's office. Once that was made clear, and after he had, she got down to business.

"Now, about your father's will..." Grimmer produced the will, and together they reviewed it. It confirmed what he'd written in his telegram to her last month, that out of her father's original thirty thousand acres, only six thousand remained. He'd sold the rest to finance the construction of the house and set himself up in business.

During their conversation she was aware of Chance standing outside on the boardwalk, leaning up against the side of the building, pretending not to watch them. She knew better. The nerve of the man!

"Well, that's that, then." Grimmer handed her his bill. It was sizable. He appeared to be waiting for her to pay him. She suspected he needed the cash to pay off the gambling debt he owed Chance Wellesley.

"There was nothing in particular described in my father's will besides the property?"

"That's right," Grimmer said. "And all the contents, of course, the livestock, the horses, et cetera. The transfer papers are all complete." He produced them, and after reviewing them she signed them.

"Yes, but I had thought he might have left me something more. Something…"

The lawyer clasped his hands together on top of his desk and leaned forward in anticipation. His paternal smile faded. For a moment he reminded her chillingly of the greedy mole in a popular children's book she read to her younger students.

"Never mind," she said, and shook off the odd feeling.

His smile returned.

She took a moment to collect her thoughts, then rose. "Thank you, Mr. Grimmer. You've been most helpful." They shook hands, and when it became apparent to him that she wasn't going to pay him his fee, she said, "As soon as I'm done at the bank, I'll see to it you get your payment."

His smile broadened. "Have a fine day, Miss Fitzpatrick."

"Goodbye."

Chance was waiting for her outside, casually twirling the watch fob hanging from his belt, trying to appear indifferent. He didn't fool her for a second.

"You're still here," she said as she breezed past him, continuing down the boardwalk toward the bank. She paused to read a handbill warning the public about a rash of counterfeit currency in circulation right here in Park County.

Chance beat her to the door of the bank and held it open for her as she entered. There were several customers in line waiting to speak with a clerk who was carefully inspecting each bill of a customer's cash deposit.

A tall, impeccably dressed gentleman who was likely the bank's manager appeared from an office in the back to offer help. He was fair-haired and clean-shaven, rather dashing, Dora thought.

"I wouldn't get my hopes up if I were you." Chance removed his hat and stepped into line behind her.

She promptly turned her back on him. "I'm sure I don't know what you mean, Mr. Wellesley."

The portly woman in front of her reeked of lavender water and struggled to keep her noisy little dog under control. Any moment Dora was going to sneeze. She opened her reticule and fished around for her handkerchief, retrieving it just in time.

"What I mean, Miss Fitzpatrick—"

The banker looked up at the mention of her name. He had the most captivating blue eyes.

"—is that Wild Bill didn't think much of banks. So if you're expecting to find—"

She sneezed so violently she dropped her open reticule. Its contents spilled out across the floor.

The banker rushed out from behind the counter, scooted the woman and her dog aside, then knelt to collect her things. Chance had the same idea at the same moment. The two men butted heads in their frenzy.

"Oh, my key!" The small brass key that had accompanied her father's letter lay at her feet.

"Allow me." The banker snatched it up a split second before Chance could get his hands on it. He secured everything else inside her reticule, then stood. It was clear from the first that Chance Wellesley didn't like him, which was reason enough to commend him to her.

"Your things, Miss Fitzpatrick." He offered her the reticule and smiled. His expression darkened as he nodded at Chance. "Hello, Wellesley. Here for another loan?"

Chance glared at him, then turned his attention to the key, which the banker had not yet returned to her.

"John Gardner, at your service, miss." He gave her a little bow, which she thought charming.

Chance muttered something rude under his breath. Dora ignored him. "I'm glad to know you, Mr. Gardner."

"You're William Fitzpatrick's daughter?"

"That's correct." It was so nice to hear her father called something other than Wild Bill.

"Although the bank does hold the mortgage on his property—your property now, as I understand from Mr. Grimmer—I'm very sorry to tell you that your father didn't keep an account here."

"Oh." She knew her disappointment showed.

"Told you so," Chance said.

She and Mr. Gardner moved closer, effectively shutting him out of their conversation.

"I didn't know there was a mortgage. Is it sizable?"

"I'm afraid it is."

Her hopes sunk.

"I hate to be the bearer of bad news, but your father had a number of creditors, and was behind on his interest payments to the bank when he died."

"I see." He'd mentioned none of this in his letters to her. Perhaps her mother had been right about his character after all.

"However, this is the key to his safety deposit box." He dropped the small brass key into her gloved hand.

A safety deposit box! Of course! That explained the strange marking on the key. Each bank had a unique identifier.

"Perhaps what's inside will solve all your problems."

"Well, I'll be damned." Chance looked over her shoulder at the key. He was so close, she felt his warm breath on her neck and detected the faint scent of his shaving soap. It was sandalwood and rather pleasant, unlike the man himself.

"I suppose you'd like to open it right away."

"Yes, I would," she said, turning her attention back to the matter at hand. "I'd also like to discuss the sale of my father's property, if you have the time."

"I'll make the time." He dismissed Chance with a glower. "I'll deal with you later, Wellesley."

Chance ignored him and followed them into the office in the back.

She whirled on him. "What is it now?" Her irritation was not lost on Mr. Gardner.

"Would you like me to intervene?"

"No. Thank you. I can handle Mr. Wellesley myself." She marched back out to the front.

Chance sauntered out behind her. "I like the sound of that, Dora."

"Of what?" She didn't bother reminding him that she hadn't given him permission to call her by her Christian name, and a nickname at that.

"Of you handling me yourself." He grinned.

"Mr. Wellesley!"

"I wish you'd call me Chance."

She'd rather burn in hell. "I have only one thing to say to you."

He hitched his hip against the hand-carved walnut partition separating the bank's customer area from the back offices and waited for her to continue.

"If you think you're going to get your hands on my father's money, you're wrong."

"What money?" He arched a brow at her, as if a point had just been scored in his favor.

In the morning light she could see the fine worry lines around his eyes and forehead, and a depth to his eyes she hadn't noticed before. The impression contradicted the roguish demeanor he seemed determined to exhibit to perfection.

She gathered her wits, ignoring the stunned expressions and hushed whispers of the bank's customers and said, "None of your business."

"Fair enough."

His acquiescence stunned her. "Fine." Before he could say anything else to annoy her, she brushed past him and returned to the banker's office.

"Everything all right, Miss Fitzpatrick?" It was plain he'd overheard their conversation.

"Just fine."

"If you don't mind my giving advice... Chance Wellesley is a gambler and a notorious ladies' man to boot. You might want to think twice about being seen with him."

"Yes, well, I appreciate your advice, Mr. Gardner." It seemed strange to her that the banker would warn her against him in one breath, then turn around and loan him money in the next. "I'd like to see my father's safety deposit box now, if it's not too much trouble."

"No trouble at all." He came around his desk, retrieved a key from his watch pocket that was secured to a heavy chain, then opened a door behind which was a set of stairs. "The vault is in the basement. After you."

The vault room was well-secured and brightly lit. She was momentarily startled by the two armed guards seated in the foyer, late-model rifles resting in their laps. The banker nodded at them, and they disappeared up the stairs.

She approached the wall of safety deposit boxes with her key.

"It's this one, I believe." Mr. Gardner pulled a long metal strongbox from one of the numbered cubbyholes set into the wall and placed it on a nearby table. "Allow me." He held out his hand for the key, his gaze fixed on hers. His blue eyes sparkled in the lamp light.

She considered that John Gardner had an honest face and a smile every bit as unassuming as Chance Wellesley's was wicked. He was her father's banker and she wanted to trust him, but if she'd learned anything from reading all those mystery novels, it was to never trust anyone where large sums of money were concerned.

She hesitated, staring at his manicured hand, then said, "I think I'd like to open it alone, if you don't mind."

He was speechless for a moment, then recovered himself. "Of course. How stupid of me. Please..." He pulled out the single chair for her to sit. She made herself comfortable. "I'll be right upstairs if you need me."

"Thank you."

She waited until she heard him top the flight of stairs and the sound of his footfalls in the room above her. It was cool in the vault room, but she was perspiring.

Debts, a mortgage and a six-thousand-acre ranch that no one wanted to buy.

She slid off her gloves and realized her hands were shaking. When she'd received her father's letter and had made the decision to relocate to Last Call, she'd liquidated her life's savings, which hadn't amounted to much, and had given notice at the one-room school in Colorado Springs where she'd taught for the past seven years. A new schoolteacher had already been hired. She couldn't go back. There was nothing to go back to.

Dora drew a breath and opened the box. What she saw inside confused her.

The box was carefully lined in newsprint and contained only two items: a tortoiseshell comb that looked oddly familiar to her and a tintype portrait she instantly recognized as her father.

There was no money.

Chapter Three

"**I**'m sorry to inform you all that the Royal Flush is closed." Dora stood in the middle of the stage at the far end of the saloon and gazed out at a sea of faces, all turned in her direction. Apparently her years of oration in the classroom transferred quite effectively to other, less scholarly settings.

The employees looked at her in confusion. The customers, on the other hand, appeared delighted and immediately rearranged their chairs to face her. With a shock she realized they mistook her announcement for the opening of a performance. After all, it was Friday evening, it was a saloon, and she was standing on the stage.

She tried a different approach. "May I have your attention, please?"

A man at the bar whistled. The customers laughed.

She ignored them and continued. "My name is Eudora Fitzpatrick. I'm William Fitz— I mean, Wild Bill's, um, daughter."

The crowd cheered. More men whistled, and some even raised their glasses to her. Tom, the piano player, whom she'd asked to stop playing a few mo-

ments ago, started up again. Delilah whispered something into the bartender's ear, then rushed to gather
up her girls.

Chance Wellesley reluctantly let one of them slide
off his lap. She felt a brief moment of victory when
he put down his hand of cards. He was the only customer, however, who did. The rest of them returned
to their gaming.

"The saloon is closed!" Though she shouted, her
voice failed to carry over the music and the chatter,
which had returned to its customary, earsplitting volume.

Delilah shrugged at her, then shooed the girls back
to work. Jim lined up a half-dozen shot glasses along
the bar, then winked at her as he filled them in one
easy motion. She noticed he didn't spill a drop.
Rowdy, whom she'd asked to stand by the front entrance and lock the outer doors once all the customers
had gone, looked to her for direction.

What was she going to do if the employees refused
to stop working and the customers refused to stop
gambling, drinking and engaging in the unmention-
able goings-on upstairs?

After the shock of discovering her father's safety
deposit box contained no cash and nothing of any
value, except for the tintype that for sentimental reasons was valuable to her, Dora had spent an hour
conversing with John Gardner. He'd confirmed
Chance Wellesley's proclamation.

Her father had died owing substantial sums of
money to nearly every business in Last Call, in addition to being three months behind on his interest
payment to the bank. Foreclosure was imminent. John
Gardner was accountable to his investors, and while

he'd kindly offered to review and possibly renegotiate the loan, it would do no good as she had no way of paying it. The only solution was to sell off the property, which Mr. Gardner had advised, as soon as a buyer could be located. He'd generously offered to ask around for her.

"What's this all about?" The voice came from behind her. It was one she recognized—and loathed.

She turned just as Chance parted the red velvet curtains draping the stage, grabbed her arm and pulled her into the darkness.

"Let me go!" How did he get back there without her seeing him? Not a moment ago he'd been sitting with his boots propped up on a card table, flirting with Delilah's girls.

"I will when you start talking sense." He maneuvered her toward the back of the stage, where she was relieved to see an open door leading to the softly lit hallway running the length of the first floor.

A minute later she was seated at the table in the kitchen, and he was making them a pot of strong coffee, rattling around the cupboards as if *he* owned the place and not her.

"What's all this nonsense about closing the place? You didn't say anything about that this afternoon."

Her afternoon had been spent avoiding his questions. He'd been waiting for her outside the bank when she'd finally emerged. She'd wrapped the tintype and the tortoiseshell comb carefully in the newsprint that had lined her father's safety deposit box and had stuffed the package into her reticule. The obvious bulge had captured Chance's attention.

"It was Gardner's idea, wasn't it?"

"To close the saloon? It most certainly was not."

She didn't like lying, but she refused to be cowed by a gambler. Her affairs were not his concern. John had, in fact, suggested closing the Royal Flush. Dora had agreed on principle. He'd also offered to assist her in inventorying and selling off anything that might be of value, using the profits to keep the interest payments up on the mortgage until the property sold.

"If you must know," she said, committed to her falsehood, "John advises keeping the saloon open until the ranch sells."

"So it's John, now."

An odd feeling fluttered inside her. The stab of jealousy that flashed in his eyes lasted only for a heartbeat.

"It's my own idea to close the saloon. I've told you."

"Close it?" Delilah burst into the kitchen, her flounces and feather boas following in her wake like a whole other wardrobe.

Jim the bartender and Tom the piano player were right behind her. They all jammed into the kitchen. A few of Delilah's girls poked their heads into the doorway.

"That's what I thought I heard out there," Jim said, "but I couldn't rightly believe my ears."

"Believe them," she said, and stood.

Chance offered her a cup of coffee, but she ignored it. Delilah took it and slugged it down.

"The ranch is for sale. In the meantime, I'm closing the saloon, selling off the garish furnishings and artwork, especially that indecent painting above the bar, and reopening the house as an establishment I know something about."

"And that would be...?" Chance eyed her.

"A school."

Delilah's mouth dropped open. Jim's eyes bugged. The piano player gawked at her, and the girls crowded into the doorway all started talking at once. Chance merely snorted as if she'd lost her mind.

"There isn't a school in Last Call." She'd confirmed that fact with John Gardner. "I plan to open one. Here."

She intended to approach the town council the first thing Monday morning to see about funding. Children were playing in the streets, for pity's sake. They ought to be in school.

"You can't close the Flush, Miss Eudora." The piano player looked as if he were going to cry. "You just can't."

"Why not?"

They all looked at each other. She had the oddest feeling they were keeping something from her, something important. Her father's words echoed in her mind.

Rest assured, your financial future is secure. I've left you something at the ranch.

When she'd first read her father's last letter to her, she'd been stunned by the prospect of an inheritance, but that wasn't the reason she'd come to Last Call. Besides, the empty safety deposit box had cured her of any wishful thinking. What her father had left her with was not a fortune but a financial nightmare.

"I'm closing the saloon, and that's that."

"Tonight?" Jim exchanged glances with Delilah.

"Why not tonight?"

"It's Friday, that's why." Chance arched a brow

at her, and she was struck, not for the first time, by how handsome he was.

She pushed the unbidden thought from her mind and said, "What's so special about Friday?"

The girls giggled. Delilah gave them a hard look and they instantly quieted.

"It's the biggest take of the week," Chance said. "Except for Saturday. At the bar in drinks and tips, at the tables in winnings, of which the house gets a five percent cut, and uh…well, you know." He jerked his head toward the doorway, where Delilah's girls continued to gawk at her.

Dora frowned, not understanding him.

"He means upstairs, honey," Delilah whispered.

"Oh!" Her cheeks blazed, and it wasn't because the kitchen was overwarm, even with half the employees of the Royal Flush crowded into it.

"The house gets a twenty-percent cut of that business. It's a damned good share." Chance didn't blink as he watched her.

"And, uh, *you're* the house, Miss Dora." Jim grinned ear to ear, as if she should be overjoyed by the notion of making a profit from the scandalous enterprise.

"I see." Dora was mortified. At the same time she was intrigued. "And, um, just how much would the house make on an average Friday night?"

"Enough to pay the mercantile in town what Wild Bill's owed 'em for the past month," Jim said.

Delilah nodded her agreement.

"That much?" John Gardner had taken it upon himself to prepare a listing of her father's outstanding debts for her. The mercantile bill was sizable.

Looking at their faces and listening to the boister-

ous crowd out front—a crowd that in one night promised to spend enough money at the Royal Flush to
settle a debt for which she was now accountable—it
was clear to her that nothing would be accomplished
tonight. So, against her better judgment, she relied on
intuition and gave in. For now.

"Very well," she said in her most teacherlike
voice. "The Royal Flush will remain open—for tonight. And, um, perhaps tomorrow night as well." If
Saturday was, indeed, the most profitable evening of
the week, only a fool would close the saloon before
then. She had bills to pay, and she was simply being
practical.

Delilah and Jim breathed audible sighs of relief.
The girls squealed as Tom drummed his fingers on
the door frame in a mock concerto.

"Good decision," Chance said. He drained his coffee cup and set it in the sink. "Bill would have been
pleased."

"Yes, well…" Somehow that thought wasn't com-
forting. Furthermore, she was sick and tired of
Chance Wellesley's meddling, and was determined to
nip it in the bud. "I do have one question for you all
before I retire."

They looked at her, all ears.

"Mr. Wellesley was not in my father's employ,
was he?"

"No, ma'am," Jim said. "Chance don't work for
nobody except himself."

Chance frowned at her, but she continued, un-
daunted. "Then why does he claim to know so much
about the operation of this saloon?"

Delilah and Jim exchanged another look. The girls
giggled, and Delilah hushed them. "Me and Jim keep

the place running,'' she said. ''Have done even when
your pa was alive. But Chance, here…well, he enter-
tains folks, if you know what I mean.''

''Oh, he's entertaining, all right.''

Chance shot her a slow smile that threatened to
melt the skin right off her if she let it. She didn't.

''He brings in a lot of business,'' Jim chimed in.
''High rollers from all over. The Flush wouldn't be
the Flush without Chance.''

No, she thought, as she studied him. It wouldn't.

He stared back, and for the barest moment dispensed with that boyish affectation he seemed to cul-
tivate like a weed. In a moment of clarity, she realized
with shock it *was* cultivated. But why?

Where had Chance Wellesley come from? No one
seemed to know. And why had he made himself a
permanent fixture at her father's saloon for the past
six months? She'd learned that fact from Tom not an
hour ago. What was his stake in her affairs—she was
certain he had one—and why had he, just now, looked
away as if he were hiding something, something he
desperately wanted kept secret?

Dora blew out a breath.

Sometimes, late at night, when she read the mystery novels she was so fond of, she'd imagine herself
as the protagonist, an amateur sleuth. Right now a bit
of sleuthing seemed in order, with Chance Wellesley
as the subject of her investigation.

''It's late,'' she said, and moved to the back door.

Chance beat her to it and held it open. ''Sweet
dreams.'' The boyish charm was back.

A blast of night air and her own determination so-
bered her. She ignored him and turned to the small

crowd of anxious faces that, she realized, were *her* employees now. "I'll see you all tomorrow."

"G'night, Miss Dora," they said in unison.

"Good night."

It *was* a good night. A wagon load of miners with money to burn showed up at the Flush round about midnight. A dozen easy hands of poker later, Chance had cleaned them out. He went to bed smiling and a hundred dollars richer, but for the second night in a row couldn't sleep.

Every few minutes he caught himself peeking out the lace-draped windows of his room to the cabin out back where Dora sat at the desk, late into the night, scribbling away in her diary. Once she glanced up at his room, but it was dark, and he took care, this time around, to stand in the shadows.

What had she found in that safety deposit box? He had to know. Whatever it was, she'd taken it with her. Tomorrow he planned to search her cabin. The fact that Bill even *had* a safety deposit box stunned him. He hadn't expected it, and he was a man who didn't like surprises.

She had mettle, he'd give her that. Standing on that stage tonight took guts, though her speech hadn't accomplished what she'd intended. The other thing that struck him was that she was practical, Bill's daughter through and through. She'd shelved those prissy sensibilities, at least for the time being, and had let the Flush ride.

"A school," he said to himself in the dark. The woman couldn't be serious.

When he finally did sleep, he had the dream. It was worse this time. He woke up in a cold sweat, the bed

sheets twisted around his legs. He was close, so close
he could feel it. The money was here. *He* was here.
It was one of them, he was sure of it. Tom? Jim?
Rowdy or old Gus? Hell, it could even be Grimmer
or Gardner. For all he knew it could be Dora Fitzpatrick herself.

Wild Bill had had a partner—a silent partner who'd
known about the money. That's why he was killed.
Chance was going to find out who it was if it was the
last thing he did.

It very well might be.

Dora Fitzpatrick was not going to close the saloon.
He'd make damn sure of it, no matter what he had to
do.

"You want me to do what?" Chance blinked the
sleep from his eyes, sat up in bed and pulled the sheet
up over his bare torso. Dawn's light streamed through
the lace-curtained windows. He'd forgotten to draw
the shades.

Dora stood outside the cracked door of his room,
key in hand, her eyes averted. "I'd like you to pack
your things." She shot him a quick glance, her gray
eyes widening at his state of undress. "I knocked, but
you didn't answer." She started to close the door.

He threw off the covers and leaped from the bed.
He caught the edge of the door before it closed. "Uh,
hang on a second. What's this about?"

She braced herself, her posture straightening, her
chin tipped high, her hand white-knuckled on the
doorknob. Their gazes locked through the two inches
of open door. She was perfectly aware that he was
bare-assed, but refused to let it show in her expression.

Her nostrils flared as she drew a breath, her cheeks blazed scarlet against her will. He'd be damned if she was pretty. She wasn't, at least not in the way he was used to women being. All the same, there was something powerfully attractive about her that he couldn't put his finger on. Maybe it was that stubborn will of hers.

"Tonight you may stay in one of the unoccupied rooms across the hall. On the opposite side of the house." She didn't blink, not an eyelash. Dora Fitzpatrick had grit.

He pulled on the door, widening the gap another inch. She held fast to the knob, fighting him. "I like this room. Why would I move?"

She tipped her chin higher, her gray eyes steel. "Because I'm telling you to."

She knew he'd been watching her last night. She knew and yet she hadn't drawn the curtains over the window. And that made all the difference.

He smiled, aware that their interaction was arousing. At least to him it was. "You *are* the proprietor, Miss Dora. So I guess I'd best move."

"Besides," she said, less sure of herself now. She looked away. Down the hall he heard Delilah and a few of the girls whispering. "Tomorrow's Sunday, and I'm closing the place for good. You'll have to be on your way."

"Now wait a second!" He jerked the door wide.

She jumped, her hand flying off the knob as if it were cattle-brand hot. Her gaze washed over his body as he stepped, naked, into the hall.

"Mr. Wellesley!" She spun on her heel and fled toward the spiral staircase.

Delilah let out a laugh. The girls giggled. They

were all in their dressing gowns and up too damned early for their own good.

"Oh, Chaaance," one of them, Lily, called from down the hall. She waved, and the girls continued to giggle. Delilah shooed them back as Dora hurried past.

He watched, grinning, as she half stumbled down the staircase into the saloon. Ten minutes later he was dressed and chasing after her.

"You're not serious about this school idea?"

She stood in the center of the saloon, hands on hips, surveying the place with narrowed eyes and a frown. Her brows pinched together as she turned a slow circle. At first he thought she was ignoring him. She wasn't, he realized. She was thinking.

"As serious as a boll weevil in a cotton field." She jotted a few lines into her red leather-bound diary, then strode to the far end of the room.

Chance followed. "What do you know about cotton fields?"

She lifted the lid of Tom's antique piano and peeked inside. "Nothing," she said, distracted. "But I know a lot about running a school. Hmm..." She plucked a few of the piano wires, closed the lid, then inspected the adjacent stage. "This will do nicely."

"Do for what?"

She turned to him and, for the first time since the incident upstairs, looked him squarely in the eyes. "For the children's performances, of course."

"You mean you teach music?" He hadn't pegged her for a music teacher.

"I teach everything." She cast him a dismissive look, then walked back to the center of the room.

"Reading, composition, mathematics, science, drama and music. Oh, and Latin."

"Latin?" The instant he caught up with her she was off again. He dogged her steps. "Who besides scholars and bookworms speak Latin."

"Read, not speak. Those urchins I saw playing in the street yesterday could benefit nicely from it, I think."

Chance shook his head. "You're not like any schoolteacher I ever met."

"That doesn't surprise me."

He laughed. Not at what she said but the way she said it, as if she knew she was different and damned proud of it. "You're set on closing the place, then?"

"You don't think I'd continue to operate a saloon?" She scribbled more notes into the diary, then scowled at the card tables in front of the bar. "We'll need desks. Perhaps these can be modified."

"Why not? A woman like you'd do a damned fine job of it."

She turned on him, one blond brow lifted in astonishment. "You're not serious?"

"As a boll weevil in a—"

"Honestly, Mr. Wellesley." She capped her fountain pen and snapped the diary shut. They disappeared into the deep pocket of her dress.

He reminded himself he wanted a look at that diary, but he'd have to wait until she was asleep. She carried it with her every waking moment.

She did an about-face, snaked between the card tables toward the stage, and hurried through the doorway into the hall. Bill had turned one of the two first-floor bedrooms into his study. She paused at the door, looking in, then continued down the long corridor toward the kitchen.

Chance knew he was in trouble. He had to convince her to keep the Flush open, to keep everybody working and the customers pouring in. If he didn't, the past six months would have been for nothing. Six months of keeping his eyes and ears open and his mouth shut, biding his time, waiting for Bill's partner to surface.

"I know why you're closing it," he called after her. "And it's not because you're a schoolmarm shocked at the idea of owning a saloon."

"School*teacher*," she corrected. She grabbed her cloak off a peg by the back door and readied herself to go outside.

He held the door for her, then followed her down the back steps. "A woman like you wouldn't be bothered by what people would think."

"A woman like me." She kept walking, past the row of cabins and the bunkhouse, toward the barns and corral.

Rowdy and Gus, busy with morning chores, tipped their hats to her as she marched by.

"A woman who's smart, who knows her own mind." He caught up with her and took her arm. She immediately pulled it away. "I like smart women."

"How fascinating."

He was losing her. He had to think of something, and fast. She skirted a pile of horse dung, rounded the corral and stopped at the edge of the meadow filling a long valley choked with spring wildflowers as far as the eye could see.

She shaded her eyes from the early morning sun

and looked out at the smattering of cattle, what remained of Wild Bill's herd.

"You're afraid," he said on impulse.

"What?" She turned to look at him.

"You heard me. You're afraid."

"Of what?" Her spine stiffened.

"Of everything." He nodded toward the house. "The saloon, the customers, Delilah and the girls. Jim, Tom, the hired hands—" He glanced back at Rowdy and Gus who'd stopped their work and were watching. "And me."

"I most certainly am not!"

"The ranch, too. It's still a ranch, you know. A hundred head or so. Angus beef. Damned fine stock."

Her cheeks blazed, not with embarrassment this time, but anger. It bothered him that after only two days he knew her well enough to know the difference. The breeze caught a tendril of her hair, freed it from the tight little bun at the back of her head, and whipped it across her face.

"John, er, Mr. Gardner told me the stock were worthless." She looked out across the valley at the cattle as an excuse to stop looking at him.

"Gardner's an idiot. This was a profitable cattle ranch once. I can tell. With a couple thousand head and the right help, a man could really make something of himself here." Without thinking, he crouched and plucked a handful of grass from the muddy ground, sifting it between his fingers as he gazed off into the distance. "Good water and sweet grass. It's a choice piece of land, Dora. Believe me, I'd know."

The words were out of his mouth before he could stop himself. He bit off a silent curse and abruptly stood, tossing the last few blades aside.

"Would you?" Dora looked him up and down. "And what exactly would a man like you know about land and cattle ranching?"

He froze, his gaze locked on hers. He'd gotten carried away, and the slip would cost him. Dora Fitzpatrick was no simpleton.

"Just what is your history, Mr. Wellesley? No one seems to know."

Which was exactly how he wanted it.

"Mr. Wellesley?" She looked at him strangely. Her gray eyes had gone soft, all tenderness and concern. He couldn't remember the last time a woman had looked at him like that.

"I, uh…"

"Were you a rancher before you went into…um, gambling?"

He looked out over the rolling green pastures flecked with spring columbine and purple sage, and thought for a fleeting moment about the man he'd once been. Dora watched him closely, and he had the uncomfortable feeling she saw right through him.

"No," she said crisply, though the canny look in her eyes contradicted her verdict. "I didn't think so."

He forced a smile and slipped easily into the pretense that had become as comfortable as a pair of old boots. She was not going to turn this around on him. He circled back to his original statement. "Trust me, you're afraid."

She looked at him, and for a heartbeat he saw in her eyes that he was right. An uncomfortable feeling gripped him. He sucked in a breath, sharp with the scents of cattle and sage and the barest hint of lilac. He hadn't noticed before today that she wore perfume.

''You don't know me,'' she said.

''No, I don't.'' He thought about the life he'd had, rich and full of promise, before the unthinkable had happened eighteen months ago. What would he have thought of Dora Fitzpatrick then? ''I don't,'' he said, ''but I'd like to.''

Chapter Four

"I want that painting removed by the time I return from church."

"Whatever you say, Miss Dora." Jim continued sweeping the broken glass, cigar butts and other evidence of the saloon's profitable Saturday-night business into a tidy pile near the swinging double doors.

Dora gazed at her reflection in the mirror above the bar and adjusted her hat. "I mean it, Jim. And I'd like you to lock the doors after I leave. The saloon is closed. No one's to be admitted."

"Yes, ma'am."

"I know you think I'm being unreasonable. But I'm certain Tom and Delilah, and the...um, girls, can find decent jobs elsewhere." She meant to retain Gus and Rowdy to take care of the place, and to help her with the conversion of the saloon into a school—if she could afford it. She wasn't certain, yet, that she could.

Jim hadn't lied. Last night's take, together with Friday's, had been enough to pay the weekly salaries of the staff, in addition to one of the outstanding bills from a local merchant. She'd have to make arrangements to pay the rest of her father's debts over time.

Surely the town council would see things her way. Last Call was in desperate need of a school, and one less saloon could hardly matter. She was certain John Gardner would help her convince them, and Sunday services at the Methodist church in town was the perfect place to begin her campaign.

"Are you ready?" Chance stood silhouetted in the entrance, morning sun at his back, casually twirling his watch fob.

"Perhaps I should have asked you to lock the doors sooner," she said to Jim.

The bartender shot him a grin.

"I've got the buckboard right out front."

Surely he didn't think she was going to church with *him?* Did gamblers even go to church? She didn't think so.

Snatching her reticule off the bar, she walked toward him. "You're supposed to be leaving today." As an afterthought she checked her pocket to make certain her diary along with her father's letter were tucked safely inside.

"Not before church. Wouldn't be proper, now would it?"

She disregarded his open appraisal of her attire as she approached, then ducked neatly under his arm and out the door. She was seated on the buckboard, reins in hand, before he realized her intent.

"Whoa!" he called as she snapped the reins.

She didn't stop, but she did look back at him. He was quite the gentleman in his Sunday best. If she didn't know better, she'd peg him for a prominent businessman or cattle baron. He wore a three-piece suit she hadn't seen before, his ever-present gun belt and a hat. She noticed his leather boots were polished to a high sheen.

She also noticed that Silas was standing by, saddled and ready, munching new grass alongside the hitching post. She frowned, first at the horse, then at Chance. He smiled at her in return, much like the cat who ate the canary.

What's he up to now? Whatever it was, she wasn't going to wait around to find out. It was already half past eight, and services began promptly at nine according to Jim. She urged the horses faster, and the buckboard rumbled down the road toward town.

A quarter mile into the trip, the ranch house just out of sight, Dora jerked the reins as the left rear axle of the conveyance hit the ground with a thud. "Good Lord!" The buckboard had lost a wheel.

A moment later the horses reared.

Chance appeared out of nowhere on Silas, ready to offer assistance. He sprang from the paint gelding and quieted the spooked team. Silas shot her a bored look as Chance offered her his hand. "Let me help you down." She was just about to take it, when he said, "Looks like you'll have to let me escort you to church after all. We can ride double on Silas."

Truth dawned as she met his gaze.

"I don't think so." Avoiding his proffered hand, she hopped to the ground and inspected both the axle and the wheel. She'd learned a thing or two about investigation from her mystery novels, and put her powers of observation to work.

As she'd suspected, neither the axle nor the wheel had given way from any natural cause. The axle pin holding the wheel in place had simply been removed. Removed by Chance Wellesley.

"You did this deliberately."

He cast her a look of pure innocence. "You don't think I'd intentionally try to make you late for church, do you?"

Oh, he was good, all right. Any troupe of players would be pleased to have him as their comic lead.

"I do." She kept her anger in check. She wasn't about to give him the satisfaction. "I am clueless, however, as to your motive."

He unhitched the horses from the buckboard, pointed them toward home, and gave them each a wallop while letting out a "Yee-ha!" that would rival any cowpuncher's. The horses took off. "They know their way back. Rowdy'll come looking for the buckboard once he sees them."

The man had no scruples. She was just about to dismiss him with a pithy insult and make her way into Last Call on foot, when her father's surrey rumbled into sight on its way to town. Aboard were Delilah and her six protégées, as she liked to call them.

"It's a long walk," Chance said. "And that church service starts on time. Ride with me, Dora."

She shot him a deadly look. Turning on her heel, she set off at a brisk march.

Delilah cackled behind her, and the girls dissolved into giggles as their surrey rumbled on, catching her up. Chance called after her. It should have given her great pleasure to ignore him, only she couldn't forget their conversation yesterday morning.

It was as if he were an entirely different person when they'd stood together looking out across the wide valley at what remained of her father's cattle.

He'd spoken passionately about ranching, the land, what a man could make of himself if he so chose. The way he'd looked when he'd said it, the longing in his eyes was what she remembered most.

"Honey, it's nearly nine."

Dora was jarred from her thoughts as Delilah pulled the conveyance to a halt just ahead of her.

"Hop up here next to me, and we'll get you to church, pronto." She shooed one of the girls to the back, and patted the seat next to her.

"Oh, no, I—" She almost said *couldn't,* but stopped herself. She didn't want to appear rude. Her mother would roll in her grave if she knew Dora had even entertained the idea of riding into town with a woman like Delilah.

"Oh, come on. Sure you can. We won't bite." She patted the seat again. A couple of the girls encouraged her.

The notion was appealing on one level. She didn't want to be late for services. If she was going to woo the townsfolk to her cause, she had to do everything right. That included being timely and courteous. Besides, John Gardner had said he'd wait for her in the vestibule. She owed it to the banker to be on time.

On the other hand, arriving early aboard a surrey with a bevy of soiled doves would not advance her cause. Nor would it recommend her to the townspeople as a suitable role model to teach their children. On the contrary.

"Thank you, Mrs...." What was the woman's surname? She never did find out.

"It's Delilah, honey. Nobody except lawyers and bill collectors call me anything else. Come on, now. Time's wasting."

Chance trotted up on Silas. The mere sight of him, and the unpleasant thought of him following her the rest of the way into town, was enough to sway her decision. Dora climbed up onto the surrey, and Delilah snapped the reins.

They were late for the service anyway, and in the end Dora was relieved. Delilah had refused to drop her off before they reached the church, so she could walk the last few blocks on her own, without the company of seven prostitutes and the gambler who rode behind them.

Mercifully, John Gardner was already in his seat when Dora entered the church. She joined him. Chance, Delilah and the girls sat in back. It astonished her that no one seemed to pay them any mind. They appeared to be as welcome as the rest of the congregation. In fact, following the service, the preacher walked right up to Chance and shook his hand. She wondered if he, like Mr. Grimmer, was another of Chance's victims at the card table.

"I'd be happy to escort you home," John said to her on the front steps of the church after the service.

Moments ago he'd introduced her to a half-dozen businessmen, some of them members of the town council. Before she could tell them of her plan to turn the Royal Flush into a school, they'd gushed on about how wonderful it was that she'd taken over her father's business, and oh, what a fine business it was, drawing all kinds of people to Last Call, and wasn't that good for the town's economy.

"She has a ride," Chance said, appearing at her side.

"With you?" John's face was stone.

"No, with us!" Delilah waved her over. She and the girls were already seated in the surrey.

"You came with *them?*"

"Oh, no, I…" How was she to explain? "I mean yes, I did, but not by design." What on earth would he think of her? It was bad enough that she owned the Royal Flush and was living there. There were still no vacancies in town.

"Her buckboard threw a wheel," Chance said. "Let's go, Miss Fitzpatrick." He took her arm and pulled her down the steps.

"Wait a minute!"

She didn't even get to wish John Gardner a proper goodbye. A few minutes earlier, before he'd introduced her around, the banker had asked her if she'd join him for luncheon in town on Wednesday. He'd said he wanted to speak with her about her father's mortgage. She'd hadn't had the opportunity to reply.

John was a nice man and wildly attractive. She was surprised he wasn't already married. She was doubly surprised he showed an interest in her, an interest that seemed to go beyond a discussion of her father's affairs, if she was reading his eyes and his mannerisms correctly.

"Wednesday, then," she called out to him on impulse.

"I'll pick you up. Noon all right?" His smile was like sunshine.

"Perfect."

Chance looked positively irritated as he helped her onto the surrey. Delilah drove them out of sight before she had an opportunity to wave goodbye to John.

"I'd watch him, if I were you," Delilah said, as

she guided the surrey onto the bumpy road leading out to the ranch.

"Mr. Wellesley?" she said, glancing back at Chance, who followed them on Silas.

"Him, too. But I meant the other one. That banker."

"Why do you say that? Mr. Gardner seems like a perfectly amiable gentleman."

Delilah arched a brow at her. "He may be, on first blush and all, but there's somethin' about the man I never liked. Can't exactly put my finger on what it is, but I'd be careful if I was you."

It was clear that, despite what the other townspeople thought of Delilah and her girls, John Gardner did not approve of them. That, in and of itself, might be the sole motive behind Delilah's dislike of the man. Dora brushed it off.

"You'd best listen to her," one of the girls whispered in her ear.

Dora slid around on her seat. "Daisy, isn't it?"

"Yes, ma'am."

"And I'm Iris," the girl sitting next to her said. "And this here's Lily—" she nodded at the girl to her left, then pointed to the back "—and Columbine and Rose." The two girls waved to her from the back seat.

"You're all named after flowers. What an odd coincidence."

They laughed, all except Lily, who was the most striking. Dora guessed her to be about her own age, twenty-five or so. A tumble of dark hair framed her delicate features and set off sharp green eyes that watched Dora like a hawk.

"No coincidence," Delilah said. "I rename each

of my girls when they first come to work for me. It's
better that way. Gives 'em a fresh start.''

Fresh start was not exactly the term Dora would
have used to describe a woman's entrance into em-
ployment at the Royal Flush. All the same, she didn't
wish to appear rude, nor did she wish to probe.

''Lily makes all the gentlemen call her by her
proper name,'' Iris said.

Delilah rolled her eyes.

''Which is?'' Dora looked to Lily herself to answer.

''Mary Lou Sugrah,'' Iris blurted.

Lily shot her a look. ''*Miss* Sugrah to you.''

The girls dissolved into giggles.

Dora twisted around farther in her seat and smiled
at the last girl, jammed into the back seat beside Rose
and Columbine. She looked younger than the others,
and had big doe eyes that lent her a fragile, almost
childlike quality. ''And what's your name?''

The girl smiled back. ''I'm Susan, ma'am. Pleased
to meet you.''

''Susan? That's not a flower name.''

Delilah snorted, and the rest of them, all except
Lily, laughed.

Rose was the first to recover. ''Miss Delilah named
her Lazy Susan, seeing as how she's so slow and all.''

''Slow?'' Dora frowned. ''At what?''

They burst into another round of laughter. Delilah
tried to hush them, but eventually gave up.

Susan leaned forward so Dora could hear her. ''I
can only manage two or three customers a night. The
other girls can double that. Why, Lily here can sometimes triple it, can't you, Lily?''

Dora's face grew hot.

"My record's fourteen, but that was in the winter. The nights are longer." Lily tipped her nose in the air and looked out across the range toward the snow-capped peaks, making it clear she was bored with the conversation.

"Oh," Dora said, trying to hide her shock. "I…uh, see."

"You girls hush now!" Delilah said. "Don't be bothering Miss Dora with your stories."

Dora turned back in her seat, grateful for the older woman's intervention.

"Don't pay 'em no mind. They're ninnies, most of 'em. Wouldn't know how to get by in this world if it weren't for me and your pa taking 'em in."

Dora considered their predicament now that the Royal Flush was closed. "Surely they can get work elsewhere. There are two other saloons right here in town."

"Don't you worry about it. They'll find a place. Won't be as nice as the Flush, and they won't be treated half as good as me and your pa treated 'em. Like daughters, is what Bill used to say."

"Did he?" The thought of it made her feel funny inside.

"Oh, not like you, of course. Bill was wild about you. Talked about you all the time."

"He did?"

"Oh, sure. He'd sneak off to the Springs just to get a look at you."

"He told you that?"

"Didn't have to. He was a fine man, your pa." Delilah abruptly lowered her gaze, then roused the horses to pick up the pace.

Dora studied her profile as she drove the surrey

toward home. Under all that face paint she was a handsome woman, and had likely been beautiful when she was young. Something about her seemed strangely familiar, yet Dora was certain she'd never seen Delilah before arriving at the Royal Flush.

"Those men that Mr. Gardner introduced me to at church…"

"Hmm?"

"They made it seem as if the whole town depends on the business my father's saloon brings to Last Call."

Delilah nodded. "It does. Boardinghouses, the hotel, the mercantile and livery, the laundry, the barber shop, the stage… Heck, even the other two saloons fare better because of us. Last Call's nothing without the Flush. It was nothing before your pa arrived, and it'll be nothing again."

"You really think so?"

"I know so, honey. I was here before your pa quit ranching. Last Call was barely a stage stop and a few shacks."

"Hmm." All the same, the town would still need a school, although most of the children lived on outlying ranches. She'd confirmed that fact at church today. "Where will you go now?"

Delilah sighed. "Don't know, exactly. But it's time for me to move on, what with…" She paused and sucked a breath. "With the Flush closing and all."

Dora had the oddest feeling Delilah had meant to say something else, but had stopped herself.

She thought about John Gardner's advice to her that first day, to close the saloon until a suitable buyer could be found. Would the bank not go under, as well, if the Royal Flush closed its doors and the town's trade dried up?

She'd hate to be responsible for an economic disaster, but she simply had no choice. She couldn't be the proprietress of a drinking establishment and gambling house. It simply wasn't proper. Besides, she had her heart set on opening a school. Now she wondered how she might fund it, if the town's enterprises dwindled. Schools were often run on taxes. If Last Call had no thriving businesses, there would be no taxes.

"What am I going to do?" she said to herself.

Delilah tossed her a sober look. "You're your pa's girl, I can see that right off. You'll do what's right. That's what he always did."

"You thought a lot of him, didn't you?"

She didn't answer, and Dora took that as a *yes*.

Glancing back at Chance, she wondered, not for the first time, what he was hiding—or hiding from. If she closed the saloon now, she'd never find out. She'd also never get to know the woman whom she'd come to believe had known her father better than anyone else.

You're your pa's girl.

Was she?

That afternoon, while the staff was assembled in the dining room sharing their last Sunday dinner together, and while Chance Wellesley was across the hall packing his bag, Dora stood in front of the walnut bureau in her father's bedroom and, for the first time since she'd arrived at the ranch, went through his personal belongings.

She realized she knew little about him except what she'd gleaned from his letters and what other people had told her. Opinions as to what kind of a man he was diverged wildly.

Her mother had called him reckless, a dreamer, a poor husband and an unsuitable father who'd abandoned them in favor of a carefree life. But that's not the impression she'd gotten from speaking with the people she'd met here, or from reading his recently discovered letters to her.

His room was neat and elegant, not at all what she would have expected. The walls were papered in a dark paisley print and trimmed in rich, burnished pine. The window coverings were velvet, a deep midnight blue. It was a man's room, a gentleman's room, by all appearances.

Excitement and fear gathered inside her as she opened the top drawer of the bureau and peeked inside. Amongst those things she expected to find—a razor and shaving brush, some handkerchiefs and neckties—was something she didn't expect.

"It can't be."

She plucked the child's toy, a small stuffed rabbit, from between the stacks of handkerchiefs and looked at it. A strange feeling welled inside her. It was *her* rabbit, one she'd had as a girl. She wouldn't have remembered it had she not seen it again, but seeing it, she'd never forget it. He'd given it to her when she was four or five, but she couldn't recall what had happened to it.

Delving beneath another stack of handkerchiefs, she withdrew something even more surprising. "Oh!" A lock of pale blond hair, tied with a piece of pink ribbon. More than anything, she wanted to believe it was her hair, that he'd kept it all these years along with the rabbit.

She laid the items out on top of the bureau, then fished her diary out of the pocket of her dress. Inside, next to the letter she kept with her at all times, she'd placed the tintype she'd found in her father's safety deposit box. She plucked it from between the pages and looked at it.

Wild Bill Fitzpatrick. The name suited him, she decided. His eyes were shining and his smile was warm. How she wished, now, that she'd known him.

In the tintype he had one hip perched on a table that looked as if it had seen better days. On top of the table was an elaborately crafted iron birdcage. No bird. Part of the image had been smudged, the lower left corner near her father's right hand. "Hmm."

She tucked the lock of hair and the rabbit carefully back between the stacks of handkerchiefs, and recalled Chance Wellesley's bold pronouncement yesterday afternoon.

You're afraid.

Was she?

She was, a little, but the fact that he, a gambler and a rogue, could look inside her and plainly see it, did more to fuel her courage than all the innate fortitude she possessed. She was no shrinking violet.

Abruptly she slammed the drawer shut.

"Whoa!"

She whirled toward the half-open door, startled by the deep timbre of his annoyingly familiar voice. Chance stood in the hallway, peering in, a dark brow arched in question.

"It's rude to sneak up on people like that." She pocketed the tintype and her diary.

"Sorry. I was just—"

Blasting past him, she closed the door to her father's room and locked it with the key she'd obtained from Delilah. She noticed Chance wasn't carrying a bag.

"Why haven't you left yet?" She gave him a quick once-over and realized he was not attired in traveling clothes. She'd specifically told him he'd have to be on his way this afternoon.

"I was just coming to talk to you about that. Now, as I see it, a woman like you, a woman alone, needs a man around to—"

She turned her back on him and made her way to the spiral staircase. As she descended, she gave a moment's thought to the repercussions of what she was about to do. They seemed minor compared to what would be lost were she to keep to her original course.

Quiet conversation drifted from the dining room as she paused at the bottom of the stairs to adjust the tidy bun that was her sole hairstyle. She smoothed her gray dress, then made her way down the long hallway.

As expected, Chance dogged her heels. She was determined, from now on, not to let him intimidate or embarrass her. If others could tolerate him, so could she. It was within her power to banish him from the Flush, but that wouldn't be good for business, and business was what she had in mind.

She stopped under the archway leading to the dining room. Chance slid past her and hitched a hip on the walnut sideboard, his gaze fixed heatedly on hers. He absently twirled his watch fob, a habit that annoyed her, and waited to see what she'd do next.

Mr. Wellesley, you're in for a surprise.

She turned her attention to the staff, who'd ceased all conversation and were looking at her with saucer-like eyes. The meal they were eating smelled delicious. She'd had nothing since breakfast and could die for a plate of Jim's biscuits and fried chicken.

"I've made a decision," she said. "The Royal Flush will remain open—permanently."

Delilah dropped her fork.

"And I shall stay on, until a buyer can be found for both the saloon and the ranch." Her school teaching could wait.

Tom let out a whoop as Jim and Delilah raised their shot glasses in a toast. She had no idea people drank whiskey with fried chicken. The girls began chattering all at once. Susan remained quiet, her soft smile beaming at Dora like morning light.

Chance didn't exhibit the victory smile she'd expected of him. His expression was bittersweet, as if he'd gotten what he wanted, but now regretted it. She feared that soon she, too, would know that feeling.

She was well aware he'd been baiting her yesterday. He wanted the Royal Flush kept open. She didn't know why, but she intended to find out. She'd also find out why a man whom she suspected was a former cattle rancher had forsaken his calling and had taken up gambling as a profession.

She stared at Chance, then Delilah. She thought about her father and her mother, and knew that in time she'd discover everyone's secrets. For the present, however, she had business to attend to. Solving mysteries would have to wait.

"There's one more thing I'd like you all to know."

"What's that, Miss Dora?" Jim, along with the others, snapped to attention.

"As proprietress, I'll be running both the ranch and the saloon—my way."

Chance cleared his throat. That cat-who-ate-the-canary smile of his was back, and frankly she was glad to see it. He was much easier to deal with this way. At least she knew what to expect.

"Whatever you say, Miss Dora." Jim exchanged loaded glances with Delilah.

"And, Jim..." She cast him a pointed look. "If I have to tell you one more time to remove that indecent painting from above my bar, I really will close this place and put you all on the next stage to Garo."

"Yes, ma'am!"

Chapter Five

Be careful what you wish for.

Chance wasn't much for old sayings, but considered this one as he bounded down the carpeted steps of the spiral staircase into an uproar. It was half past seven in the morning, a time when all self-respecting gamblers, bartenders, piano players and whores should be asleep.

"That's right," Dora said as she directed Tom and Jim, who were moving the piano closer to the bar. "Just a few more feet."

The two men shot him pained glances, grunting under the weight of the instrument.

"Perfect!" She smiled at them. "Now, rearrange all the card tables as we discussed. And get rid of that painting!"

"The danged thing is heavy as sin, Miss Dora." Jim wiped his balding pate with a bar towel.

"It's the frame," Tom said. "Carved walnut. Your pa ordered it special last year, all the way from Kansas City."

"Yes, well, it's lovely, but…"

"Come on, Tom." Jim waved him toward the bar. "Let's put the pretty lady away."

Chance grinned. True to her word, Dora Fitzpatrick had taken charge and was running things her way. God help them all. He'd like to think it was his influence that had changed her mind about keeping the saloon open, but he knew there was more to it than that. Something had happened between yesterday morning when they'd had their conversation and yesterday afternoon.

When he'd caught her unaware in her father's room, cradling that toy, he'd read a vulnerability in her eyes that had stunned him. Right then and there, he'd realized that somewhere under that prim, self-righteous exterior was a woman with feelings.

Shaking off the image, he waited until Tom and Jim had removed the painting and carried it out to the hallway, then grabbed a cup of coffee from behind the bar. Iris and Rose hemmed him in, scrub brushes in hand. He maneuvered around them and approached their new taskmaster.

Dora acknowledged him with a polite but cool nod.

He gave her one of his smiles in return. "First time I've ever seen any of these girls on their knees doing something besides…well, you know." He left the rest to her imagination.

Behind the bar, Iris and Rose giggled.

Dora didn't raise a brow, didn't so much as flush. He admired her fortitude. "Those floors are filthy," she said. "They haven't been scrubbed in months. Someone has to do it." She turned on her heel and whipped open her diary, running a finger down a neatly printed list. When he tried to read over her shoulder, she snapped it shut. "Do you mind?"

He shrugged, amused, and downed another swig of coffee.

"Oh, Delilah, over here." Dora rushed to help her with an overflowing bucket of soapy water.

"Kitchen's nearly done. Don't know where Lily's got off to, but Columbine and Daisy are working like miners in there."

"Good. There was enough dirt and grease caked on that stove to conceal buried treasure." Dora relieved her of the heavy bucket. Water sloshed over the rim onto Bill's favorite Persian carpet.

Chance winced, set his cup down and stepped in. "Here. Let me help you."

"No need."

"I insist." He grabbed the bucket handle, covering her hand with his. It was the first time he'd touched her bare skin. She flashed her eyes at him.

They were almost blue, but not quite. When she let her guard down, which wasn't often, he recognized that same soft intelligence he'd noticed the night he'd secretly watched her writing in her diary.

"All right, then." She allowed him to take the bucket, her gaze still fixed on his. "As long as you're up, I suppose you might as well make yourself useful."

A lock of her hair had come loose and lay lightly across her cheek. He had a powerful urge to touch her, to reach out and tuck it back behind her ear.

"Yes, well…" Unnerved, she looked away, as if she'd read his thoughts. "You may set the bucket right here."

Watching her, he placed the bucket on the floor next to the bar in front of a cigar store Indian statue Bill had picked up somewhere. Dora dropped to her knees, grabbed the scrub brush from the soapy water and went to work on the statue.

"You never stop, do you?"

"Hmm?" She glanced up at him. "What do you mean?"

"You." He took in the rest of the staff, hard at work, carrying out her directives. "Them. All this."

Tom and Jim were moving furniture around, and the girls were cleaning. He spied Rowdy and Gus out front sweeping the porch, and now Delilah was perched on a chair, polishing the cut glass crystals of the chandelier that hung above the center of the room.

"You get a bee in your bonnet about something, and you don't stop till it's buzzing."

"If by that you mean I'm committed to carrying out my plans, then yes, you're correct, Mr. Wellesley."

"Chance. If we're going to be living here together, you really ought to call me Chance."

She arched a brow, then turned her attention to her work, scrubbing harder. "We're not—" she cleared her throat "—living together, but if you insist on making the Royal Flush your home, I suppose we can drop the formality of using our surnames when we're in private."

He suppressed a smile. He'd never insisted, as he recalled, he'd just dragged his feet. And once she'd decided to keep the saloon open, she hadn't exactly tossed him out on his ear. She'd allowed him to stay because he was good for business—at least that's what she wanted him to think.

But there was more to it than that. She wanted him to stay because, despite her better judgment, she liked him. It was as simple as that. He'd felt it when he'd touched her hand, and again when he'd looked into her eyes and discovered that subtle vulnerability that hit him in the gut like a punch.

He could use that to his advantage. He meant to use it, to use her. All his months of watching and waiting were finally about to pay off. Wild Bill Fitzpatrick had hidden a fortune somewhere before he died. His daughter knew where it was. Only she didn't know she knew.

"But now that we *are* in private, Dora—" he glanced at her troop of dedicated workers "—or nearly so, what exactly are your plans?"

"Oh!" She dropped the scrub brush and sat back on her heels. "Will you look at that."

"What?"

She placed her hands against the base of the wooden Indian and pushed, putting all her weight into it.

"What are you doing?"

"Look!" She plucked a bank note from the floor. "It was underneath the statue. Why, it's a hundred dollars!"

Delilah visibly paled. She scrambled down from the chair on which she was perched, forgetting the chandelier that was now swaying overhead. Tom exchanged a look with Jim. They all crowded around her, elbowing Chance out of the way.

Iris and Rose popped up from behind the bar, then called for the other girls to come out from the kitchen. Lily appeared on the balcony at the top of the stairs. She stood there, looking down at them.

Chance was ready for what came next.

"It's just the one bank note, I guess." Dora inspected the floor after the men muscled the statue out of the way. She had a strange look on her face, as if she were trying to remember something that was just beyond her recollection.

"Let me see that." Chance reached into the throng and snatched the bill from her hand. Holding it up to the morning light, he studied it.

"Give it back to me. It's not yours." Dora moved in closer, peering at the bill alongside him.

"Maybe not," he said, satisfied at how the little scene was playing out. "But it won't do you any good, either."

"What do you mean?" She took it from him and frowned, holding it up to the light and studying it as he had.

"I mean it's counterfeit."

"What?"

Delilah and the girls exchanged looks. Tom's mouth dropped open. Jim merely shrugged.

"It's a fake," Chance said, watching their reactions, Dora's in particular. "Counterfeit currency. Surely your friend Gardner warned you about that kind of thing."

"Well…yes, he did, but…" Her frown deepened. "How do you know it's not real?"

"I just do."

She looked at him hard, as if she were trying to see beneath the surface, as if she knew there was something more there. There had been, once, but that was a long time ago, and he'd been a different man.

"But how?"

He shot her a smile. "It's my business to know." Which was the first true thing he'd told her about himself since the moment he'd laid eyes on her.

"You mean because you're a gambler."

He didn't answer, and she walked away, still frowning, snapping the crisp hundred-dollar note between her fingers.

They all returned to their chores. Only Lily remained, still and silent on the balcony, watching as Dora slipped the counterfeit note between the pages of her diary, right beside the letter she was so fond of reading over and over. A letter he knew was from her father. A letter he meant to read tonight.

Dora lay awake in the dark, in the narrow bed in the cabin behind the house. She'd deliberately left the lace curtains open so she could see the second-floor window of the room from which Chance had been asked to move. Only he hadn't moved. He was intent on keeping an eye on her, and she knew why.

His light had been out for hours, which was unusual. And he'd acted strangely the rest of that morning and the whole of the afternoon. She'd retired early, following the light supper that Jim had laid out in the kitchen for the staff. Monday nights in the saloon were busy, and she hadn't seen Chance since.

She was about to see him now.

A shadow passed her window. She tensed, recognizing the set of his shoulders, that strong profile, his unfashionably long and tousled hair. She'd deliberately left her door unlocked to make it easy for him.

But she was no fool. She'd also made certain the small, pearl-handled derringer she'd found in her father's desk that afternoon was tucked conveniently under her pillow. She'd never used a gun, but she knew how. The mystery novels she'd devoured had described the process in detail.

When she heard Chance try the doorknob, she

knew her hunch had been right. He'd been eyeing her diary from the moment he'd discovered it wasn't the bible he'd been so certain she carried on her person at all times.

Unless Chance had told them, she was fairly certain the rest of the staff believed it *was* a bible. She'd done nothing to alter their perception, and had made sure never to let them see her writing in it. She wasn't usually so secretive, but intuition, which she rarely relied on, told her in this case the idea was prudent.

Moonlight reflected off the brass knob as it turned. Dora rolled quickly onto her side, hunkered down between the sheets and pulled the covers up to her nose. She snapped her eyes shut as the door swung silently open.

A draft of night air washed over her. She drew a breath infused with leather and sandalwood shaving soap, and knew he was in the room with her. Her skin prickled beneath the fine-weight cotton of her nightgown.

His footsteps were nearly imperceptible. The door clicked shut, and she felt rather than heard him pause, waiting to see if she'd awaken. She lay still as stone, forcing herself to breathe slowly, deeply, mimicking sleep.

Thank heavens he couldn't hear her heartbeat, which thumped inside her like the bright snap of the snare drums she'd once heard in a rare Denver performance of John Philip Sousa's band.

Her father's last letter to her lay on the desk by the undraped window, the parchment a soft silvery gray in the moonlight. She'd left it there on purpose for him to read. Her diary, however, was in bed with her, under the pillow next to the derringer.

Some things she had no intention of sharing. The letter, on the other hand, had revealed little to her that was tangible, and if Chance Wellesley could decipher more from her father's words than she had, so be it. That was her plan. Two could play at this game. She would be the one keeping a close eye on him from now on.

If there was money hidden somewhere on the ranch—and she was beginning to think there was— she was determined to find it, even if Chance Wellesley had to lead the way. That hundred-dollar bank note she'd discovered under the statue this morning had not been the first. She'd found others while poking around the house, but hadn't tipped her hand, so to speak, until today.

She'd wanted to gauge their reactions, all together and all at once. The opportunity had presented itself, and she was pleased with the results. She was not pleased, however, to learn the bill was counterfeit. Chance had been right.

That afternoon she'd gotten hold of a Colorado Springs newspaper that a customer had left in the saloon. A half-page article expounded on the rash of counterfeit currency being circulated in the West, and included detailed descriptions of what to look for.

The article had also discussed the new breed of lawmen, agents of the United States Secret Service, who were charged with ridding the country of false currency and bringing counterfeiters to justice.

Dora held her breath and risked a peek from beneath her lashes.

Chance stood at the desk with his back to her, silhouetted in the moonlight, his hand on her father's letter. Silently he picked it up and, tilting it toward the silvery light, began to read.

Who are you? she wondered as she watched him in the dark. He took his time, sliding the pages one behind the other as he read and reread them. If there was something there, some clue that wasn't obvious, she suspected he was just the man to recognize it. Chance Wellesley had a shrewdness about him that wasn't apparent on the surface. One had to look to see it—and she was looking.

He replaced the letter on the desk, careful to refold and position it exactly as it had been when he'd entered the room. She watched him as he moved to the bureau by the potbelly stove that provided the tiny cabin with heat.

Quietly he slid open each drawer and rifled through her things. He was looking for the diary, or perhaps he was looking for the contents of her father's safety deposit box. The tintype was tucked safely away between the pages of her diary. It was precious to her, and she wouldn't risk losing it.

The tortoiseshell comb, on the other hand, was still wrapped in the newsprint that had lined the box. She had no reason to hide it from him. He discovered it in the third drawer, unwrapped it and looked at it briefly, then returned it to its place amongst her stockings. Likely he thought it was hers.

Her eyes widened as he selected one of her stockings from the drawer and held it up to the light. Her anger surged as he rubbed the thin, dark wool between his fingers. How dare he handle her undergarments? When he had the audacity to brush the top of the stocking across his upper lip, letting it linger there, she let out a muffled squeak.

Chance whirled on her.

She snapped her eyes shut and rustled around in the bed, emitting more squeaks and sighs, feigning a dream. She wasn't the only one who could act.

She heard the drawer of the bureau slide closed, and Chance's nearly silent footfalls on the pine flooring as he moved quickly to the door. Another draft of night air washed over her as he slipped outside and she heard the doorknob turn behind him. His shadow was visible as he moved along the back of the house toward the steps leading to the kitchen.

She'd done it!

Dora breathed relief. She leaped from the bed and shot to the window. She watched as Chance crept up the back stairs and went inside. A new cat was in town, she thought mischievously, and the canary had no idea she was on the prowl.

"Three ladies. Read 'em and weep, boys." The marshal laid out his cards, raked in his winnings and beamed them a smug grin.

The men at the table groaned. One of them threw in his hand, then wandered upstairs with Lily to forget how much money he'd lost that night.

Chance gave the marshal a halfhearted smile. "Seems to be your night, Max." He gathered up the cards and began to shuffle. "Go again?"

"Nah, it's past midnight. Best get home or the wife'll skin me alive."

"Boys?" Chance said to the rest of them.

Grimmer looked like he wished someone would do him a favor and put him out of his misery. "Not me. I'm busted."

Chance knew it was true. The attorney played

poker with him twice a week, and never went home until all his money was spent. Mortimer Grimmer had a bad gambling habit, which was why he'd continued to hound Dora for the pittance her father owed him for handling his business affairs.

The other players murmured sentiments similar to the attorney's. Chance glanced at the other tables, thinking to pick up another game, but his heart wasn't in it.

The marshal shot him a look as he rose from his chair. "Never seen you lose so many straight. You okay?"

"Hmm?" He'd only been half listening. For a moment he thought he'd seen Dora in the shadowed hallway off the kitchen. "Uh, yeah. Right as rain."

The truth was that he was distracted, and had been for the past week, since the night Dora Fitzpatrick arrived at the Royal Flush.

Jim wandered over from the bar and set a fresh glass of beer in front of him. As he gathered up the empty glasses and full ashtrays, he said, "Never seen her over here before, this time of night." The bartender nodded at the shadowed figure in the hall.

Chance hadn't, either. Since she'd decided to keep the place open, Dora had made it a point to steer clear of the saloon when business was bustling. That meant most evenings. She'd said that while, legally, she was the proprietress of a drinking establishment, she had no intention of flaunting it, particularly during those times when other, even more scandalous commerce was being conducted. He smiled, remembering. Never in his life had he met a woman who referred to gambling and whoring as commerce. He also recalled the shocked look on her face when Delilah had suggested she join them all one evening for a drink.

"I'll be right back," Chance said. "Hold the table for me."

"You got it."

He nodded to Grimmer and Max, who were just leaving, then snaked his way around the crowded card tables toward the hall. It was busy for a Thursday night. Most of the girls were upstairs, and there were already lines forming outside the bedrooms.

Tom was playing up a storm on the piano, and in a few minutes Delilah would take to the stage and offer up a song. The woman surely could sing. He recalled how Wild Bill would stop whatever he was doing just to listen to her.

Jim handed off his load of glassware to one of the local waifs Dora had hired to wash dishes in the evening. Chance had to give her credit. In a matter of days she'd whipped the place into shape. The floors shined, the draperies and Persian carpets smelled fresh, and the chandelier gleamed along with every spittoon in the place. The customers, delighted with their sparkling surroundings, even began using them instead of the floor. The Royal Flush was, at last, the showplace it was always meant to be. Wild Bill would have been proud of his daughter.

But what was she up to now?

She'd been dogging his steps for days. In the beginning, he'd been the one following her. Now the shoe was on the other foot. She'd shown an inexplicable interest in him lately that didn't add up. Not that he disliked her interest. He liked it, and that was reason enough for him to be cautious.

He opted for the long way around, moving quietly into the hallway off the far end of the saloon. He paused a moment, allowing his eyes to adjust to the dim light. Dora stood not ten feet from him, her back turned, her arms outstretched like a tightrope walker. In one hand she clutched her diary, in the other a fountain pen.

What the devil was she doing?

She paced off the steps from the center of the hallway to its end near the kitchen. Then she flipped open the diary and scribbled an entry. He realized she was about to turn. The door to her father's study was open. He ducked inside where it was dark and waited.

"One, two, three…" She was counting her steps. Now why would she do that?

He'd learned almost nothing from his discreet visit to her cabin a few nights ago. Nothing, at least, that had revealed any more than he'd already known about Wild Bill Fitzpatrick and the money, and who his partner might have been.

"Five, six, seven…"

Her stocking had smelled faintly of lilac, of her. He drew a breath and could still smell it. He didn't know if it was the power of his imagination or the fact that in a few more steps she'd be standing next to him.

It occurred to him that Bill might not have brought her in on his shenanigans, after all. His letter to her had been cryptic. Chance knew there were other letters, but Dora kept that damned trunk of hers locked, and he'd need more time alone in her cabin if he was going to read them.

"Nine, ten…"

In the end he *would* read them—and her diary. What worried him was that he felt bad about it.

You've gone soft, Wellesley.

The end justified the means. That's what he'd told himself the past eighteen months, and that's what he believed. It was the reason he'd been able to do some of the less savory things he'd done. It was the reason he'd be able to do what he was now about to do to Dora Fitzpatrick.

"Twelve."

He stepped out of the darkness and grabbed her.

"Oh!" She dropped her pen and diary and turned into his arms. "Chance!"

She *was* wearing lilac, and it hit him like a shot of whiskey straight up.

"You're up late," he said.

"Um…yes."

He held on to her, and to his surprise she didn't try to get away.

"What were you doing just now?"

"Doing?" Her breath was warm on his face as she looked up at him in the dark. "Why, nothing. Just, um…"

He ought to let her go and grab the diary. That had been his plan. He ought to, but…

She did try to get away, then, as if she'd suddenly read his thoughts, as if she knew how damned good she felt in his arms. She tried, but he wouldn't let her go.

"Kiss me," he said, on impulse.

Her sharp intake of breath, the immediate tension in her body were signs that should have stopped him. But he didn't stop.

"No!" She struggled as he pulled her closer! Her hips tilted into him.

"One kiss," he said. "You know you want to."

"I…I *don't* want to."

"I do." He tilted his head and kissed her.

Chapter Six

It was her first kiss.

She'd read about kissing, of course. After all, she was a schoolteacher. It was important for her to have a command of all subjects. Only she wasn't the one in command in this particular situation.

Chance pulled her firmly against him, his hands snaking around her waist and up her back. His lips were warm, his tongue hot as it teased the tightly pressed seam of her mouth, seeking entrance.

She couldn't breathe. She couldn't think.

Instinctively she'd closed her eyes and had placed her hands against his chest. At first she'd pushed at him, working to extricate herself from his grip. She wasn't pushing anymore. Her hands slid upward and came to rest around his neck.

The tinny piano music and men's laughter, the pungent scents of beer and cigar smoke drifting from the saloon, all faded from her awareness. All her senses were trained on him now.

Chance deepened the kiss, and she gasped. He made a throaty sound, taking her response as acquiescence.

You know you want to.

His words burned in her mind. She *had* wanted to, and wanted it still. She gave herself up to the moment and dared to kiss him back. It was the singular most exciting thing she'd ever done in her life.

Heat suffused her body. And his.

He backed her against the wall, his fingers tangling in her hair, releasing her tight bun into a golden cascade that spilled nearly to her waist. Fisting a handful of it, he rolled his hips suggestively into hers. She realized with a shock that the situation had moved far beyond anything she'd ever read about in books.

"Mmm."

"Oh!" Her eyes flew open.

His gaze flashed heat in the dim lamplight spilling from the kitchen at the end of the hall. She'd never seen him this way. So intense, so serious, so…

He abruptly broke the kiss.

She sensed a change come over him, a hesitation in the way he held her, as if he wasn't sure what he was doing or why, which was precisely how *she* felt.

"Well, well, what have we here?" Lily stood, hands on slim hips, silhouetted in the doorway at the opposite end of the long hall.

Chance instantly transformed his conduct. He jerked Dora tightly against him, the roguish grin that was his trademark flashing like lightning across his face. "Just having a bit of fun."

"Fun?" Dora pulled out of his grasp, and he laughed softly.

"If it's fun you're wantin', Chance honey, come on upstairs with me." Lily crooked her finger at him.

"I thought you were already…engaged, or I would have earlier."

"Not now I'm not, but I'd like to be—with you."

Dora was mortified. She retrieved her diary and pen from the carpet where she'd dropped them. As she tried to move past Chance, he caught her arm.

"Join us?" he said, affecting his most devilish grin.

She felt suddenly sick to her stomach. Mustering her pride, she spun on her heel, her nose in the air, and marched back down the hallway toward the saloon. The sound of his laughter burned in her ears.

To her shock, Delilah was waiting for her at the end of the corridor. Dora wondered how long she'd been standing there and what, if anything, she'd seen and heard.

"I want *you* to come with me."

"I really don't have time right now, Delilah. I was reviewing my father's books and I noticed that Jim's been ordering way too much whiskey for this time of—"

The older woman grabbed her shoulders. "It's past midnight. The books and the ordering can wait." Delilah steered her toward the entrance to the back of the stage and into the tiny dressing room where the girls kept costumes for special occasions. After lighting the lamp, she pointed to an upholstered stool. "Now sit."

All the fight had gone out of her. Dora did as she was told.

"I saw what went on back there."

"Between Chance and Lily? I suppose as long as he pays like everyone else, it's all right. But we're running a business here, and—"

"Between Chance and *you*."

Dora sucked in a breath, denials and explanations

poised on her lips. Delilah arched a neatly plucked brow at her. Nothing that went on at the Royal Flush got past the woman. Dora exhaled. "Oh."

"I'm gonna give you some advice."

"I really don't need you to mother me." Her own mother would have been shocked at her behavior a minute ago. Her advice would have been to spend a day in church on her knees, praying for enlightenment and forgiveness. She didn't think Delilah's advice would be quite as self-condemning, but the gist of it would likely be the same.

"I think you do. And whether you want it or not, I'm giving it, so listen up."

Dora folded her hands in her lap and gave Delilah her full attention.

"Your father thought a lot of that man."

"Of Chance?" It was the last thing she'd expected her to say.

"Yes. And so do I. Most of the time, anyway. Not that he hasn't pulled some harebrained stunts around here, like what he did back there."

"You mean with me." It was painfully clear Chance had been toying with her.

"I mean that little act with Lily."

"Oh." Now she was truly confused.

"But make no mistake, underneath all that charm and affectation lies a real man. A man with a heart. Even if he's lost his good sense."

Dora had no idea what she was talking about.

"But you watch yourself around him, you hear."

That piece of advice she understood clearly. "I plan to."

"Well, good. Now get yourself off to bed. I suspect

you'll have us all up early again tomorrow, prettyin'
the place up.''

Dora stood and gave her a small smile. Delilah was
the one with the heart. It occurred to her that the older
woman had a lot to lose with the saloon changing
hands. Never once had she suggested Dora keep it.
"Not too early," she said. "I'm exhausted."

Delilah winked at her. "That man's kiss does
things to a woman—so they say."

"That's not what I meant." Dora followed her out
to the dimly lit hallway. It was empty. Chance and
Lily had gone upstairs. She felt a brief stab of anger,
followed by jealousy and self-reproach, a volatile fusion of emotions she'd never before experienced in
her twenty-five years.

"Maybe not," Delilah said, "but that doesn't mean
I'm not right."

Chance leaned back in the saddle and tried to rub
the kink out of his neck.

Silas turned and looked at him.

"What do you know about it? You're a gelding,
remember?" He fished a carrot he'd nabbed from the
kitchen out of his pocket and handed it to the horse.

Silas munched away as Chance looked out across
the range, a wash of spring color thriving under sun
and sky. Melting snows fed the South Platte river, a
silver ribbon in the distance, where a handful of cattle
grazed. The wind felt good on his face. He needed a
sobering up after last night, but not because he'd been
drunk.

He'd been reckless.

Afterward, he'd gone upstairs with Lily to convince
himself—and Dora—that he'd felt nothing more than

animal lust when he'd kissed her, nothing beyond desire when she'd kissed him back.

But that was a damned lie.

And was the reason he now found himself riding aimlessly in circles on Silas, considering his next move. "What do you think, boy?" he said to the paint, who'd been with him since the beginning, his only confidant these past months.

Silas threw his head back and whinnied.

"Yeah, I like her, too, and that's a problem."

His interest in Dora Fitzpatrick was both distracting and dangerous. Distracting for him, and dangerous for her, which was why he had to nip it in the bud. He'd come too far to do otherwise.

Hoofbeats pulled him from his thoughts. He turned in the saddle, his hand jerking to his gun belt, then relaxed when he spied two familiar figures. Gus raised a gloved hand in greeting as he and Rowdy trotted past, heading in the direction of the stray cattle he'd seen by the river.

Chance didn't know much about either of them, except that they'd worked for Wild Bill a long time, long before he'd sold off all but six thousand acres of what had once been a sizable spread, long before he'd opened the Royal Flush.

Neither of them were high on his list of suspects, but he hadn't ruled them out. He hadn't ruled anyone out—not yet. It was too soon, and there was too much he didn't know.

While Silas finished his carrot, Chance pulled a hundred-dollar bank note out of his breast pocket—a counterfeit note, the same one he'd stolen from the top drawer of Dora's bureau when he'd visited her cabin four nights ago.

A dozen times over he'd done the arithmetic in his head. There was close to fifty thousand dollars in real currency unaccounted for at the Royal Flush. The question was who knew about it and who didn't? The answer would lead him straight to Wild Bill's silent partner and the men he'd been hunting, men who were going to pay.

Dora followed him around like a shadow, thinking he knew something she didn't. Smart woman. But was she stupid enough to be involved in her father's corruption, or was she merely an innocent tossed into a deadly situation she knew nothing about? In his gut he knew the answer to that question.

Here was his dilemma, then.... He had to draw Wild Bill's partner in, and at the same time keep Dora out of the way—for her own good. He was playing a dangerous game, and when he'd encouraged her to keep the saloon open, he hadn't counted on her being underfoot. He also hadn't counting on caring. He did care, but only because he didn't want her hurt. His feelings had nothing to do with last night. He'd be damned if they did.

Letting his eyes drift closed for a moment, he remembered how good she'd felt in his arms. He could still recall the play of her tongue against his, the passion he'd unleashed in her and had barely tasted before he'd come to his senses.

Dora Fitzpatrick was a spinster schoolteacher who'd never been kissed, until he'd kissed her. For her own good and his, he had to get her out of here. But how?

Silas stirred beneath him. Chance was instantly on his guard. A wagon rumbled up the road from Last Call. Spurring the paint into action, he trotted toward it and intercepted Jim Parker with his weekly load of supplies.

"What's the news from town?"

Jim pushed his hat back on his head and scratched his bald pate. "The marshal's wife's not speaking to him again. Grimmer's trying to sell that dappled nag of his. Oh, and I saw that banker buying a new suit of clothes at the mercantile this morning. Looked mighty fine in 'em, too."

"That so?"

He'd felt a stab of satisfaction earlier that week when Dora had postponed her luncheon with John Gardner to Friday. Today. She'd been busy ever since, turning the Royal Flush upside down, and turning him inside out. He ought to be encouraging her relationship with the banker. At least it would keep her occupied. But he hadn't encouraged it, and the reason bothered him more than he wanted to admit.

"Room's open at the hotel." Jim arched a brow at him. "First one in a month."

"Dora know that?"

"Not yet."

"Good. Don't tell her."

The bartender frowned.

Dilemma solved, Chance thought. Part of it, anyway. His mind was already working. He urged Silas to pick up the pace. "I know just the person to break the news."

"I am *not* moving to town. I can't possibly afford it." Dora narrowed her eyes past Lily to the bar, then widened them again in shock. "And how on God's green earth did that painting get back on the wall?"

She'd had the nude portrait removed days ago. She

spun on her heel toward Jim, who was sweeping up some broken glass by the piano.

"Don't look at me, Miss Dora. I had nothing to do with it."

"Me, neither," Tom said, as he maneuvered the piano out of the way, as she'd instructed, so Jim could get behind it with his broom.

She swept her gaze across the saloon, seeking out other likely suspects. It was midmorning, and the first customers of the day had begun to arrive.

She noticed Chance, who looked as if he'd been up for hours, leaning casually against the railing of the spiral staircase twirling his watch fob, one booted foot hitched on the step behind him.

Dora shot him a murderous look.

He shrugged.

Tom's attention drifted from the piano and the broken glass as Susan came out of the kitchen to see what all the commotion was over. The girl had obviously been baking. She had flour on her nose.

"If you lived in town," Lily said, "the painting wouldn't bother you."

"*We* wouldn't bother you," Susan said.

Dora stood close enough to Tom to hear him sigh, to see the light in his eyes as he watched the petite chestnut-haired girl. Susan seemed oblivious to her effect on the smitten piano player.

"You don't bother me," Dora said, after recovering herself. "Don't be silly."

"Well, some of us don't, I guess." Lily downed a shot of whiskey she'd poured herself from the bar. "Then again, I suspect some of us do."

She'd had just about enough of Lily's attitude. She told herself her feelings about Lily had nothing to do

with what had transpired last night between the two
of them and Chance. She wasn't in the least bit jeal-
ous. The thought was ludicrous.

The schoolteacher-turned-proprietress in her took
over. "What bothers me is when the staff depletes the
house's supply of liquor." She snatched the open bottle from off the bar and cast Lily a disapproving look.
"Liquor meant for paying customers."

A couple of miners who'd just come in sidled up
to the bar. Dora nodded at Jim. He handed his broom
to Tom and scurried past her, relieving her of the
whiskey bottle before taking his place behind the bar.
"What can I get you gentlemen?"

"There," Dora said, more to herself than to anyone
present. All was right with the world again. "Back to
work," she said to Lily and Susan. "You, too, Tom."
The piano player was still mooning.

Lily deliberately brushed her as she passed.
"You're worse than Delilah." Dora took that as a
compliment. She'd come to respect the older woman
as a hard worker and a shrewd businesswoman.

"I think you're wonderful," Susan said. "And I
don't want you to move to town. Lily don't, neither.
Not really. She's just being stuck-up."

Lily snorted, then transformed herself in time to
give Chance a seductive smile and a little pat on the
shoulder as she sauntered past him and up the stairs.
Chance arched a devilish brow in response.

It has no effect on me, no effect at all.

Despite her inner proclamation, Dora's blood
boiled every time she thought of the two of them
together. It boiled over when she thought of how
Chance had deliberately led her on last night, had
made a fool of her.

She'd made a fool of herself.

It would never happen again. Not if he were the last man on earth.

"Things is good here, now," Susan continued. "Ain't they, Tom?"

Tom's face lit up like the state Christmas tree. "They sure are, Miss Susan. They sure are." He swept the broken glass into a dustpan and followed her into the kitchen.

For a fleeting moment last night, she'd thought she'd read in Chance's eyes a hint of what she'd just seen in Tom's. Ridiculous, she told herself, and turned her back on the lot of them.

She had no idea what had possessed her in that darkened hallway. The devil, her mother would have concluded, if she'd been alive. And in this case, Dora was inclined to agree with her.

"You're in fine form today." Chance ambled past her and took his customary seat at one of the gaming tables. Jim set a beer down in front of him before he even had time to order.

Dora stopped the bartender with a look.

"Ma'am?"

"You allow Mr. Wellesley to run a tab, do you not?"

Jim shot Chance a quick look. "Well, uh, yes, Miss Dora. It's customary."

"Is it?" She looked down her nose at the gambler. He looked a bit disheveled this morning, and she recalled that he'd been out riding. "And where do you keep track of the amount Mr. Wellesley owes us?"

"Keep track?" Again, Jim looked to Chance for support. None was forthcoming. Chance merely sat there, looking smug. "Well, I pretty much keep track of it in my head. And, well…at the end of the week, Chance here pays me what's due.''

She considered that not once since she'd arrived had she ever seen Chance Wellesley drink anything stronger than beer. Never had she seen him consume whiskey. That seemed odd to her, given his profession, but beer wasn't free, and that was the point.

''So, you tell him the amount, and he pays you.''

Jim's face flushed. ''Well, not exactly.''

''I tell him the amount and then I pay him,'' Chance said. ''I keep track of it. Jim trusts me. Your father trusted me, too.''

It was exactly as she'd suspected. Who knew how much money he'd already swindled them out of. She reached into the deep pocket of her dress and pulled out a small black book. She handed it to the bartender. ''I'd like you to start keeping track of exactly how much Mr. Wellesley drinks during the week.''

Jim looked speculatively at the journal. ''Whatever you say, Miss Dora. Though I don't rightly think it's necessary.''

''Well, I do.'' She affected her iciest look and aimed it in Chance's direction.

He visibly shivered, then grinned. ''While you're at it, you might want to keep track of some of the other things I consume around here.'' He rocked back in his chair, propping a boot up on the table, then cast a glance over his shoulder to the balcony above, where Lily was just disappearing into one of the bedrooms.

She felt the color rise in her cheeks. The high-buttoned neck of her dress seemed suddenly too tight. She ground her teeth behind tightly pressed lips, determined not to let him bait her. "I'll get Delilah to do that."

Jim took the hint, and scurried back to the bar where more customers were gathering.

"You know, Lily's idea isn't half bad." Chance rocked his chair backwards, precariously far. One nudge would knock him to the floor.

Dora was sorely tempted. "What idea?"

"You moving to town. Away from all this… objectionable commerce." She followed his glance to the bar where Tom and Jim were, again, removing the nude portrait.

"You'd like that, wouldn't you?"

He was truly an enigma. At first he'd all but dared her to keep the saloon in operation and to remain here on the premises. Now he seemed to be invested in her departure. She wasn't fool enough to believe Lily had come up with the idea on her own.

"Not necessarily," he said, looking her up and down in a manner he knew annoyed her.

She fished her diary out of her pocket and opened it to the page she'd been penning earlier that morning in her father's study. "Perhaps you're the one who should move. Your living expenses are about to increase. As of today, I'm raising your rent to fifty dollars a week." She snapped the diary shut and marched from the room.

Chance pursued her, as she knew he would.

She made a beeline for her father's study, opened the door with the key she'd had ready in her hand, and allowed him to follow her inside. The draperies were open, and the room was bright and cheery, like the matter-of-fact demeanor she put on for his benefit. She took her place behind the desk, sat up straight in her father's leather chair and gave him her full attention.

"Fifty dollars a week is larceny."

"I know it is. However, that's the new price on the room you occupy, or any room you wish to occupy at my saloon."

"So it's your saloon now, is it?"

The look she gave him said the answer to his question should be obvious. "That includes full board, of course."

He harrumphed.

"In addition…" She opened the heavy ledger sitting atop her father's desk and flipped to the appropriate page. "The house's cut of your gambling profits has increased to—" she ran her finger along the entries made in ink in her father's hand "—twenty percent." It had been five percent.

Chance swore. "Seven percent and not a penny more."

"Fifteen."

"Ten."

"Done," she said, and closed the ledger.

He stormed to the window and looked out. She noticed, not for the first time, how broad his shoulders were in relation to his slim hips. She also noticed he'd taken to wearing two guns in his gun belt instead of one.

"Why?" he said, and turned to face her.

"Because I need the money and because you can afford it." Which was true. "I've seen you play cards. I know how much your winnings are on a good night."

"What about the bad nights?"

She arched a brow at him. "You don't have many of those." Last night had been an exception.

For the hundredth time since then, she thought about his hands on her, his heat, the way he'd looked at her just before he kissed her. It was as if he knew he shouldn't, but couldn't help himself. It had been one of those rare moments since she'd met him over a week ago that she'd felt she was seeing the real Chance Wellesley, the real man.

A man with a heart.

She hadn't forgotten Delilah's words.

His behavior since had nullified her instincts about him. And now, standing here in the light of day, looking into his eyes, she was confused.

"You don't like me much, do you?"

This was not a question she'd expected. "I...don't trust you. There's a difference."

He looked thoughtfully at the objects in her father's study—an old cattle brand mounted on the wall flanking the desk, a collection of Chinese puzzle boxes scattered across the walnut credenza, stacks of books on the floor—and as he did so, his expression changed.

She perceived a longing in his eyes she'd seen only once before, that morning on the range when he'd talked of ranching, the land, of what a man might make of himself if he had the chance.

His gaze settled on hers. "You're right not to trust me. I—"

"Yes?"

He paused, as if some terrible struggle were going on in his mind. Without thinking, she rose and came around the desk. He stood there, rigid, and before she realized what she was doing, she took his hand in hers.

He looked down at their hands, entwined.

She was aware of her beating heart, of the room growing warmer. He grazed her palm with his thumb, tenderly, with affection, and the sensation of it sent a shiver clear up her spine.

Then, without warning, as if he'd been dreaming and had all of a sudden come awake, he laughed. His face lit up, his eyes flashed mischief. She tried to draw her hand away as the man withdrew and the rogue appeared.

His fingers tightened over hers. "I've been known to lead women astray." To punctuate the point, he lifted one dark brow in a scandalously suggestive manner.

Dora pulled herself together. "Yes, well..." She yanked, and her hand was freed. She shook it to revive her circulation. "This woman is miraculously unaffected."

As she started around the desk, Chance caught her arm. "You're lying."

Now it was her turn to arch a brow. "You're the one who's lying, Mr. Wellesley."

"Chance," he said pointedly. Her words had wiped the smile from his face. His grip on her tightened.

She dug her heels into the Persian carpet and looked him square in the eye. "I don't know who you are, but make no mistake, I will find out. I'm not a saloon girl to be toyed with."

"I can see that." His eyes glittered with new appreciation.

"Furthermore, you will let go of my arm, and you

will not put your hands on me again. Is that under-stood?''

''Miss…uh, Fitzpatrick?''

Startled by the unfamiliar voice, her gaze flew to the open door.

''It's me, Miss Fitzpatrick. John Gardner.'' He stepped into the room, and in a heartbeat appraised the situation. His gaze settled disapprovingly on Chance. ''Everything all right here?''

''Right as rain,'' Chance said, and released her.

Dora breathed. She dismissed the gambler with a nod and turned her full attention on the banker, who was the finest figure of a man she'd ever seen, present company included.

Hat in hand, he was dressed in a dark woolen suit and brocade vest, the color of which set off his eyes, the most brilliant of blues. His boots were polished to a high sheen, completing the picture of a perfect gentleman.

Noting Chance's scowl, she smiled. ''Mr. Gard-ner…John. I wish you'd call me Dora.''

''Dora, then,'' he said, and beamed her a smile so sincere it would have made angels weep. ''I'm here to escort you to luncheon.''

''Your timing is perfect.'' She sidestepped Chance, walked to the door and took the banker's arm. ''More than perfect,'' she said, and cast the still scowling Chance a haughty look as she and John Gardner quit the room.

Chapter Seven

"I respectfully disagree," John said, after chewing thoughtfully on a forkful of roast beef. "You should move here to town, to the hotel, away from that place."

"That place, for better or worse, is mine," Dora reminded him. She was actually rather proud of the improvements she'd made to the operation in just a few short days.

"Hopefully not for long."

"You've located a buyer?" She ought to have been thrilled, but a tiny pang of alarm gripped her, and she suddenly lost interest in her food.

"Not yet, but I expect to hear something soon from the inquiries I made last week on your behalf."

She felt a palpable relief, which was ridiculous she reminded herself as she dug in to her mashed potatoes. Her objective was to sell the ranch and the saloon as soon as possible. Wasn't it?

She glanced at the other customers in the hotel dining room. Mr. Grimmer, her father's attorney, was lunching alone at a table in the back. The marshal's wife, along with a few of her friends, sat across from her. The woman cast her a most unfriendly look.

"Don't mind her," John said. "She's angry that her husband's been spending so much time at the Flush. It's not your fault."

The marshal was, in fact, a good customer, and had complimented her the last time he was in on how good the place looked. *Spruced-up* was the term he'd used. Dora was inclined to think it *was* her fault he'd been spending more time in the saloon, as had a number of their other regular customers.

In addition to the visible improvements she'd made to the saloon, she'd had several discussions with the staff about how to improve service to their customers. After all, the whole point of her short proprietorship was to make money—as much as possible—to not only defray the debt her father had incurred, but to make the saloon an attractive target for potential buyers.

She'd be well on her way had not a number of new creditors appeared. Once word had spread that she was making good on Wild Bill's debts, anyone who'd ever lent her father a nickel had come out of the woodwork. The ledger she kept of the saloon's outstanding debts was growing, not shrinking.

"Don't you like your roast beef?"

She realized John had put down his fork and was looking at her. "Oh…um, yes." Spearing another bite of meat she said, "It's wonderful." It wasn't quite as flavorful as Jim's pot roast, but she'd never say that.

It was kind of the banker to have asked her to luncheon to begin with. She'd gone on the premise that they'd mostly be discussing her father's affairs. Otherwise, it wouldn't have been proper. Never in her life had she been out with a single gentleman sans chaperone.

Not that she'd been abiding, by any stretch of the imagination, by what was and wasn't considered proper behavior for a young woman these days. She reminded herself she was a saloon owner, and while technically she wasn't living on the premises, she slept fifty feet away in a cabin out back.

"I'm glad you're having a good time," John said. "I've looked forward to our meeting all week." His eyes sparkled as he watched her.

Dora felt a bit guilty. "So have I," she said, though she'd postponed their luncheon by two days. The excuse she'd given him was that she'd had pressing matters to take care of at the ranch, which was true.

She'd wanted to keep her eye on Chance Welles-ley, to find out if her father's letter had sparked any insights she'd missed. She was certain now, after finding more bank notes—real and counterfeit—that the "something" her father had left for her at the ranch was money, and that Chance was after it.

She told herself that postponing her luncheon with John had nothing to do with Chance kissing her in the darkened hallway, or the fact that she'd shamelessly kissed him back. Nothing whatsoever. It had been a freak incident, one that had turned out badly and would never be repeated.

All the same, she couldn't help recalling how closely Chance had held her, how his lips had felt on hers. Two short hours ago in her father's study, for a fleeting moment he'd looked at her as if she were the most desirable woman on earth. No man had ever looked at her that way. No man had ever made her feel as if—

"Dora?"

She snapped to attention. John was looking at her quizzically.

"Um...did you say something?"

"Yes." He gave her a bright smile. "I said I think you look stunning in that hat."

"Oh!" His compliment caught her off guard. The hat had been her mother's and was a bit old-fashioned, even for Dora, who didn't cater much to the latest styles. "Thank you," she said, feeling suddenly self-conscious.

He was flirting with her, and she hadn't been attentive enough to even notice, until now. She'd been preoccupied thinking about Chance.

When the waiter came, John paid the bill, then stood and offered her his hand. "Shall we?"

When she took it, and his fingers closed over hers, she didn't feel the same excitement she'd experienced with Chance in the study, when he'd brushed his thumb across her open palm. She reminded herself she was wearing gloves now. Yes, that had to be the difference.

John Gardner was everything Chance Wellesley was not—a respectable member of the community engaged in a respectable business. He safeguarded people's money, not swindled them out of it.

As he helped her into her cloak and rested his hands lightly on her shoulders, she thought about something she'd never dared think about before, except on the rare occasion when she succumbed to a brief fantasy fueled by the novels she read.

She thought about marriage.

Marriage and children and the kind of life she suspected all maiden schoolteachers dreamed about at some point. She looked into John Gardner's eyes as he held the door open for her, and knew beyond a doubt that he was thinking about it, too.

"Walk a while with me? It's a lovely day."

"I'd like that," she said.

As they strolled down the street past the livery and the mercantile, she thought about what it would be like to settle down in a town like Last Call.

John tucked her arm securely under his. "Still considering opening a school?"

"At the saloon, you mean? No." She'd made a promise to the staff that she'd keep the Royal Flush open until a buyer was found and the transaction completed.

"What about here in town? I think it's a fine idea."

She glanced at the children playing in the street with a couple of stray dogs. Friday afternoon shoppers went about their business, ignoring them for the most part. The marshal and his deputy, lounging in a couple of rockers that were permanent fixtures on the boardwalk outside the town jail, tipped their hats to her and John as they passed. She noticed the minister and his wife across the street chatting with passersby, and a couple of young boys up to some kind of mischief on the second-story porch over the barbershop. The target of their waywardness appeared to be two school-age girls playing jacks on the boardwalk below.

Last Call had potential, she decided. It wasn't as big or as sophisticated as Colorado Springs, but was much more in need of her services from the look of things.

All the same, she said, "I'd planned on leaving once the saloon is sold. There's really nothing to keep me here."

John paused in front of the bank and looked at her, his blue eyes infused with heat. "Isn't there?"

All of a sudden she felt confused and unusually warm, despite the crisp spring chill in the air and a light westward breeze.

"Don't answer," he said. "Not yet. Think about it a while. And think about this…" He opened the double doors leading into the bank and she entered. "I've spoken to my investors, and they've agreed with my proposal to renegotiate your father's mortgage—over a longer term and at a reduced interest rate."

Dora was so stunned, for a moment she couldn't speak. "But…why would they do that?"

John smiled at her. "I told them I'd back the loan myself."

"But—"

"Just until a buyer can be located. They've even agreed to loan you a bit of cash to get your school going, with the provision that it be located here in town, of course."

"Of course, but—"

"Don't say no. Think about it." He grasped her shoulders with an air of proprietary confidence that made her uneasy.

She took a step back, out of his arms. "Why would you do this?"

It was Friday, payday, and the bank was crowded with townsfolk. The last customer in line at the counter turned and said, "Seems pretty clear to me."

Dora gasped.

"Wellesley," John said, his smile fading.

"Howdy, Gardner." Chance tipped his hat to the banker, then settled his gaze on her. "One piece of advice, Dora."

Recovering herself, she stood tall, chin tipped high, and looked down her nose at him—well, as best she could, given that Chance was at least half a foot taller than she.

"Beware of Greeks bearing gifts." He cast John a sideways glance.

He was supposed to be encouraging her to move to town, not warning her against the one element that, all else failing, might make the idea appealing to her. The problem was that he didn't trust Gardner.

An even bigger problem was that he cared.

For the next three days Dora avoided both the banker and him. She'd sat with Mortimer Grimmer and his wife at church yesterday, and had openly declined Gardner's invitation to join him at the hotel for Sunday supper. Instead, she'd eaten with the staff in the dining room at the Flush, complimenting Jim's cooking and evading Chance's gaze.

"She found another one!" Iris rushed over to his table. "There, behind the bar."

Chance glanced at the faces of the wet-behind-the-ears cowpunchers who'd come over from Garo to play cards with him that afternoon. Without preamble he folded his hand. Lucky for them. "I'm sitting this one out, boys." He motioned to Rowdy who stood at the bar taking a break from his chores. "Keep my seat warm, why don't you?"

"Sure thing, Chance."

The two traded places. Chance leaned across the bar and glimpsed Dora on her hands and knees, her rump stuck up in the air like a Christmas roast. He resisted the urge to comment. He had a harder time resisting the natural response of his body as he watched her.

"This one's a fifty," Dora said, holding the bank note up for inspection. "And it's real!"

If she'd been in on her father's misdeeds, she wouldn't be advertising the sudden appearance of stray bank notes. More and more he was convinced she knew nothing about Wild Bill's business dealings.

"Let me see that."

She glanced up at him. "Oh, it's you." Scrambling to her feet, she held the fifty-dollar bill closer to the light from the wall sconce flanking the blank spot on the wall where the portrait of Wild Bill's favorite whore had hung. "I'm perfectly capable of distinguishing counterfeit bills from real ones."

"Gardner give you a lesson the other day?"

He was kidding, but she took him seriously. "He did, in fact. We spent quite a long time together at the bank after you left."

She was lying. Not a minute after he'd made his withdrawal and had left the bank, Dora had come out with Gardner on her heels. Chance had watched them covertly from the corner.

Despite Gardner's insistence, she'd refused to let him take her home in his buggy. Gus had brought the wagon in to pick up a load of supplies for Jim, and she'd ridden back to the Flush with the ranch hand. So much for Gardner's effect on her. Chance smiled, recalling the banker's murderous look in his direction, the moment Dora and Gus were out of sight.

"I'll be right back," she said, returning him to the present. She stuffed the fifty-dollar bank note into the pocket of her dress and shot him a look before heading toward the kitchen. "Please don't disturb anything."

"Who me?"

The second she was out of sight, he leaped over the bar and landed in a crouch, like a cat, on the other side. Jim, who stood close by polishing Wild Bill's collection of silver whiskey flasks, eyed him.

Another bank note was barely visible, wedged between the shelving attached to the back wall of the bar. The moment Jim went about his business, Chance reached for it. When he pulled, two more bank notes fluttered to the floor. He quickly scooped them up. They *were* real, he realized, and stuffed them into the pocket of his vest.

Dora's booted feet came into view. "Mr. Wellesley!"

"Chance," he said, smiling up at her. "You caught me red-handed." She extended her palm and waited. He fished the bank notes back out of his vest pocket and handed them to her.

"Where, exactly, did you find them?"

Jim came over and knelt beside him, his eagle eyes inspecting the burnished pine shelving of the bar. Delilah appeared, as well, along with Tom and two of the girls. Too bad there was no way to tell whose interest was purely innocent and whose wasn't.

Chance shrugged. "Just laying there, like the other one."

This time *he* was lying, and she knew it.

Someone else besides him knew about Wild Bill's money, and if he had to spend the rest of his life playing cards at the Royal Flush to find out who, then so be it.

"I'd like to make something clear to all of you," Dora said, looking directly at him. "Any money found on the premises, regardless of how little or how much, belongs to the house. Is that clear?"

The others murmured their agreement.

"Chance?"

It was the first time she'd ever called him by his Christian name. He didn't think she even realized it. For a moment it threw him off balance—literally.

"Steady there, partner." Jim placed a hand on his shoulder.

Chance got to his feet and stood there for a moment looking at her. She *was* pretty, he decided, and smart as a whip. "Clear as the South Platte on a summer's day."

"Good." She glanced at the spot on the wall where the painting had hung and frowned.

"Something wrong?"

"Um…no." She shook off whatever was bothering her, and her icy demeanor returned.

Chance prayed that no more stray bank notes would turn up while she was around. It just made the situation worse. The money was a draw for Wild Bill's partner, and he didn't want her finding it. He wanted her out of the way before she got hurt, and before he did something stupid he'd regret.

"So, are you going to take Gardner up on his offer?"

His question had the desired effect.

She blushed.

"What offer?" Delilah asked.

"Oh, it's nothing. John—I mean Mr. Gardner—offered some funding should I choose to open a school in town."

"You're thinking of stayin' on, then?" Jim's expression was cool, his eyes hard to read. Chance took it all in.

"Well, perhaps, but…"

Delilah arched a painted brow at her, and Dora's face flushed a deeper shade of pink.

"I—I'm not really sure at this point."

"A school would mean you'd have to move to town," Delilah said. Chance wasn't sure about her, either. Hell, any one of them could have been Bill's partner. Or maybe it wasn't any of them. Damn it!

"Not necessarily. Not yet, at any rate."

"She's got other reasons to move to town," Chance said, hoping to provoke her.

"You do?" Lily, who'd come down from upstairs, looked at her with renewed interest.

"I most certainly do not." Dora brushed past him and made for the kitchen.

"I knew you'd see things my way."

His words stopped her in her tracks, as planned. She turned, her embarrassment cooling to anger.

"I'll never see things your way, Mr. Wellesley."

"Oh, I don't know. We saw eye to eye here a few nights ago, didn't we?"

She stormed off, and he censored his smile. If he was lucky, she'd be gone that afternoon. Days ago, when he'd first learned of it from Jim, he'd paid the hotel clerk in town to hold their only available room. His investment was about to pay off.

Her trunk sat packed and ready in her cabin for the whole of the next day, until she'd gained enough consensus in her own mind to finally unpack it again.

"I will not let him drive me out," she said to herself as she placed the last of her woolen stockings back in the bureau. "No matter how irritating he becomes."

Furthermore, she'd decided once not to toss him out, and she'd keep to her decision. Chance Wellesley brought business to the saloon. She'd continue to use him to insure the Flush turned a profit. She'd also continue to watch him. He was here for a reason, and more and more she grew to believe that reason was her father's money.

She would find it first. She was determined.

And unbeknownst to him, Chance Wellesley was going to help her.

She'd lain awake the past three nights thinking about John Gardner's offer—or offers, if she'd read his behavior toward her correctly. The banker was prepared to personally back a new loan in her name that would solve all of her financial woes. She should have "jumped on it" as Mr. Grimmer had put it when she'd told him of the banker's proposition at Sunday services.

But she hadn't. In fact, she hadn't yet responded. She'd purposefully evaded John's company ever since. "Why?" she'd asked herself over and over, and each time couldn't fathom a answer that appealed to her rational mind.

John had made no attempt to mask his affection for her. He was helping her because he cared. She ought to have been thrilled. In her diary she'd made a list of all his admirable qualities, qualities any woman would treasure in a friend—and certainly in a husband.

Late one night while she was doodling in the margins, she'd caught herself listing all of Chance's cor-

respondingly disreputable characteristics beside them.
Why she would compare the two men, even subconsciously, worried her. In the end, she'd torn the sheets out of her diary, crumpled them up and tossed them onto the fire in her father's study.

The fact remained that she was, for no good reason, leery of accepting John Gardner's help. She told herself Chance Wellesley had nothing to do with her feelings. The notion was ridiculous. If anything, his warning made John's offer even more appealing. Greeks bearing gifts, indeed.

Still, she wasn't prepared to bind herself financially to John. She had a feeling that in this case financial ties implied other, more intimate connections, and she simply wasn't ready to make that kind of commitment.

She was ready, however, to stand on her own, to take charge of her destiny. She knew that destiny would be greatly improved should she uncover the location of her father's money. So again she reread his letter, looking for clues, and for the dozenth time she studied the tintype and the tortoiseshell comb wrapped in newsprint.

"It's here," she said, tucking the mementos safely away in the top drawer of the bureau. "Somewhere."

Her diary in hand, Dora locked the door to her cabin behind her, and set off in search of Rowdy and Gus, her father's longtime ranch hands. She intended to interview the entire staff, faithfully record their remarks, then sift through the evidence, much like the sleuths in the Wilkie Collins installment mysteries she loved so dearly.

Rowdy was more than willing to answer her series

of carefully prepared questions. Gus, on the other hand, seemed to disapprove of her sleuthing.

"Nope," Rowdy said. "Your pa never asked me to dig no holes, exceptin' for these here fence posts."

Gus retwisted a length of barbed wire around the post they'd just repaired. "Why you so interested in post holes?"

"I'm not," she said. "Did he ever ask you to dig any other holes?"

"He didn't," Gus said. "But Chance did."

Dora froze, her pen poised in midair.

"I thought that book there was a bible." Rowdy tried to read her handwriting upside down.

Dora tilted the diary so he couldn't see. "No, it's not a bible. It's a journal." She hadn't wanted them to know, but she could hardly be expected to commit all their remarks to memory.

"Hmph." Gus knocked his wide-brimmed hat backward off his forehead. "Whaddya know."

"When, exactly, did Mr. Wellesley ask you to dig this hole?"

"'Bout six weeks ago," Gus answered, looking over at Rowdy.

Dora continued scribbling. "Do you know what the hole was for?"

"Sure," Gus said.

"You do?"

Rowdy looked at the ground and kicked nervously at the dirt with the toe of his boot.

"Well," she said to Gus, who seemed to enjoy dragging things out. "What was the hole for?"

"For your pa's coffin."

Dora stopped breathing.

Rowdy shrugged. "Chance said he deserved a

proper funeral. Bought the coffin himself out of his own money. Had it made special in Garo.''

"Chance did this?" She glanced across the yard, past the bunkhouse to the small hillock where her father was buried.

"Yes, ma'am," Rowdy said. "Me and Gus whitewashed the little picket fence around the plot up yonder. That was Chance's idea. For the fence, I mean. The headstone, too."

"What headstone?" She narrowed her gaze at the small wooden cross ringed with flowers.

"It ain't here yet," Gus said and spat, then went back to work on the barbwire fence.

Rowdy shrugged. "Chance ordered it from that company makes fancy monuments. You must know the one—in the Springs. Should be here in a couple a weeks, I reckon."

She did know the place, and knew for a fact that the hand-carved marble headstones were very expensive. "I see," she said, but she didn't see. Why would Chance Wellesley have done all this for her father? "Yes, well…" She finished penning their comments and snapped the diary closed. "Thank you for your time."

"You need any help, Miss Dora, you just say the word."

"Thank you, Rowdy. You, too, Gus."

"Ma'am." They tipped their hats in unison as she took her leave.

The girls were next on her list. Dora didn't think she'd have time to interview all of them in one day, but she'd at least make a start. So far, nothing her father's two ranch hands had told her was very helpful in discovering the location of the money. If anything, she'd have to broaden her search.

She climbed the spiral staircase to the second floor. The saloon was busy for a Wednesday afternoon, and some of the girls were already working. Chance was playing cards with a couple of locals, and watched her as she moved along the balcony toward the upstairs parlor, which would be empty this time of day.

Lily sat beside him at the gaming table, draped across the marshal's lap. She gave Dora a little wave and a smile. Dora nodded politely in return. Their exchange was not lost on Chance who, much to her annoyance, let out a chuckle. A moment later the marshal spread his cards across the table and wiped the grin from Chance's face. Max raked in his winnings.

Now Dora was the one smiling. "Serves him right," she muttered under her breath, then disappeared into the upstairs parlor.

Susan was already there, waiting. "Howdy, Miss Dora."

"Susan," she said and tentatively took a seat on the red velvet chaise in the center of the room.

"You're wantin' to know about your pa, aren't you?"

"That's right. What can you tell me about his affairs?"

"Affairs? You mean business dealings? Money and such?"

Dora nodded.

The petite, dark-haired girl sat beside her on the chaise. Her big brown eyes lit up when she spoke. "Not too much, Miss Dora. But I liked him, your pa."

Dora faithfully penned Susan's words into her diary, but suspected the girl wasn't going to be of much help.

"I once heard him say that a bank ain't no place to keep money. Does that help?"

"It does. Thank you." Dora had already figured that out for herself. All the same, Susan genuinely seemed to want to help, and Dora didn't wish to appear ungrateful.

Susan looked around the room, and Dora's gaze followed as the girl inspected every nook and cranny with narrowed eyes.

"What are you looking at? Or for?"

"Oh, nothing."

If Susan had firsthand knowledge of her father's actions, Dora needed to know. She was taking a risk, but could see no other way. "Did my father ever talk about where he *did* keep his money?"

"Oh, no. I never rightly heard him say." Susan inched closer on the chaise and looked at her with those big doe eyes as if she were about to impart a secret. "But I know he spent a lot of time in his study. A lot of time. And he got mad if Delilah or one of us girls went in there with a dust rag."

"Really?" Now here was something of interest. Dora scribbled madly into her diary.

Susan smiled. "I told 'em all it wasn't a bible. I was right, wasn't I?"

"Yes." She tipped the red leather-bound journal away, so Susan couldn't read what she'd written, not that the girl seemed to be looking.

"I knew I was right. Nobody exceptin' a preacher carries around a bible. Not even schoolteachers. Even straitlaced schoolteachers like yourself."

"Straight...laced?"

"You know. Proper-like."

Dora was familiar with the term, and knew it wasn't a compliment.

"I said, 'Lily, Miss Dora's not so prudish as you make her out to be.'"

"Lily thinks I'm prudish?"

Susan glanced at the long, tight sleeves and high-necked collar of Dora's hopelessly outdated gray dress.

"No, don't answer that." Dora straightened her spine, banished Lily's criticism from her mind and poised her pen. "Let's get back to the money."

"You think your pa left you some money? Here?"

Dora stopped breathing and looked at her. Susan's eyes were wide with curiosity, nothing more.

"I don't know. Perhaps."

"What will you do with it if you find it, Miss Dora?"

"I never said there was any money. I was merely speculating."

"But if there is…what would you do with it?"

She considered Susan's question. "One of the things I've longed to do for years is open my own school."

"That would be wonderful. And you'd do it here, of course, in Last Call."

"Well, I don't know about that." She thought again about John Gardner's offer. Intuition told her it was for much more than a bank loan, though he hadn't been bold enough to state it.

Yet.

"And you'd teach reading and writing, and what else?"

"Lots of things. It would depend on the interests and capabilities of my students."

"You're good at readin', I suppose?"

Dora thought it was a strange question. "Why, yes, of course. I'm a teacher."

Susan bit her lip and looked away.

"What is it?"

The girl shrugged. She reached into the pocket of her dress—a lovely peach taffeta that set off her delicate features—and produced a folded paper. A letter, Dora realized.

Susan handed it to her. "I wouldn't dare to ask it, normally speakin', of a proper lady like you. But seein' as how you've been so nice to us, Miss Dora— to me, especially—" She gestured to the letter. "Would you mind?"

"You want me to read it?"

Susan nodded, blushing. "I usually ask Delilah, or one of the other girls, but it just came today."

Dora opened the carefully folded pages and took in the neat script. "You want my opinion on what it says."

"No. Well, um…yes, that too. But what I really want is to know what it says."

Truth dawned. "You…can't read."

Susan shook her head. "Never went to school."

Dora didn't know why it surprised her. Lots of people couldn't read. That was precisely the reason she'd wanted to become a schoolteacher in the first place. Her mother had encouraged it because it was a respectable calling for a woman, and one that typically had nothing to do with men.

Dora had had her own reasons for pursuing education as a career. Quite simply, she loved books, losing herself in a world of adventure and excitement. For as long as she could remember, she'd wanted to share that love with others.

God knows her mother hadn't shared it. Adventure and excitement were the devil's work, according to Caroline Fitzpatrick. Dora grinned, reflecting on her surroundings. She was living a bit of that adventure and excitement now, here in the most notorious saloon in the county—a saloon she owned.

"Mother would roll in her grave."

"Hmm?"

"Oh, sorry." She snapped the crisp pages of the letter in her hands. "Of course I'll read it to you. And later, if you like, I'd be happy to teach you to read."

"You would?"

"Of course."

Without warning, Susan threw her arms around Dora's neck, practically knocking her off the chaise. She hugged the girl in return, a tiny flame of satisfaction curling inside her. This was the other reason she loved teaching. The joy it brought to others.

Together they read the letter, Susan following the words on the page with her finger as Dora read aloud.

"It's from an orphanage in Denver," Dora said.

"I know." Susan beamed her a smile more brilliant than the afternoon sun streaming through the lace-curtained windows of the parlor. "I have a son."

Chapter Eight

He'd tried everything he could think of to get her to move to town, including becoming so obnoxious even he couldn't stand it. Nothing seemed to rattle her.

"I don't see the point." Chance slung a hip on the edge of Wild Bill's walnut desk and twirled the watch fob the old man had given him two days before he was murdered.

"The point is…" Dora looked up from the *New England Primer* from which she and Susan were reading. "Everyone should know how to read." She nodded at the girl to continue.

"Even whores?" Dora had already asked him once not to call Susan, or any of the girls, by that—how had she put it—derogatory term. He only did it to needle her, and he suspected she knew that, given the black look she gave him from behind the desk.

"Yes," she said crisply. "And gamblers. Swindlers and horse thieves, too."

He grinned. "I'm touched that you think so highly of me as to place my profession in the same category with swindlers and horse thieves."

"If the shoe fits, Mr. Wellesley…" She arched a

pale blond brow at him, then went back to her teaching.

"Ouch," he said, and wandered across the room to the fireplace.

"I can come back later, if you like, Miss Dora." Uncomfortable with their bantering, Susan looked ready to make a break for it.

"No, I think we should continue." Dora's gaze pinned his from across the room. "Despite the interruption. Read on."

Susan continued, stumbling over the letters Dora had taught her to recognize.

Chance watched as Dora's attention—and her gaze—strayed to the high, paneled walls of the study. She cocked her head, peering from one carved walnut panel to the next, as if she were looking for something that didn't meet the eye head-on.

The location of the money.

He'd seen her questioning Gus and Rowdy yesterday afternoon, and had heard from Lily that she was interviewing the girls. Dora was searching for it, all right, and didn't seem to care who knew. But he cared. He had to. If she wasn't careful, she'd get her head blown off just like her father had.

He toyed with Bill's collection of Chinese porcelain on the mantel, and considered that if he'd been a better man than he really was, the kind of man he used to be, he'd make it his number one priority to see that didn't happen.

But he wasn't that man, not anymore, and he had other priorities. One, in particular, that had nothing to do with Dora Fitzpatrick—at least not yet it didn't. It wouldn't, if he could figure out how to keep her from getting mixed up in things that would eventually get her killed.

He'd tried almost everything in his bag of tricks, and nothing was working. Charm, intimidation, taunting, sincerity—she seemed immune to his entire repertoire. He looked up and caught her watching him.

What's it going to take, Dora, to get you to stop?

She didn't look away, and for a moment he thought again of their kiss. Once, a long time ago, she might have been the kind of woman he'd have gone for, despite her plain looks. She was smart and self-sufficient. She knew her own mind, and even if no one else agreed with her, she was tenacious enough not to back down if she thought she was right.

He admired that about her.

His father would have liked her. His mother and sister, too, God rest their souls.

She didn't have to teach Susan to read, but here she was, up early in her father's study, doing exactly that. Despite everything—the risk to her reputation, the clash with her Christian values, and the plain hard work involved—she'd kept the saloon alive, had made it thrive. She'd done it for the staff and for the town. He knew that now. He felt it as he looked into her eyes.

She reminded him a lot of Wild Bill—goodhearted and generous to a fault. She was that and more. Everything he, himself, wasn't. All the more reason he needed to stay away from her.

Why hadn't she taken Gardner up on his offer? Why hadn't she moved to town? She could have done both of those things, and still she could have looked for the money. But she hadn't. She was still here, despite his and the banker's best efforts to sway her view.

He held her gaze, and she his. And then it hit him like a brick upside the head.

She was here because of him, because *he* was here.

"Lord," he whispered, and broke her stare. He turned toward the fireplace, and in the mirror above the mantel he saw her watching him.

Once, only days ago though it seemed like months, he would have used her naive interest in him to his advantage. In fact, he'd planned on it. But now everything was different. When he was near her he felt hot around the collar, as if his suit were suddenly too tight, too close to his skin.

He didn't feel in control anymore. On the contrary, he felt out of control, not himself at all. And his reasons for being here, knowing with certainty what his life would come down to in the end, made being out of control not an option.

Tense, he dropped to a squat and grabbed a couple of logs, thinking he'd build a fire—not so much to warm the room, as it was a fine spring day out, but to give himself something to do so he wouldn't think about it anymore.

"Chance?"

The sound of his name on her lips sent a rush of heat clear through him.

"Are you all right?"

He positioned the logs, then hunted for kindling. "Right as rain," he said, giving her his stock answer.

A heap of ash and blackened logs in the back of the fireplace crowded his new creation. He grabbed the whisk broom and brushed the heap forward. A crumpled-up piece of paper, singed at the edges, cart-wheeled onto the hearth.

He snatched it up, and a second before tossing it toward the wicker wastepaper basket by the desk, he recognized the fine ivory vellum. It was a sheet torn from Dora's diary.

"What you got there, Chance?" Susan asked.

"Sheet of paper." He uncrumpled it and smoothed it out against the mantel.

"What is that?" Dora rose from her chair, frowning.

"Are you going to read for us, Chance? Miss Dora can teach you, too."

He quickly perused the page, then shot them both a grin. "I know how to read."

Dora came around the desk, alarm flashing in those steely gray eyes of hers. "Give me that."

"No." He started to read aloud what she'd written, a long listing of neatly penned qualities on the left, under the name of one John Gardner, banker. "Trust-worthy?" Chance shook his head. "I don't know about that one, Dora."

"Susan." She turned to the girl. "Please leave us."

"Well, sure, Miss Dora, but…"

"Now!"

"Yes, ma'am."

Chance laughed as Susan shot from the room like a frightened doe. His smile transformed into the grin he'd perfected on Dora's behalf, for just such an occasion.

"Chance Wellesley, of all the low, ill-mannered—"

"Gentle?" He shot her a look. "I've got news for you, Dora. Any man of yours who's gentle is in for a long, hard ride of it."

"Uncouth—" Her frown deepened. "What do you mean 'man of mine'? That's not what that list is about. It's simply my way of—"

"Lascivious?" He looked at the word again. "What the hell does that mean?" It was under his name, not Gardner's, at the top of a significantly longer list of characteristics, all of them negative, scribbled in the right-hand margin of the page.

"Lewd," she said, and snatched the crumpled paper from his hand.

He tried to grab it back, but she balled it in her fist and hid her hands behind her. A second later he had her pinned, backed against the mantel, his face inches from hers. Her nostrils flared, her eyes were silver daggers. Never in his life had he wanted to kiss a woman more than he did at that moment. His lips descended on hers.

"Am I gonna have to toss a bucket of water on you two to keep you apart?"

Chance jumped back at the same moment Dora let out a squeak.

Delilah stood in the open doorway, her arms crossed over her ample bosom. Susan lurked behind her in the hall, her brown eyes wide as saucers.

"No," Dora said, quickly adjusting her dress and patting her hair, which had all but come undone. "I have the situation completely under control."

Delilah smirked. "Glad someone does, 'cause he sure don't, do you, Chance?" She winked at him.

Normally he would have grinned in response, but this time he didn't think it was funny. Delilah was right. His good sense was going to hell in a handbasket. The problem was, he was enjoying the trip.

A minute later Dora had the fire going and tossed the list onto the flames. "There," she said. "That's that."

"Damned right." Chance straightened his vest and grabbed his hat from the desk where he'd left it when he'd come in. The forgotten reading primer lay on the floor. He picked it up and handed it to Dora. Their gazes locked, and for the hundredth time that day he told himself to back off.

"You two had better watch yourselves," Delilah said, eyeing them. "At least in front of the girls." She gave Susan a scoot, and she disappeared down the hall. "Lord, do they love to gossip. Especially that Lily. Who knows what that banker'll do when he gets wind of this."

Dora's face blanched.

"Don't worry," Chance said. "He'd never believe it. A gambler and a schoolmarm?"

"School*teacher,*" Dora said. "And yes, I completely agree with you. The idea is preposterous."

"It's a doozy," Delilah said, and shook her head at the two of them.

For two straight days she'd managed to keep an eye on Chance, while at the same time avoiding any prolonged interactions with him. It hadn't been easy. The man took pleasure in baiting her.

She was certain, now, that he was deliberately trying to get rid of her. While she'd never actually seen him poking around the ranch or the saloon, snooping in places he had no business being, she was convinced he was here for one reason alone—to find what her father had left her.

She recalled her listing of his character flaws; she could recite them by heart. Chance Wellesley might be a lot of things, but one thing he wasn't was stupid. If *he* was here looking for the money, it had to be real.

Chance's canny persistence, the appearance of stray bank notes, a few rumors she'd heard in town, and her father's penned innuendo all added up to one thing—a fortune hidden somewhere on the premises.

The question was where?

Drawing the heavy velvet draperies aside in the saloon, she peeked out the window at the progress Rowdy had made with a shovel in the front yard. The grassy area from the oak tree to the well was peppered with holes. On her instruction, he'd been digging. However, she hadn't told him why he was digging. She suspected he thought she was crazy.

Gus had been over the barn, the bunkhouse, the cabins and other outbuildings twice over, tapping the walls with a hammer, looking for loose boards, again on her instruction. What she'd really hoped he'd find was a secret panel. So far, he'd turned up nothing more than a long list of repairs that needed attention.

Rowdy had been more successful. So far he'd found nearly a dozen coins, including several double eagles, likely dropped by customers who'd had more to drink than they could handle. It wasn't the fortune she'd hoped for, but it was something.

She'd been over her father's study, his bedroom and the upstairs parlor a dozen times, and had turned up nothing more than dust bunnies.

Dora sighed.

"Still at it?"

She turned at the sound of Chance's voice.

He leaned up against the bar and motioned to Jim for a cup of coffee.

"Still at what?" She noted he was dressed more formally today than usual.

"Cleaning." His tone of voice implied he knew she was doing more than that.

"I beg your pardon?"

"You're barking up the wrong tree, Dora."

The man had more catch phrases than suits of clothes, and he was a definite clotheshorse. She ignored him.

It was Saturday morning, and shortly the first customers of the day would begin to arrive. Tom had just sat down at the piano across the room to practice a new piece she'd heard him working on yesterday. She hadn't yet interviewed him, and thought now would be a good time.

She sidestepped Chance. "Tom?"

The piano player swiveled toward her on his stool. In her haste to get away from Chance, she tripped on the edge of the Persian carpet. A heartbeat later he was there, but she refused his help.

"You okay, Miss Dora?" Tom rose from his stool.

"Fine," she said, rubbing her calf where she'd banged it against a chair. "Oh, shoot! I've run my stocking." She lifted her petticoat higher to inspect the damage.

"And a fine stocking it is, too." Chance shot her a lusty look.

While she'd grown immune to his vulgar taunting, knowing full well it was an act he put on to unnerve her, his mere mention of her stocking made her see red.

"If you ever have a hankering for more midnight plundering of my undergarments, Mr. Wellesley, I suggest you satisfy your fetish elsewhere, unless you'd like to find out just how good I am with a derringer."

Chance gawked at her, thunderstruck.

Good. She was glad he knew that she'd been aware of his invasion of her cabin that night. Perhaps he'd not think her so naive from now on.

Tom's eyes widened. Dora scowled at him, too. He swiveled back around to face his piano and instantly broke into a chorus of "Hangtown Ladies." She was grateful, and used the diversion to get her temper under control.

Another diversion presented itself, for which she was also grateful. Mr. Grimmer strolled into the saloon along with the marshal and a couple of local business owners. Chance, who'd recovered his composure before she'd recovered hers, was only too happy to oblige them in their quest to see who could lose the most money on this fine Saturday morning. Chance ushered them to his regular table, and cast her a curious look before sitting down.

Dora turned her back on them all. "Tom?"

"Yes, Miss Dora?" He continued his playing at a softer volume.

"Can you tell me what you know about my father's business dealings?" She opened her diary and plucked her fountain pen out of her pocket.

"Sure," he said. "But I don't know much. Just that he owed nearly everybody in town."

"Yes, I'm aware of that."

Tom looked up from the piano. "Some of them bills got paid, of course."

"Really?" That was hard to believe given the mountain of debt she'd inherited along with the saloon. "How?"

"Chance paid 'em. From his winnings, I guess. Did it all the time, only no one's supposed to know about it."

Now it was Dora's turn to look thunderstruck. "Why on earth would he have done that?"

Tom wasn't listening. She followed his gaze across the room to where Delilah was shooing Daisy and Susan toward the bar. Jim had just poured a couple of seasoned miners shots of rye. Tom stopped playing the piano when one of them put his arm around Susan.

"Tom?"

His face flooded with color, the vein at his temple pulsed, as he watched the miner paw her. Susan smiled at the man and made small talk, but it was clear to Dora—and to Tom, she realized—that Susan would rather be anywhere else in the world than in the grip of a man who was about to pay her to have relations with him.

Delilah cast Tom a disapproving look. He visibly shook off his anger and began to play again. This time the tune was somber.

"You're in love with her, aren't you?" Dora was guessing.

Tom didn't answer. He kept his eyes on the sheet music positioned in front of him, though it was plain to see that wasn't the tune he was playing.

"Have you told her?"

His bunched shoulders relaxed a little, and he shot her a quick glance. "No."

"You should, you know."

"Won't matter."

"Why do you say that?"

He drew a breath and moved into a love song, a lament Dora recognized and loved. "She won't have me. She won't have no one."

"Why not?"

"I reckon 'cause she thinks she's spoiled now. You know—" he glanced over at Susan who was leading her customer up the spiral staircase to one of the bedrooms above "—from working here."

Dora felt like the lowest of hypocrites. Here she was reaping profit from an enterprise she openly scorned, and that had likely ruined the life of one of the sweetest girls she'd ever met.

"She told you that?"

"Didn't have to. I just know."

He continued to play while Dora reflected on a situation she was now determined to put right. She hadn't spoken to anyone about the conversation she'd had with Susan in the upstairs parlor. While she very well might be betraying a confidence, intuition— which she'd begun to listen to more and more—told her she was making the right move.

"Do you know about Susan's child?"

Tom stopped his playing and looked at her. "I do, but she don't know I do."

"And?"

He drew himself up out of his melancholy slouch and said, "I think we ought to go get him, that's what I think."

"You mean take him from the orphanage in Denver."

"Damned straight. Her kin forced her to give him up after he was born, so I heard. Then they turned her out. She showed up here eight months ago, and Delilah and your pa took her in."

Susan hadn't revealed these details to her. Dora let the new information sink in. "I think you should tell her you know," she said at last. "I think it would ease her mind."

"You do?"

"Yes."

Tom broke into a lively melody, his fingers flying over the keys, light as a whisper. Chance looked quizzically in their direction, and Dora promptly ignored him. Still, the notion that he'd helped with her father's debts and had taken it upon himself to insure William Fitzpatrick had had a Christian burial plagued her.

Who are you?

"Might ease his mind, too," Tom said, tipping his chin toward Chance. "Then again, might scare the bejesus out of him."

"What?" Dora said.

"You tellin' Chance you're sweet on him."

Gardner had dredged up one lame reason after another to ride out to the Flush nearly every day this week. A couple of times he'd even bought a round of drinks, though he'd come in the late mornings when business was slow, and he, himself, only drank sarsaparilla.

Chance had had just about of enough of him.

"Gardner," he said, when the banker sidled up to the bar for the fifth day running.

"Hello, Wellesley. Buy you a drink?"

"Sure. Why not?"

Dora was just coming in from the kitchen with a tray of clean glassware for Jim. The local girls she'd hired to wash dishes were in the upstairs parlor reading with Susan and Columbine. The place was turning into a damned school despite the fact it was still a saloon.

"Miss Fitzpatrick! Dora." Gardner removed his hat. He tossed her a smile that turned Chance's stomach.

Over the past week he'd made some quiet inquiries into the banker's background, but had come up with next to nothing. That, coupled with Gardner's dogged interest in Dora, put him on his guard. He continued to tell himself—every damned hour if he had to—that his suspicions about Gardner had nothing to do with the irritation he felt each time the banker captured Dora's attention.

She still hadn't taken him up on his offer of a new loan, and she still hadn't moved to town to be closer to him. All the same, when Gardner had showed up yesterday out of the blue to take her to church, Dora had changed her plans so she could ride with him. Not that her interest in Gardner ate at him. It didn't, goddamn it.

He downed the beer Gardner bought him in one gulp. "Hit me again, Jim." He turned to the banker. "This one's on me. How about something stronger than that toilet water you're drinking?"

Dora shot him a nasty look.

"Oh, no," Gardner said. "I don't drink hard liquor."

"Not even beer?" Even the street urchins Dora was so intent on teaching drank beer.

"Not typically. It, uh, clouds my judgment."

"Well, that's a new one."

Dora cleared her throat in that huffy schoolmarm style that usually prefaced a lecture of some kind. "I think that's admirable. Think what a better world we'd live in if others—" she arched a blond brow in his direction "—followed your example, John."

Chance snorted. "My judgment's just fine, thank you very much."

She made an impertinent little sound in the back of her throat that he found annoying and fetching all at once. He noticed she was dressed for hard labor, in that same old ugly gray dress.

Maybe she was going to help Gus with his hammering or Rowdy with his digging. Half the damned ranch was covered in holes. Just yesterday Silas had stepped in one of them and nearly busted an ankle. Chance had ended up in the dirt.

"I was thinking, Dora, that perhaps you'd like to join me in town for supper one night."

Chance turned his attention back to Gardner. He was openly courting her, despite the fact that she hadn't really encouraged it. She hadn't discouraged it, either, he reminded himself.

"Another beer, Chance?" Jim's hand was poised to pull him another draft.

"Go ahead, Mr. Wellesley," Dora said. "It couldn't possibly make your judgment any worse than it already is."

The look they exchanged was not lost on Gardner. The banker knew he and Dora were at odds half the time, and in heat the other half, thanks to Lily's blabbing all over town what she'd seen in the hallway that night.

"Set me up," he said to Jim.

"About our supper…" Gardner looked expectantly at Dora.

"I'd like that," she said, flashing her eyes in Chance's direction to gauge his reaction. He didn't give her the satisfaction of seeing him scowl. "But why don't you come here?"

"To the saloon?"

"To the *ranch*," she said. "Jim fries a melt-in-your-mouth chicken, and you haven't yet tried my scalloped potatoes."

"You can cook?" Chance hadn't seen her at work in the kitchen except for cleaning.

"Of course I can cook. It's just that I haven't wanted to intrude on Jim's domain."

The bartender brightened right up. "I'd be pleased as punch for you to try out those potatoes, Miss Dora."

Pleased as punch? What the hell kind of place was this turning into?

"And I'd be happy to sample them," Gardner said. "May I bring some wine?"

"You mean you don't drink sarsaparilla with supper, too?" Chance couldn't help himself.

Dora glared at him. "Wine would be lovely," she said to Gardner. "Thursday. Seven o'clock."

"I'll be here."

Chance watched as she gave the banker a little smile, then floated back to the kitchen and closed the door.

"You're one smooth operator, aren't you, Gardner?"

Wisely, Jim left the two of them alone, moving down the bar to serve other customers.

"What's your problem with me, Wellesley? You haven't liked me from the get-go."

"No problem. I just can't figure your motive."

"What motive?" Gardner met his gaze, didn't back off an inch.

"You and her." He cocked his head toward the kitchen.

"I would have thought it was perfectly obvious. I care about her."

Gardner's bald statement caught him off guard.

"She's a fine woman, though I don't expect someone like you would know the difference." Gardner glanced at Lily, who'd taken the opportunity, now that Dora was gone, to slide her arm around Chance, making him feel uncomfortable under the circumstances.

Chance brushed her off.

"She's not a woman to be trifled with." Gardner drew himself up, and Chance did the same. They were nearly the same height, dead on the same age, he'd discovered from his brief investigation.

His hand moved instinctively to his gun belt. He noticed the banker didn't wear any weapons. None that were visible, at any rate. This was a side of John Gardner he hadn't seen before. He decided to test it.

"It's money, isn't it?"

Gardner laughed.

"That's what you're after. Admit it." He'd never really considered the banker on his list of murder suspects. Gardner wasn't a man who easily blended in with the crowd at the Royal Flush. If he'd been there the night Wild Bill was shot, someone would have seen him. That didn't mean he couldn't have hired an anonymous gun to do his dirty work for him.

That didn't mean he wasn't Wild Bill's partner.

He locked eyes with Gardner.

"To begin with..." The banker's voice was chillingly calm. "I don't believe the saloon or the ranch will ever amount to anything, and I don't like it that Dora does. It's a wild-assed fantasy keeping her from making the right decisions where business is concerned."

"Is it?" He couldn't tell if Gardner really believed that or if he was just feeding him a load of bull. He'd also never heard the banker swear before. The words had rolled off his lips naturally, as if he always talked like that. He had a new appreciation for Gardner—and new suspicions.

"Stay away from her," Gardner said.

"Is that a threat?" His hand closed over the walnut grips of his Colt.

Gardner didn't breathe, didn't move a muscle. He also didn't back down. Chance had to give him credit.

"Just how well did you know Bill?"

"Dora's father?" The banker smiled, a slow smile that spread like a disease across his unblemished face. "Well enough."

Chapter Nine

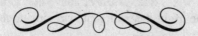

"No!" Dora crossed her arms over her chest and looked pointedly at Delilah.

"Yes." Delilah positioned her in front of the oval mirror flanking the dressing table, while Columbine and Rose held the velvet gown up in front of her.

"See? It's beautiful."

"It's scandalous," Dora said.

"The violet lights up your eyes. Don't it, girls?"

The others, all except Lily, enthusiastically agreed. An hour ago they'd sent Susan out to the cabin to fetch Dora upstairs to Delilah's room. Had she known the purpose of the summons, she'd never have come.

"What's wrong with what I'm wearing?" She'd changed out of her simple gray dress into a high-necked black frock she reserved for special occasions.

"It's fine," Delilah said, "if you're in mourning." She grimaced at the sturdy woolen fabric.

"But you ain't," Susan said. "You're entertainin' a gentleman. You want to look pretty, don't you?"

Dora looked at her reflection in the mirror and frowned.

"Not that you ain't pretty," Susan said quickly. "You just need a little…"

"Help." Daisy moved up behind her and, gazing into the mirror, framed Dora's face in her hands. "Just a little."

"And we'd best be quick about it," Susan said. "He'll be here in less than an hour!"

The *he* was John Gardner, and while Dora should have been excited about their evening together, she now wished she'd agreed to dine with him in town, as he'd originally proposed. Dining here, under the scrutiny of her employees—not to mention Chance— wasn't as appealing as it had seemed when she'd first suggested it, despite Jim's fabulous fried chicken, which she could already smell cooking downstairs.

Delilah started in on the buttons of Dora's black frock. "The first thing we need to do is to get you out of this old thing."

"But—"

"No arguments, now. Trust me this once." Delilah's eyes held a maternal affection so genuine, Dora couldn't help but comply.

"All right," she said. "I'm willing to try it on, but I'm not guaranteeing I'll wear it."

Seconds later she was stripped of the black frock. Lily plucked it off the bed as if it were a smelly dishcloth and dropped it ceremoniously onto the floor by the door.

"I knew it!" Delilah said. "I knew you had a fine figure underneath those frumpy clothes."

Dora felt suddenly self-conscious, standing there in front of them all in her undergarments.

"Someone else knows it, too," Susan said.

"Mr. Gardner, you mean." Dora blushed. She'd caught the banker looking at her the other day.

"I was talkin' about Chance." Susan shot her a mischievous grin. Lily snorted.

Before she could reply, Delilah spun her around so Columbine and Rose could lower the two-piece velvet gown over her head. There must have been two dozen tiny hooks up the back. As Delilah began to fasten them, Susan stepped in and matter-of-factly scrunched Dora's chemise down into the top of her corset, exposing the tops of her breasts.

Dora gasped at the result. "It's far too small. Look at the bodice!"

"Scanty is a better word for what it is," Rose said, "but that's the point, isn't it?"

"It's perfect." Delilah turned her toward the mirror and, together, they looked at Dora's reflection.

"I can't wear this."

"You can and you will. It's lovely."

The gown itself *was* lovely, a rich violet velvet, that set off her creamy skin and gray eyes. It had thin straps rather than sleeves, and was beaded across the bodice in a swirling pattern that disappeared into the nipped-in waist. The style was more old-fashioned than the fancy gowns the girls wore in the evenings in the saloon, but that was one of the things Dora liked about it.

"It's yours?" she asked Delilah.

The older woman nodded. "I can't wear it now, of course. Piled on too many pounds over the years. But it's always been special to me."

"A man bought it for her," Iris said, a knowing look in her eyes.

"Only she won't say who," Rose added.

Dora wondered if the man had been her father.

"You'll need gloves," Delilah said, her eyes shining with emotion.

"Here." Susan and Daisy helped her into a pair of long black evening gloves.

Delilah opened the carved walnut box on top of her dressing table. "And some jewelry."

"Oh, no. I don't typically wear jewelry."

"How about this?" Delilah chose a simple black satin ribbon trimmed in lace. "It's just enough to draw some interest." She fastened it around Dora's neck before she could protest.

"I've got news for you," Lily said. "It ain't the ribbon he'll be lookin' at." She flashed her eyes at Dora's ample expanse of exposed bosom.

Dora refused to be embarrassed. She did look good, she decided, staring at her reflection in the mirror—perhaps for the first time in her life—and she intended to enjoy it.

"Now for some lip rouge." Columbine was already opening various jars on Delilah's dressing table.

"Absolutely not," Dora said. "This is where I draw the line. I will not wear paint on my face."

"She's right." Delilah told Columbine to put the tops back on the jars. "Decent women don't wear lip rouge. You all know that."

The implication, of course, was that Dora was decent while the rest of them were not. She felt a stab of pity for Susan, who lowered her eyes and brushed a hand across her lips. The others, Lily in particular, seemed unaffected by Delilah's proclamation.

Dora didn't know how to feel. Three weeks ago if someone had told her she'd be fawned over like Cinderella going to the ball by half a dozen ladies of the night in an upstairs bedroom of a saloon—and that she'd enjoy it—she wouldn't have believed them.

Her whole world had changed since then, she reminded herself. Having dinner with a gentleman who was interested in her was the least scandalous of some of the things she'd recently done. She ought to let herself enjoy it.

"Now for the hair." Susan narrowed her eyes in thought as three of them descended on her at once with pins and hairbrushes.

"What's wrong with my hair?"

"Nothing," Delilah said, "if you'd fix it right."

"Nobody except schoolmarms and preachers' wives do their hair like this anymore." With one flick of her wrist, Susan released the tight chignon that was Dora's everyday hairstyle.

"I *am* a schoolmarm, I mean teacher. Remember?"

"Not tonight you ain't," Susan said. "You're a woman."

"And he's a man," Rose added.

They all giggled.

"Not much of one if you ask me." Lily flopped onto Delilah's bed and affected a bored expression.

"You hush now," Delilah said. "John Gardner's not the only man who'll be seeing her tonight."

Dora looked at her, but Delilah wouldn't meet her gaze. Dora had no intention of appearing in the saloon, if that's what Delilah had meant, though she would have to brave the roomful of men for the few seconds it would take her to descend the spiral staircase.

"If we only had some pretty combs…" Susan continued to work on Dora's hair.

"Oh," she said, recalling the lovely tortoiseshell

comb her father had left her in his safety deposit box. She'd meant to wear it tonight, but had been called upstairs before she'd had a chance to fix her hair.

Waving the girls away, she retrieved her black frock from the floor where Lily had dropped it, and fished the tortoiseshell comb out of the pocket.

"Here," she said, dropping it into Delilah's hand. "Will this do?"

Delilah's breath caught. "Where'd you get this?"

She hesitated before answering. Delilah looked as if she'd seen a ghost.

"Looks familiar," Susan said.

"My, um, father left it for me in his safety deposit box at the bank. It must have been dear to him." She looked at Delilah, whose blue eyes shimmered in the lamp light. "Do you know to whom it belonged?"

Delilah fingered the comb as if it were a rare treasure. She clearly knew something about it. Dora would remember to ask her about it later. The comb looked strangely familiar to her, too—it had ever since she'd first laid eyes on it.

"Beats me," Delilah said abruptly, and tossed the comb to Susan. "Pretty, though. It'll look good on you."

Susan and Rose fashioned her long blond hair into a charming upsweep, leaving a few wispy tendrils, which they curled with a hot iron, to frame her face. The comb was the perfect accent. Delilah was right. It did look good on her. In fact, when the girls stepped away and allowed her to see herself in the full-length mirror, Dora was stunned.

"I hardly recognize myself."

"That's a good thing," Lily said. Delilah thumped her.

"All right you girls, downstairs with you." Delilah opened the door and ushered them all out. "It's Thursday night, and rumor has it some old boys from the Springs'll be up this way to try their luck at cards. I expect you to console them when they lose."

Dora followed her to the door, thanking the girls for all their help. At last she turned to Delilah. "I can't thank you enough." On impulse Dora hugged her.

"Oh, it's nothin'. I'm glad you finally saw things my way."

"I don't know why I was so reluctant."

"Probably 'cause you ain't never spread your wings before. A girl like you—smart and pretty with her whole life ahead of her—it's time for you to fly." Delilah winked at her. "Even if just for tonight."

She hadn't spread her wings, she realized, until the day she'd made the decision to follow her heart instead of her head, and had come to Last Call to learn about her father.

"Hell's bells, Miss Dora!" Tom stood in the hallway. His eyes bugged out like a Chinese pug's.

Chance was just coming out of his room across the hall. Dora sucked in a breath and steeled herself for his appraisal. He stopped dead when he saw her. As his gaze washed over her, gooseflesh rose on the bare skin of her upper arms.

"Hell's bells, indeed," he said.

She expected him to make some lewd comment, or to toss her one of his devilish smiles. He did neither. He simply stared at her, his eyes smoldering, as she walked purposefully to the staircase, head held high, and descended into the saloon.

* * *

He told himself it was just the dress, or the way they'd fixed her hair. Maybe it was the way she carried herself, knowing he couldn't take his eyes off her. In the end he decided it was just her. It didn't matter what she wore, that old gray sackcloth or dressed to the nines, she'd gotten under his skin.

Gardner arrived promptly at seven. Dora was waiting for him. She made a brief appearance in the saloon to welcome him, turning the heads of all the men in the room, then led him to the dining room at the back of the house, where Jim had already laid out their supper.

It was to be a *private* supper, Delilah reminded him as he strolled too casually into the kitchen under the pretense of snagging himself one of Jim's fried chicken legs. Glancing down the hall he saw her, a vision in violet, her gloved hands resting on the frosted glass panels of the sliding dining room doors. She was about to close them. Gardner stood behind her, glaring at him.

Chance pinned her with his gaze and nodded a greeting. She froze. It would be harder, he told himself, if she cared for him, even a little. That was the last thing he wanted or needed. All the same, deep down, he craved her acceptance and her affection like a drug.

A little over a year ago, his rage and his pain exhausted, his vengeance unfulfilled, he'd wandered into an opium den in Fairplay and didn't leave for nine weeks. He knew what addiction was, and he was addicted now—to her. Only this was worse. If he didn't get her out of his system, she was the one who'd be hurt. Looking into her eyes, he knew it as surely as he knew the sun would rise tomorrow.

Gardner slipped a hand boldly around her waist and grinned at him. It had been a long time since Chance had allowed himself to feel the kind of anger which had driven him to the unalterable course he was now set on. He felt that anger now as he turned his attention to Gardner.

His dilemma was that he couldn't trust his instincts anymore, not where Dora was concerned. The twisting in his gut that intensified when Gardner laid hands on her only made things worse. He could no longer separate his irrational feelings for her from his very rational suspicions about Gardner's relationship with her father.

Dora flinched, ever so slightly, at Gardner's touch.

That was the only encouragement Chance needed. "If you need me," he said to her, "I'll be right out here."

Her gray eyes widened, in surprise or indignation, he wasn't sure which. She recovered herself and visibly shook him off, turning her head toward Gardner, smiling at the banker as if he were everything in this world she could possibly want.

Chance knew acting when he saw it. After all, he was the master.

Flashing him a smug look, Gardner reached past her and closed the sliding doors. Chance stood there, watching their silhouettes behind the frosted glass panels, until Delilah pulled him away.

John Gardner ate three servings of her scalloped potatoes. He was so stuffed from the meal, he had to decline even a tiny slice of Jim's preserved peach pie. Dora indulged, just to have something to distract her from the banker's intense staring.

He'd told her eight times over the course of the evening how beautiful she looked, and while his attention wasn't unwelcome, it made her nervous in a way that the attention of the only other man who'd ever really noticed her—namely Chance—did not.

If you need me, I'll be right out here.

"Brandy?" Jim said as he cleared away the last of the dishes and silver.

"Not for me." Dora raised a gloved hand to her mouth, covering a feigned yawn.

"None for me, either," John said. "It's late. I know you get up early, Miss Dora, and I should be getting back to town."

She smiled at him, relieved. Their evening together had been the longest three hours of her life. Why, she couldn't pinpoint, except that her feelings, which should have followed the sensible conclusion that John Gardner was a worthy suitor, did not match his.

"It's been a lovely evening," he said as he rose and came around the table to take her hand.

Jim made a quick exit.

"I enjoyed it, too."

"Perhaps we can do it again sometime—soon."

Dora didn't answer.

"May I escort you to church on Sunday?"

It would have been impolite to have said no, so she agreed. He opened the sliding doors into the hallway and was surprised to see Jim already standing there with his hat and coat. Dora was surprised, too.

"Shall I walk you out?" she asked.

"It's raining." Chance stood at the opposite end of the hallway near the open door leading to the back of the stage. The sounds of Tom's piano and Delilah's mezzo-soprano drifted from the saloon.

"I'll be fine." She turned to take John's arm.

"No, no, you'll catch cold." John's gaze was riveted to Chance. "Stay here. I can see myself out."

Jim handed him his coat and his hat, as if to punctuate the point. As soon as the banker was gone, Chance returned to his card game in the saloon. Dora watched him for a moment from behind the spiral staircase, until Lily planted herself in his lap and his arm slid neatly around her waist.

"Nice evening?" Delilah said, coming up behind her and spooking her half to death.

"Oh! Um, fine."

Delilah had that motherly, let's-have-a-talk look in her eyes, but Dora wasn't up to it. Not tonight. After thanking Delilah and Jim for their part in ensuring Mr. Gardner had had a pleasant time, she retreated to her cabin.

So many things suddenly weighed heavy on her mind, not the least of which were her own confused feelings about John Gardner, about Chance and her own future. She slid the tortoiseshell comb out of her hair and turned it over in her hands, studying it.

Her father might have left her any number of things in his safety deposit box—gold, stocks, even another letter describing in detail where he'd hidden the money that seemed to be on everyone's mind but that no one openly talked about—but all he'd left for her was the comb and a tintype of himself. They were clues, she was sure of it. They had to be!

She smiled, thinking it ironic that she'd always liked a good mystery, but now that one presented itself in real life, in *her* life, she was at a loss to solve it.

Again John had pressed her to move to town and

accept his help. Again she'd put him off. Leaving the
ranch now would all but guarantee she'd never discover her father's true legacy to her. Looking at the
tintype, at the warmth in his eyes and the calmness
of his expression, she had the strangest feeling that
perhaps his legacy wasn't money at all.

Carefully she rewrapped the comb in the sheet of
newsprint and tucked it along with the tintype under
her stockings. As she changed out of her borrowed
evening gown into a long cotton nightdress, she pondered the other mystery on her mind.

Chance.

In the past three weeks she'd learned no more
about his history than she'd already discovered her
first day in town with him. He was an enigma. On
the surface he was a charmer, always jovial and styl-
ishly uncouth. But beneath the facade, in those rare
moments of clarity, she perceived two warring fac-
tions within him, one intent on keeping secret some
terrible truth, the other desperate to reveal all.

She slid between the cool sheets of her narrow bed
and sighed. Perhaps she was making too much of him,
reading into the situation something that only existed
in her mind. Maybe he really was just a scoundrel,
one with a soft spot for her father.

She lay awake into the wee hours of the morning
thinking about him. When at last she gave in to her
insomnia—and her craving for another piece of Jim's
fried chicken—she got up and put on her dressing
gown, donned a pair of slippers and stole across the
yard to the back porch.

The kitchen was dark. Inside she could still hear
Tom's soft playing in the saloon, but the rest of the
house was quiet. Tom was a night owl and often

stayed up late practicing new music. She decided not to disturb him.

She was just about to light the kerosene lamp on the kitchen table, when she heard someone out in the hall. The last thing she wanted was to run into Chance. She flattened herself against the wall near the stove and listened. Light footfalls and the occasional squeak of a board sounded down the corridor.

The footfalls stopped, and Dora held her breath. There would be no repeat of their kiss in the dark. She'd be a fool to let something like that happen between them again. She edged toward the back door, determined to make her escape before he caught her.

Another sound stopped her in her tracks, a dull scraping along the floor. Intrigued, she crept back to the doorway leading to the hall and peeked out. Someone was there, a man, but it wasn't Chance. She could tell because the shadowy shape wasn't nearly as tall as the gambler's six feet.

She stood silent for a moment, allowing her eyes to adjust to the dim light.

The man knelt, then grunted as he picked something up from the floor. Dora realized it was a box. *What on earth…?* She was about to step out into the corridor and make herself known, when he raised his fist.

''Oh!'' She muffled her cry with the back of her hand.

He paused, then raised his fist higher and landed one firm beat on the walnut paneling of the hall, midway between the dining room and her father's study. To Dora's utter astonishment, a portion of the wall gave way, opening inward on silent hinges. The man disappeared into the darkness beyond, and Dora was left standing there, alone, her heart pounding.

Of course!

Since the day she'd decided to continue operating the saloon and had begun to fix the place up, the length of the hallway had always bothered her. It seemed too long—much longer than the combined dimensions of each of the three rooms off of it. In fact, she'd even measured it and had made a note of the discrepancy in her diary. That was the night Chance had kissed her. How could she forget?

On impulse she crept down the corridor and stared into the black void. It was a secret passageway leading down. Did she dare descend? She heard rustling below. Her breath caught in her throat as soft light flayed open the darkness of what appeared to be a secret basement. The man had lit a lamp.

She reminded herself that this was her house now, and her basement, secret or otherwise. Still, she took care to descend the steps as quietly as possible, though it hardly mattered as the man was making an awful racket.

Tom's playing continued, drifting down the hallway from the saloon. She didn't know whether he could hear the noise or not, or whether he'd be able to help her if she got herself into trouble.

Who was down there, and what in God's name was he doing?

She reached the bottom, a blind turn, and stepped onto soft dirt. The air was cool and musty, like a wine cellar she'd once been invited to see at a fancy house in Pueblo when she was a girl.

The racket was louder now. She inched around the blind turn and stopped dead. The room wasn't nearly as large as she'd expected. Crammed with boxes and old furniture, it seemed at first blush nothing more than a basement storeroom.

The man had his back to her. In the lamp light she immediately recognized him. His bald head sheened with perspiration, the muscles of his bare forearms bunched as he lifted the box.

"Jim."

He jumped at the sound of her voice and promptly dropped the box. He jumped again when he turned and saw her standing there in the shadows.

"Miss Dora!"

She stepped into the room, her narrowed gaze moving over every darkened corner and inch of wall, each trunk and box and stick of dated furniture. She arched a brow when her eyes settled on the nude portrait of her father's favorite whore, leaning against a stack of dusty boxes.

"What are you doing?" She nodded at the box he'd dropped when she'd startled him. A cold apprehension curled inside her.

The bartender shrugged. "Just putting away some old bottles. Empties." He knelt and opened the lid of the box. "Delilah likes me to save her some for the girls' potions and such."

She remembered Delilah's dressing table, crammed with both store-bought and homemade toiletries and colognes.

"Oh." His answer seemed reasonable.

"You're up awfully late, Miss Dora. Or early, depending on how you look at it."

"Yes." Something about the storeroom seemed off to her, but she couldn't put her finger on exactly what it was. "Why haven't I seen this before?"

"The cellar?" Again he shrugged. "Don't rightly know. It ain't a secret. I don't come down here much. There's rats."

A shiver shot up her spine as she whirled, checking the space around her.

"Tom and me kill 'em when we find 'em. Your pa used to borrow the marshal's cat—well, until the marshal's wife got wind of it and put a stop to it. It's some special variety, a Maine Coon, I think she calls it. Won some prizes in the Springs."

He was rambling, and she had the strangest feeling he was hiding something, not that Jim had ever given her any reason to doubt he was anything other than a loyal employee.

Again she peered into the darkened corners of the basement, then looked up to examine the low ceiling.

"I know what you're thinking, Miss Dora."

She frowned, distracted, and turned her attention back to Jim.

"You're thinking this is where it is."

"Where what is?"

He shot her a candid look. "The money."

Chapter Ten

"That's right. A high-stakes poker game." Chance set his coffee cup down on the card table, kicked back in his favorite chair and waited for Dora's reaction.

"When?"

"A week from tomorrow. Saturday night."

He'd decided on it last night while she and Gardner were together behind closed doors, and after a couple of old boys from the Springs who'd made the trip to Last Call just to play cards with him cleaned him out.

He was tired of waiting for Wild Bill's partner to surface. He'd gather up all the rotten apples in one barrel in one night, leak the rumor about Bill's secret fortune, and see if he could get the most rotten of them to show himself.

"But why?"

"Why not?" he said. "The house's cut of the profits will be sizable. I assume you could use the money."

It would mean she could postpone taking Gardner up on his offer of renegotiating the mortgage the bank held on the ranch. While he wanted her out of the way, he was convinced Gardner was up to something besides just being neighborly, and he didn't like it.

"Sizable if you win, you mean."

He grinned at her. "Where's your faith in me?"

"I thank the Lord daily that, up until now, I haven't had to put my faith in you for anything."

He winced, clutching at his heart as if he'd just been shot.

"All the same, I like the idea," she said. "It's good for business. I'll ask Jim to lay in more supplies." She fished her diary out of her pocket, pulled her fountain pen from behind her ear and began scribbling.

He smiled to himself.

She paused. "What are you up to?"

"Nothing." He tipped his chair back precariously far. "Just trying to make a living, like everyone else."

He could tell by her expression she didn't entirely believe him.

"There's something you're hiding."

"There's a lot I'm hiding. Come on upstairs with me and I'll show it to you."

As expected, she snapped the diary shut and marched off, but not before he recognized a flash of pain in her eyes, wedged there between embarrassment and irritation.

"Damn it." He'd hurt her. "Dora, wait." He followed her out through the kitchen, down the back steps and into the yard.

She kept walking.

He knew it was more than just his base comment that had upset her. He'd made plenty of those over the past few weeks, by design, and to her credit she hadn't let him scare her off. No, this was different. He was off balance, too. He'd lost over two hundred dollars at cards last night—a first—while Dora had kept company with that banker.

Chance grabbed her arm. "Wait."

She whirled on him.

Suddenly he was at a loss for words.

"Well?"

Looking into her eyes, he felt a burning in his gut he hadn't felt in...hell, maybe never. "I'm sorry. I was just joking."

She held his gaze, her face flushed, her nostrils flaring prettily, then all at once the fire in her eyes died. "You've made that quite clear, on more than one occasion."

The most glaring evidence being that night in the hallway when he'd kissed her, then had made light of the whole thing after Lily caught them together. Remorse twisted inside him.

"You...think I don't want you?"

"Of all the ridiculous—" She wrestled out of his grasp and fled toward the barn.

Gus and Rowdy were inside, watering the horses. The two ranch hands exchanged looks as Dora shot past them toward the last stall, nowhere else to go.

"Give us a minute, boys," he said.

"Sure, Chance." Rowdy set his bucket down, and he and Gus retreated outside, leaving them alone.

"These stalls are filthy." She made a show of inspecting them, kicking up soiled straw with a booted foot, and furiously making notes in her diary. He noticed her hands were shaking.

"You think I don't want you," he repeated, moving toward her.

"Mr. Wellesley, our conversation is over. I have work to do."

"Dora." He placed his hand over hers, stilling her pen.

She wouldn't look at him. So he looked at her, seeing beyond the dowdy gray dress and severe bun. Underneath she was a woman on fire.

"You're wrong," he said.

She dropped the pen and the diary and spun toward the last stall, where Silas stood watching them. The horse approached her and she reached out to him, stroking his face and neck.

He did want her, more than he'd ever wanted any woman. It was the damnedest thing. He couldn't explain it to himself, and he certainly wasn't going to explain it to her. But if he stood there a second longer, this close to her, he was going to take her in his arms and show her he hadn't been joking at all.

Don't do it, Wellesley.

"Good boy," she said to the horse, continuing to stroke him.

If things had been different, if he'd been different, he could tell her right now who he really was and why he was here. He could tell her how he felt about her. But that wasn't an option. There'd be no happy ending to look forward to, even if she did return his feelings.

It took every ounce of will he could muster to turn away from her. He plucked her diary and pen from the ground and handed them to her. She glanced at him only briefly, then dusted them off and dropped them into her pocket.

"You may have your card game," she said quietly,

continuing to stroke Silas's neck. "But once it's done, I'd like you to leave."

If things went the way he expected them to go, if Wild Bill's partner showed himself, he'd be leaving anyway, one way or another.

"Ma'am," he said formally, then headed for the door, which Rowdy had left open.

Word of the high-stakes card game spread fast. By midweek there wasn't an extra bunk to be had within ten miles of the Royal Flush. Delilah had crowded all six girls into one room for the week, to free up a few extra beds at the saloon for high-paying customers.

For days Jim had been busy behind the bar and in the kitchen in preparation. Dora had hired extra help from town to ease his workload. Three wagon loads of groceries and liquor had been delivered already, and Jim expected more. Dora checked off the supplies as they arrived, and had Jim keep a careful watch on inventory.

The local merchants with whom the Flush did business, and who were still owed thousands of dollars, suspended their "no credit" policies in honor of the festivities, after Dora had promised to pay each of them an equal share of her profit for the week toward her father's outstanding debts.

The town was alive with new business, and everyone was in a good mood. Everyone except Chance.

Dora had thrown herself into the preparations, working night and day, determined to keep her mind on business and off the things Chance had said to her last Friday in the barn. It didn't work. He was on her mind more than ever, and as she spent more and more time in the saloon, helping out, there'd been frequent opportunities to exchange the odd greeting or look.

You think I don't want you. You're wrong.

Nothing he could have said to her would have stunned her—or thrilled her—more than those words. At night in bed when her mind drifted, she replayed the scene in the barn over and over, only her actions, and the outcome, were different. She'd recognized the look in his eyes when he'd made that declaration, she'd known that with the slightest encouragement from her 'he would have taken her in his arms.

In her nighttime fantasies she'd given him that encouragement—a look, a touch, a word—and he'd kissed her just as he'd kissed her that night in the hallway. And she'd kissed him back.

"Miss Dora?"

Jim's voice jolted her back to the present.

"Um, yes?" She closed the icebox door, which she realized she'd been holding open for the past few minutes, staring blankly at the contents in cold storage.

"Mr. Gardner's here to see you."

She wasn't expecting him, and yet she wasn't surprised. He'd come calling twice since their supper last week, and each time she'd had Delilah or Jim make some excuse as to why she couldn't see him. She knew she couldn't put him off forever. He needed to know whether or not she'd accept his offer of financial help. She was ready to give her answer.

"Tell him to wait in my father's study." She checked her reflection in the small mirror over the kitchen sink. "I'll be along in a moment."

Jim shot her a blank look, tossed his bar towel onto

the counter, then quit the room, presumably to do as she'd asked.

Ever since the night she'd discovered the secret staircase leading down to the basement, she'd had an uneasy feeling about him. All along she'd suspected that some of the staff knew about the money hinted at in her father's letter, but not until that night had anyone spoken openly to her about it.

Since then, she hadn't had a good opportunity to explore the underground storeroom, and with the upcoming card game Jim had packed it full of liquor and other supplies.

"Oh, yoo-hoo…" Lily arched a thin dark brow at her from the kitchen doorway. "Lover boy's here, and dressed to kill."

"Yes, I know. Thank you."

Lily shook her head, surveying Dora's hair and outfit. "He come with flowers, too. God knows why."

She'd had just about enough of Lily's ill-mannered taunts. The girl was so uncivil, she didn't know why Delilah kept her on. Out of all of them, Lily was the smartest and had the most business sense. Maybe that's why they all suffered her bad behavior. Dora was inclined to boot her, too, as soon as the week was over.

She'd had a flurry of second thoughts after she'd given Chance his notice in the barn, which was absurd. Whatever he might have been in his old life, he was a gambler in this one, and she'd been acting like a smitten schoolgirl instead of a schoolteacher.

All of it ended, now.

She patted her hair, smoothed her dress, and brushed past Lily without so much as a nod.

Dora marched down the hall toward her father's

study. The man waiting for her was a gentleman, she reminded herself. He deserved her full attention. Chance Wellesley was hereby banished from her mind.

"Dora." John smiled as she entered the room.

"Oh!" Lily was right. He did have flowers, the most beautiful roses she'd ever seen. She wondered where he could have gotten them this time of year. It was still early spring in the high country and too chilly for them to bloom.

"These are for you."

"They're lovely." She took them and set them into a porcelain vase on her father's desk.

She'd learned over the past weeks that her father had been fond of Chinese art and artifacts. His study was peppered with small collections of figurines and porcelain.

"Thank you. You've been too kind."

John took her hand and guided her to the Queen Anne chair by the window. "It's not kindness. It's..."

She sat down, noticing his agitation. He looked around the room, distracted, and his cheeks were flushed, as if he'd been out riding on the range. She knew for a fact he'd come in the buggy.

"I would have asked your father first, had he been alive, but he's not."

She wished more than anything he was alive. She realized, these past few weeks at the ranch, that her mother had completely misrepresented the kind of man her father had been. She didn't know why. But she was sorry she hadn't had the opportunity to know him.

"Asked him what?"

To her utter astonishment, the banker dropped to his knees. When he took her hand and looked into her eyes, she knew instantly his intent.

"Marry me, Dora."

A little squeak escaped her throat.

"Marry me now, today."

She could hardly breathe. "I—I thought you were just being friendly, making me the offer of the bank loan."

He squeezed her hand tighter. "You won't need the loan if we're married."

"I...don't think I need the loan anyway." She shrugged, surprised at her own feelings, or rather, lack of them. "This card game will bring in enough business that I'll be able to catch up on my father's interest payments to the bank. I think I can stay current until a buyer's found for the ranch."

"Forget the loan, then. I want you with me, in town."

"I can't move to town. Not yet."

"Why not?" He brushed his thumb over her open palm, much as Chance had done almost on this very spot, not so long ago.

She hadn't shared with John her feelings about her father, her need to discover what he was like, why he and her mother had been estranged all these years and yet he'd continued to watch over her as she'd grown up.

She poured it all out now to him, and he listened attentively, kneeling there on the Persian carpet before her, holding her hand.

"A lot of people cared for my father, don't you see? He was a good man. I know that now. I didn't before. There's more I'd like to know, I just need time.''

''How much time?''

She shrugged. ''I don't know.''

''Somebody killed him,'' John said. ''That somebody could come after you. Have you thought of that?''

She hadn't thought of that, likely because it didn't make any sense. She told him so.

''He's right.''

Both of them turned at the sound of Chance's voice. He stood just inside the room. Dora was certain she'd closed the door behind her when she'd come in.

''You shouldn't be here,'' he said.

At first she thought Chance's comment was directed at John. She was wrong. He was looking directly at her.

''We agree on something at last.'' John got to his feet, but didn't let go of her hand.

She pulled hers away, uncomfortable under Chance's dark scrutiny. ''You said no one knows who killed my father.''

''That's right.'' He flashed his eyes at the banker. ''No one does.''

''So how do you know I'm safe in town?''

She had both of them there. They didn't answer.

''Besides, I have nothing to do with why my father was killed. How could I? I wasn't even here. Why would this person come after me?''

Chance eyed John. ''Maybe you have something he wants.''

''What could I possibly have that—'' Then it

dawned on her. "You mean his money. That's why he was killed."

It was the first time she, herself, had ever spoken openly of what her father had hinted at in his letter to her.

Chance's expression darkened.

"That's ridiculous," John said. "Your father didn't have any money. If he had, I would have known about it."

"Why you?" Chance said, moving closer.

John shrugged, as if it were obvious. "I was his banker."

Dora stepped between them, just in case.

"Is that all you were?" Chance's eyes blazed murder.

At first she'd thought his only reason for staying on was to find the money, or to swindle her out of it if she found it first. But some things didn't make sense. His obvious affection for her father, his growing animosity toward John, the way he looked at her when they were alone...

Why had Chance goaded her into keeping the saloon open all these weeks, but now suddenly wanted her gone, tucked safely away in town?

"I think you should leave now," she said to John, taking his arm and moving him toward the door. "I'll see you Sunday at church."

"You'll think about my offer?"

"She doesn't need a loan." Chance glared at him.

John paused in the doorway and looked at him. "That's not the offer I was referring to, not that it's any of your business."

Dora felt her face grow hot as Chance turned his gaze on her.

"I see," he said.

"Do you?" John shot him a smile. "Good."

For a heart-stopping moment she thought Chance was going to lunge at him.

"Sunday, then," John said to her.

She followed him from the room, her spine prickling as Chance's gaze burned into her.

His Colt was in pieces on the bed when a soft knock sounded outside his room. His rifle was handy, so he grabbed it before he got up to see who it was.

"It's me," a small voice said on the other side of the door. "Dora."

Surprised, he turned the key in the lock and cracked the door.

"Are you going to shoot me?" She looked pointedly at his rifle.

"I don't know," he said, lowering the weapon. "Think it would do any good?"

He was still irritated by what he'd witnessed between her and Gardner yesterday in the study. They hadn't spoken of it since.

"Probably not. May I come in?"

Now he was doubly surprised. Dora Fitzpatrick, schoolteacher, entering a man's room alone—his room—while the man himself was in residence.

"Sure." He pushed the door wide and gestured for her to enter.

Her eyes registered first surprise, then suspicion, when she surveyed the weapons on his bed. "What's all this?"

He shrugged. "Just cleaning my gun."

"You mean guns. I count three. And two knives."

She moved to the bed and gingerly lifted his buck knife off the coverlet.

"My father gave me that when I was a boy. It's a good knife." It was the first time in eighteen months he'd mentioned any of the members of his family to anyone.

She studied the weapon with new appreciation, noting the carved ivory handle. "You knew him, then?"

"My father? Sure."

"I wish I'd known mine."

They could hear the sounds of Tom's piano and men's voices below them in the saloon. Lily's seductive laugh was like a melody. Dora's expression darkened when she heard it. Risking her rebuke, he closed the door. She said nothing.

He wondered why she'd come. He'd seen little of her since the incident in the study. It was better that way, for him and for her.

Before he could caution her, she touched the tip of the knife blade with her finger. "Ow!"

"Give me that." He snatched it out of her hand and re-sheathed it, then noticed the drop of blood on her gray dress. "You're bleeding. Here, let me see it."

"It's nothing," she said, and sucked at the cut. "That's a very sharp knife."

"Sit down." The only chair in the room was heaped with clothing he hadn't had a chance to cart downstairs for one of the girls to launder. "Here." He cleared a spot for her on the bed.

She cast him a nervous look.

"You're already in here with me. If I'd wanted to do anything inappropriate, I'd have already done it. Go on, sit down."

For the first time since he'd met her, she did as he asked.

"Give me your hand."

"No, it's really—"

He didn't wait for her to finish. He grabbed her hand and peeled the fingers back to look at the cut. She was right. It wasn't bad. "You ought to know better than to touch a blade like that." He fished his handkerchief out of his pocket and pressed it to her finger.

"I'll be fine. Thank you." She tried to pull her hand away, but he held on.

"You'd be better off in town for a few days. Even Gardner thinks so."

"I have a feeling his reasons for wanting me there are quite different from yours."

Recalling one of Gardner's reasons, the one that made his blood boil, he let her hand go.

"Who are you, Mr. Wellesley?"

"You know who I am."

"I know you're not just here to play cards." Her steely eyes cut into him as neatly as his blade had nicked her finger.

"I am here to play cards. Saturday night. There's a thousand-dollar ante. Winner takes all."

"Why now? You could have held a card game like that anytime, long before I arrived here."

He leaned against the bureau and reached for his watch fob, twirling it as he studied her. "I didn't have a mind to, until now."

"I see." She rose from the bed and surveyed his room.

"This is the first time you've been in here. Why now?" he said, repeating her own words.

"Because now I have a mind to."

He knew she'd say that, and he laughed. She didn't, but he could see the muscles in her jaw relax.

"And because I have a question for you."

"Shoot."

She glanced at the guns he'd been cleaning on his bed and said, "What will you do with him once you find him?"

"Who?"

"My father's killer."

He looked at her, stunned. He dropped his watch fob, and it hung there by its chain, forgotten. He quickly recovered his composure. "What makes you think I care?"

"Everything that's happened here the past three weeks. And things I've been told happened before I arrived."

He knew she knew about the money he'd put up to pay for Bill's funeral. He smiled at her, but could tell she wasn't buying his nonchalant dismissal, no matter how artfully accomplished.

"Don't get me wrong," he said. "Bill was a fine man. It was a damned shame what happened to him."

"This morning I went into town. I talked to the marshal about that night."

"Max? Good. He was here. He could tell you what little there is to tell."

"He said that you went crazy, tore the saloon and the ranch apart, trying to identify the shooter, that you questioned every person here that night."

The room was too damned hot. He walked to the window and opened it. The cool breeze felt good on his face. He rubbed a hand over his beard stubble and carefully considered his next words. "Max and I are friends.'' He shrugged for effect. ''That was just my way of helping out.''

''For a gambler, you're awfully helpful.'' She came right up to him and looked him in the eyes. ''If that's what you really are.''

He met her gaze and relived the kiss he'd stolen from her in the hallway. He wanted to kiss her again. She was thinking about it, too. He could see it in her eyes. Her effect on him was dangerous, especially now, when she was so close.

''Ah, hell,'' he said, and pulled her to him. Before he could change his mind, he kissed her hard. She didn't resist, and that scared him. He drew a breath and marshaled his will, but in the end she was the one who backed away.

''I'll be downstairs,'' she said. ''If there's anything you'd like to tell me.''

There was a lot he'd like to tell her, but now wasn't the right time. He followed her into the hall, catching up with her at the top of the spiral staircase.

Delilah was just coming up. ''A couple of Southern gentlemen here to see you.''

Chance didn't know any Southern gentlemen, but that didn't mean much. High rollers with money to burn were coming in from all over to play cards with him. ''Tell them I'll be right down.''

''They want Miss Dora.''

''What for?''

Delilah lifted a painted brow at him. ''Cause *she* runs this place, not you.''

''What do they want?'' Dora asked.

''Rooms. I told 'em we didn't have none left, but they're awfully nice-looking gentlemen.'' Delilah winked at her. ''It'd be a nice change for the girls.''

Dora descended the staircase into the saloon. Chance and Delilah followed. He recognized the two men instantly by their manicures and fine clothes. Each sported a set of Smith & Wesson .44 caliber revolvers with walnut grips and engraved nickel finishes that would have set a working man back a year's wages.

"Lee Hargus, ma'am." The younger looking of the two removed his hat and gave Dora a once-over, then a polite smile. "And this here's my brother, Dickie."

"Mr. Hargus," she said, nodding first at one, then the other.

The older one said nothing. He was tall and had a cool air about him that Chance didn't like.

"Delilah says you'd like a couple of rooms."

"That's right."

"You're here for the game, then?"

Dickie's blue eyes narrowed. His brother hitched an elbow on the bar and took in the scene around him: drinks flowing, every table packed with card-playing men and every girl working, even Susan. Tom's piano music was lively, and the atmosphere downright festive.

"That's right," Lee said. "We're here for the game."

"I've got two rooms left, but I'm afraid they'll cost you."

"Money's not a problem." He gestured for Jim to pour him a drink.

"Wonderful. They're right across the hall from Mr. Wellesley's."

Lee leveled his gaze at Chance. Dickie's blue eyes followed.

"Wellesley," Lee said, giving him a different kind

of once-over than he'd given Dora. "Sounds familiar."

Chance felt the muscles in the back of his neck and shoulders bunch. His Colt was still upstairs on the bed in pieces.

"Yes," Dora said. "Our Mr. Wellesley has quite a reputation."

"I thought you were saving those rooms," Chance said, and shot her a pointed look.

"Hmm? No, I wasn't saving them. In fact, the rooms are ready now."

"Good." Lee downed his shot of whiskey, then smiled at her. "Let's go."

"Dora." Chance took her arm, making it clear he wanted to speak with her alone.

Her annoyance with him showed. "Excuse me, gentlemen," she said to the brothers. "I'll be right back." She followed him into the kitchen.

The second he had her alone, he said, "I don't like those two. Send 'em packing."

"Why don't you like them? They seem perfectly agreeable to me. Besides, they've got money. They're exactly the kind of men you were hoping to attract."

She was right, but for reasons she knew nothing about.

"Upstairs I asked you if there was anything you'd like to tell me. Is there?"

He said nothing.

Irritation charged with a healthy dose of rebellion shone in her eyes. "Fine." She marched back out to the saloon.

"Dora, wait."

She paused under the staircase. "Well?"

He'd come too far to jeopardize things now. Grinding his teeth, he bit back a curse.

Their interaction wasn't lost on the Hargus boys.

"Oh, don't mind them," Lily said, slinking up beside Lee and wrapping her arms around his neck. "They're like two polecats in a burlap sack. You never know if they're gonna spit at each other or—" She flashed Dickie a look and smiled. "Well, you know."

Lee smiled pointedly at Dora. "Ma'am?"

She shot Chance an angry look, then said, "Yes, Mr. Hargus. You and your brother are most welcome here at my establishment." She gestured to the staircase. "I'd be happy to show you to your rooms."

Chapter Eleven

The Hargus boys were trouble from the beginning.

Dora sat in the upstairs parlor with Susan, the *New England Primer* open on her lap. The door was cracked, and neither of them could concentrate with the commotion going on outside.

"Dickie prefers blondes," Rose said. "I heard his brother say so last night. So there!"

"That ain't true." Daisy's voice quavered. "He asked for me this morning when he got up, didn't he?"

"Delilah said he asked for me!"

"There they go again." Susan cast Dora a look.

Where was Delilah when she needed her? The girls, all except Susan, had been fighting over the Hargus brothers since they'd arrived. If Dora let this new round of bickering go on a moment longer, she'd have a full-blown catfight on her hands. She set the primer aside.

"What are you going to do?" Susan followed her out into the upstairs hall.

"I'm going to have a little talk with them."

She'd speak with Columbine and Iris later. Lily

was another matter altogether. She'd corralled both brothers in Lee's room a little over an hour ago and hadn't come out since.

"Good luck," Susan said.

It was Friday afternoon and the saloon was packed with men drinking and gambling, trying to win enough money to play in the high-stakes poker game Chance had set for tomorrow night.

Dora peered over the balcony, surveying the scene below. Cigar smoke drifted up from the first floor and hung in the air like a cloud. She blinked a couple of times to clear her eyes.

"You mean she's still in there with 'em?" Daisy said.

Rose screwed up her face in a nasty smirk. "Yes, she's still in there, but you can't hear anything except whispering going on."

The two girls put their ears to the door of Lee Hargus's room, their eyes wide with curiosity. Dora grabbed them by the ruffles fringing the low backs of their brightly colored dresses and pulled.

Daisy jumped. Rose swore.

"You two ought to be downstairs," Dora said.

"But Lily's—"

"I don't care what Lily's doing. Delilah will skin you two alive if she sees you're not working." Dora still wasn't comfortable with their profession and never would be, but if they were downstairs mingling, at least they wouldn't be fighting over the Hargus boys.

"What about her?" Rose frowned at Susan. "She's not working."

"I am so," Susan said, flashing her copy of the

New England reading primer at them. "I'm working to better myself."

Daisy snorted.

"That's enough." Dora maneuvered them toward the staircase. "I've made the same offer to each of you. You can either improve your skills in reading, writing and arithmetic, here with me, or..."

"Or what?" Rose said, grinning.

Dora refused to be embarrassed. "Or continue to make a living on your backs. It's your choice." There. She'd said it.

Rose and Daisy exchanged looks.

"It's mighty kind of you to offer, Miss Dora, but I'm not too good at arithmetic." Daisy shot Rose a conspiratorial smile. "On the other hand, I *am* good at—"

"All right, that's enough." Dora clapped her hands as if they were students and she the teacher. "Downstairs with the both of you."

She and Susan watched as the two of them glided downstairs and began chatting with customers. Dora breathed relief. She had no idea where Delilah was. She'd have to speak to her about these Hargus brothers, and about keeping the girls in line.

"Are we done, then?" Susan glanced at her primer.

Dora was pleased by how quickly Susan's reading skills were improving. Each day they read from the *New England Primer* and from the letters Susan had received from the orphanage where, under pressure from her family, she'd placed her baby son.

Dora had made some inquiries and discovered it would be a simple matter for Susan to take her child back—if she were married.

Susan's attention strayed, her gaze fixing on something below them in the saloon. Dora realized she was staring at some*one*. Tom.

The piano player looked up, and Susan froze. He smiled at her, and when she smiled back he stumbled over his piano keys, botching the piece.

Both of them laughed.

Dora patted her arm. "Why don't we pick up again tomorrow where we left off?"

"All right," Susan said, not really hearing her. She handed Dora her primer and started down the staircase.

"Go on! Get up there. All three of you."

What on earth...?

Chance, who for some reason wasn't playing cards, herded the young girls Dora had hired to help in the kitchen toward the staircase. Susan backed up onto the balcony as they thundered up the steps, all chattering at once.

"And stay up there, till you get some sense. You hear?" Chance frowned at them, then cast her a quick look before returning to his regular table.

Dora looked to Susan for an explanation. She had none.

"What's all this about?" Dora said to the girls.

The eldest of them, who was thirteen, said, "He's madder than a hatter at us now, Miss Dora."

"Why?" She couldn't imagine what the girls could have done to provoke him.

"He says we should get some schooling from you."

"He did?" She was both surprised and intrigued.

"Yes, ma'am. Chance—er, Mr. Wellesley, I mean—says we ought to be hauled out to the barn and whipped if we ever says something like that again.''

''You said it, not us.'' The youngest of the three poked her in the arm.

''Said what?''

They exchanged glances, then looked to Susan for help.

''Well?'' Dora said.

''Oh, heck, I said it.'' The eldest girl looked Dora in the eyes. ''I said if we worked hard, in a couple more years maybe we could be like Miss Susan here.''

''And Miss Lily,'' the other girl said. ''I want to be like her.''

Dora was taken aback. ''You said that to Ch—I mean Mr. Wellesley?''

''Yes, ma'am. When he come into the kitchen to wash his hands.''

The youngest girl's eyes went wide. ''We thought he was gonna whip us right then and there.''

''He should have.'' Dora crossed her arms over her chest and gave them her most disapproving look. ''That's not why I hired you.''

The eldest looked appropriately contrite. ''He said you'd straighten us out.''

''Did he?''

All three of them nodded.

''Here, take Susan's primer and go on into the parlor. There's another one on the settee. I'll be along directly.''

One of them grabbed the primer and they all took off like shots.

Dora looked over the balcony into the saloon.

Chance glanced up from his card playing, and for a brief moment held her gaze.

"What do you make of that?" she said to Susan.

"Of Chance scolding those girls?" Susan shrugged. "Typical."

"Of Chance Wellesley?"

"He scolded me once, too. Well, not scolded so much as advised. He told me I didn't have to stay here if I didn't want to. That he'd see to it I got a decent job somewhere else."

"Did he?" Now she was truly stunned.

"Sometimes you've gotta look extra close, Miss Dora, to see what a man's really like." Susan was staring at Tom again, her brown eyes shining.

"Yes," she said, her gaze drifting to Chance. "Perhaps you're right."

The Hargus boys were either lying or they just plain couldn't count. Chance glanced at his hand— full house, aces high—then resumed his stare-down with Lee.

"I'll see you." The Southerner grinned at him, then slid a stack of double eagles in his direction.

Chance laid out his hand. The twitch at the corner of Lee's mouth was nearly imperceptible as he glanced at Chance's cards. His green eyes cooled as he folded his hand. The other men at the table grew suddenly quiet.

Jim shot Chance one of his trademark want-me-to-get-the-shotgun glances from behind the bar, but Chance discreetly waved him off.

Lee laughed, then leaned back in his chair, motioning one of the girls over from the bar. The other men at the table relaxed as the Southerner called for another round of drinks.

"You're good, Wellesley," Lee said. "It's refreshing to find a man who lives up to his reputation."

"Which you heard about, I presume, all the way down in... Where'd you say you and your brother were from again?"

"Arkansas. Our daddy's got a farm right outside Doddridge. Nice quiet place. You'd like it."

Chance collected his winnings, sweeping bills and coins into a leather pouch that, tonight, was fat with Lee Hargus's money. Most of the bills were counterfeit. He could tell just by feeling them. Instead of calling him on it, Chance said, "Arkansas... That's a long way to come to play cards."

Lee shrugged, his grin sliding to the side of his face. "What else we got to do, right boys?"

The other men at the table laughed, then raised their glasses.

Chance got to his feet.

"The night's still young, Wellesley." Lee began shuffling a new deck. "One more hand."

Chance declined.

"He's savin' himself for tomorrow night," one of the others said. "Can't say as I blame him. It's the biggest game ever been held at the Flush. Just look at the place. There's men here from all over, just trying to win enough to buy in."

"A thousand-dollar ante." Lee let out a long, low whistle. "Gotta be a mighty confident man."

Rose slid onto the Southerner's lap. "Ooo," she said. "You seem mighty confident to me."

Everyone laughed.

"Wild Bill would have been a happy man," Rose said, "had he seen the place running like this."

The men at the table raised their glasses in memory of William Fitzpatrick. All except Chance, who didn't have a drink in front of him, and Lee Hargus, who didn't even twitch.

"Did you know him?" Chance asked.

"Me?" Lee slid his hands around Rose's waist. "No. Can't say that I did. Heard he was a good man, though."

"He was."

Lee's smile faded. He raised his glass and tossed his whiskey back in one swallow.

"Boys," Chance said, nodding to the men at the table. "Hargus." He turned his attention back to Lee. "I'll see you tomorrow night."

"I look forward to it."

As Chance snaked his way through the crowded tables toward the bar, he searched each face, as he'd done every night at the Royal Flush for the past six months. Some of the men he knew, most of them he didn't. Some of them even looked familiar. He told himself it could be anyone, but in his gut he knew the man was here, now, watching and waiting. Chance had been watching and waiting for months. It was time he finally did something.

"I don't know about those two," Jim said, when Chance approached the bar.

"Who?"

"You know who. Those Hargus boys."

"Give the gentlemen a chance to settle in. They've only been here a couple of days." Delilah cast Dickie, who lounged against the piano listening to one of

Tom's love songs, a lusty look. "Besides, I like 'em. Especially that tall, quiet one."

"You would," Jim said. "That way you can do all the talking."

"And the bossin'," Lily said as she swished past on her way upstairs with an extremely drunk client.

"Oh, hush." Delilah smirked at them both.

Jim grinned at her, then the two of them went back to their respective duties—Jim making sure every customer's glass was filled with the most expensive whiskey he could talk them into, and Delilah making sure if they were lonely, they weren't lonely for long.

Chance stood there taking it all in, reflecting on what he knew for sure and what he only suspected. Grimmer, Wild Bill's lawyer, was here again tonight, sitting at his regular table with the marshal. He still hadn't crossed the rotund little man off his list.

Nor was he sure about Tom or Jim, or even Delilah. He watched as she herded a couple more girls toward Lee Hargus's table. For some reason she'd taken those Southern boys under her wing, and he didn't like it. It occurred to him that in all these months he'd never been able to find out Delilah's last name. It had bothered him from the first day he met her. It bothered him more now as he watched her swoosh across the saloon toward the piano and fawn over Lee's older brother.

"Get you a drink, Chance?" Jim leaned across the bar to catch his attention.

"No, not tonight."

"Staying sober from now on, huh?"

"Ever seen me drunk?"

Jim looked at him funny. "You know, come to think of it, I never have."

That was because he'd been sober for the past year, ever since Wild Bill Fitzpatrick had saved his life by hauling him out of that opium den in Fairplay. Bill hadn't known him from Adam, but he knew a man with a death wish when he saw one, and Bill was too good a Samaritan to let another man do himself harm.

"I'm going upstairs," Chance said.

He climbed the spiral staircase, surveying the scene below one last time before turning toward his room, which was near the corner and not visible from the saloon.

He fished out his key, but didn't use it to unlock the door of his room. He used it to unlock the door of the room next to his, the room in which Lee Hargus had taken up residence.

A few minutes later he found what he was looking for, and his suspicions were confirmed. The train-ticket stubs he held in his hand revealed that Lee and Dickie Hargus had left Texarkana for Colorado Springs nine days ago, two days *before* Chance had announced the high-stakes card game.

The Hargus boys could count, after all. They weren't stupid, they were lying.

"I don't believe it," Dora said.

"It's true." Delilah sorted through the old gowns in the back of her walnut clothes cupboard as Dora plopped onto the bed, more confused than ever.

"You mean to tell me that Chance has never...not with *any* of the girls? Not even Lily?"

Delilah shot her a look. "Especially not with Lily. The woman grates on him. I can tell."

"Yes, well, she grates on all of us, doesn't she."

"Here," Delilah said, and waltzed toward her bearing an evening dress of dark blue silk. "You'll look dandy in this one."

"I told you. I'm not appearing in the saloon. Especially tonight." It was half past nine, and the high-stakes poker game had already begun. It was quieter than a Sunday church service downstairs.

"Like it or not, you own this place. It's a big night for the Flush and for you. For all of us. You should be there."

Dora held the gown up in front of her. It wasn't nearly as scandalous as the violet velvet she'd worn for her evening with John Gardner, but it was still a bit sensational. She decided she liked it.

"Why hasn't Chance been with any of them?" she asked as she looked at her reflection in Delilah's oval mirror.

"Beats me. That's for you to find out."

"Me? What makes you think I'd ever ask Chance Wellesley something so personal?"

Delilah snorted. "If you ask me, you two ought to be gettin' a *lot* more personal with each other."

"Oh, stop."

"That man wants you. He needs you. I can tell."

Now it was Dora's turn to snort. "Yes, I'm sure he does. Like an incorrigible boy needs a good ear-twisting. Besides, you're wrong. That night in the hallway…" She recalled their kiss for the thousandth time. "He went upstairs with Lily. You were there. You saw them."

"I saw that Lily was madder than a hornet when I went up directly after. Chance sent her to bed. Alone."

"She told you that?" A thrill curled inside her.

"She didn't, but Susan did the next morning."

Dora held the blue silk up in front of her again. It was very sophisticated, perfect for a woman of her age. In fact, looking at the cut of the gown more closely, she didn't think it was too daring at all.

"You know," she said to Delilah, "I think I will make an appearance tonight. Why not? I do own the place. I might as well enjoy it—just this once."

"Now there's your pa's girl talkin'." Delilah beamed her a smile.

"You really think so?" She'd like to believe there was something of him in her.

"I do. Now, get dressed and get on down there. You want to see Chance whip those Hargus boys at cards, don't you?"

She did. The more she got to know Lee and Dickie Hargus, the less she liked them. "Go ahead," she said. "I'll be right down."

All eyes turned to Dora as she glided down the spiral staircase into the saloon. The first thing she noticed was that the painting of the nude woman had been resurrected from the basement storeroom and was hanging above the bar. Someone—likely Jim—was going to get a piece of her mind, but later.

The second thing she noticed was Chance's expression, a tense fusion of worry and desire. Her gaze locked with his. All that she'd discovered about him over the past few weeks forced her to view him in an entirely different light.

She knew he didn't want her here, not tonight. He'd made it clear he was concerned for her safety, given the heated emotions that accompanied this kind of event. But she didn't entirely buy his argument, and had the nagging feeling he had other motives for wanting her gone. That afternoon he'd made one last effort to send her to town, but she'd refused to leave.

John Gardner had also come out to the ranch that afternoon to plead his case—that she should be nowhere near the Royal Flush tonight. Anything might happen, he'd said. As her gaze drifted over the crowd, she noticed that nearly every man in the room wore a gun.

Despite her momentary anger about the painting and her muddled feelings about Chance and John, she forced a smile and nodded politely at her customers as she descended into the throng.

Every man in the room who hadn't already removed his hat, did so now. Well, at least she was respected, if not entirely respectable.

"Shall we continue?" Chance said, and turned his attention back to the game.

Tom sat at his piano, but wasn't playing. Susan stood nearby. The rest of the girls, including Delilah, were working the crowd. Rowdy and Gus were busy outside tending to customers' horses, and Jim, as always, was behind the bar.

She wondered if this was the way things had been the night her father was shot. That's how Chance had described it—a packed house. Everyone who was anyone in Last Call had been there. Everyone except John Gardner.

"Hello, Dora."

She turned at the sound of his voice. "John!"

He'd been waiting for her behind the staircase in the doorway leading to the hall. The three young girls she'd hired from town were busy in the kitchen behind him.

"You didn't think I'd leave you alone out here tonight, did you?"

She hadn't really given it any thought. "I, um..."

To be honest, she hadn't given *him* much thought since their evening together a few nights ago. Just this afternoon he'd renewed his proposal of marriage, and again she'd put him off, asking for more time to consider his request.

He smiled and took her arm, stood there with her as if they were already married and he owned the place. Chance glanced up from the game and for a chilling heartbeat locked eyes with him.

"I, um, need to check with Jim to make sure he's got things in hand." She unwound her arm from John's and hurried behind the bar.

"Miss Dora, you look pretty as a picture." Jim looked her over appreciatively and smiled.

Dora flashed her eyes at the nude portrait. "Speaking of which..."

"Now don't go blaming me. I had nothing to do with it. I went out to the kitchen about an hour ago to see how the girls were getting on, and when I came back it was just there. Honest."

She arched a brow at him, unconvinced. "We'll talk about it later."

Dora took charge as men clamored for more drinks, the girls fell behind in the kitchen, and the lines outside the upstairs bedrooms dwindled. Even Lily's charms couldn't sway much interest away from the high-stakes game.

The hours flew past. Men joined and eventually left the table after they'd "busted," as Jim put it. By midnight only five players remained: a politician from

Denver, a rancher from Fairplay who'd apparently been very lucky, the Hargus brothers and Chance.

For the first time all evening, Dora dispensed with her busywork and decided to watch. John leaped from his chair and offered her his seat as she approached the nearby table he shared with a couple of local merchants, Mr. Grimmer, and the marshal.

Chance dealt another hand, and the crowd fell silent. Dora held her breath, counting over ten thousand dollars in bills and coin on their table. Lee Hargus looked at her and smiled. She watched the muscles in Chance's face tighten.

"Heard a rumor this afternoon," Lee said to her, after glancing at his hand.

Dora couldn't imagine why he'd address her during the game. Uneasy under his scrutiny, she remained silent.

"Folks say your daddy was a swindler."

"What?"

Whispers spread like wildfire through the crowd.

"What are you talking about?"

"Come on," John said. He took her hand and pulled her to her feet. Dora stood fast, refusing to leave with him.

Lee pushed a short stack of hundreds to the center of the table, nodding to Chance that he was in. "Heard he was taking in currency and giving change in counterfeit. Right here in this saloon."

Dora had never heard anything so ridiculous. "I have no idea what you're talking about." She looked to Chance for an explanation, but he didn't even acknowledge her. He stared at Lee, his hands clenched into fists under the table.

"Heard the real money was stashed somewhere here." Lee glanced around the room.

For a chilling moment no one said a word.

Then Chance laughed. It was the last thing she or anyone else expected. He slapped his cards down, rocked back in his chair and reached for his watch fob. "Wild Bill a swindler? He wouldn't know how to begin. Hell, it was a miracle he was able to keep this place running on his own."

What an odd thing for Chance to say about her father. Dora looked at him, confused.

The Denver politician tossed his cards into the center of the table, folding his hand. "I heard Fitzpatrick had some kind of business partner, helped him keep this place afloat."

Partner? Her father's letters had said nothing about a business partner.

Lee eyed the politician, interested in this new piece of information.

"Is this true?" Dora looked to Jim and Delilah for confirmation.

The two exchanged glances. Delilah shrugged. "Well?" she said to Jim.

John placed a shaky hand around her waist and tried, without success, to draw her away from the table. She removed it, then shot him a look. His frustration was evident, but that didn't concern her now.

"I've got news for you, Mr. Hargus." She straightened her stance and looked down her nose at Lee. "My father never would have swindled anyone, least of all his customers."

"She's lying," Dickie said.

It was the first time in two days Dora had heard

Dickie Hargus utter a word. The Southerner sat statue-still, blue eyes cool, his expression unreadable.

The marshal's hand slid toward his gun belt.

Chance flashed him a look, and he backed off.

For what seemed like an eternity, the only movement in the room was the lazy swirl of smoke curling off Lee's cigar.

Placing his cards facedown on the table, the Denver politician said, "Maybe she's in on it."

"I beg your pardon?"

She noticed the tic at the edge of Chance's mouth. Lee's smile faded. The rancher pushed back his chair, sweat beading on his forehead. At any moment Dora thought he might bolt from the room.

Her gaze was suddenly drawn to the pewter watch fob Chance wore each day, suspended from a chain attached to his belt. It was an unusual shape, not like any fob she'd ever seen before. It struck her as odd that a man like Chance would wear such a decoration. He didn't even own a watch.

"There's nothing to be in on." With his usual self-assurance, Chance began to twirl the pewter fob.

Dora stared at it, mesmerized, its motion hypnotic. Chance toyed with the object incessantly, yet tonight she had the strangest feeling she'd seen it elsewhere, out of context. As the revolutions accelerated, the room felt suddenly overwarm. Dora's head began to pound.

Of course!

"Miss Dora, look out!"

Dickie Hargus drew his gun, so fast it was in his hand before the piano player's warning registered. With a shock, she realized Chance had drawn his, the watch fob abandoned on its chain. The marshal reacted next, then every man in the room was on his feet.

John grabbed her hand. It occurred to her that he was the only man there who wasn't armed. He tried to pull her to safety toward the bar, but she dug her heels into the Persian carpet.

A heartbeat later, Chance moved in front of her, directly into the path of Dickie's aim. ''Hold up, Hargus.''

In those inscrutable blue eyes, Dora read the Southerner's intent and braced herself for the outcome.

Chapter Twelve

If he could have relived the past few weeks, he'd have done a lot of things differently. To start he would have sent Dora Fitzpatrick back to Colorado Springs the very first night he met her.

Chance locked eyes with Dickie. Lee moved into line with his brother, flaunting one of his .44s. No one breathed.

"Boys?" the marshal said.

Chance felt Dora's hands light on his back, her warm breath tickled his ear. "Don't."

He'd lied to her and used her, manipulating her into keeping the saloon open to give him more time. Worse than that, he'd endangered her life. The end justified the means. That's what he'd made himself believe the past year. Now he wasn't so sure. Staring into Dickie's cold eyes, he realized he'd become as ruthless as the men he was hunting.

"Chance?" Dora said.

Wild Bill's partner was here. Chance could feel it.

Earlier that week as men arrived from all over, Chance had discreetly spread the rumor that Wild Bill

Fitzpatrick had been cheating his customers. Only it wasn't a rumor, it was the truth.

For nearly a year Bill had been taking in real currency at the Royal Flush and making change in counterfeit. Coins were heavy, and distances far, and in recent years more and more men were paid in bank notes instead of gold. Bill had capitalized on that fact and had squirreled away a fortune in the process. A fortune he'd kept secret from his silent partner, a counterfeiter and money launderer with whom Chance had unfinished business.

The marshal narrowed his eyes at each man circling the table. "The card game's over."

For a heartbeat no one moved.

Lee was the first one to put away his gun. "Suits me," he said, then smiled. "I was losing, anyway."

Chance squared off with Dickie.

"I mean it," the marshal said.

It occurred to Chance that, for gamblers, the Hargus brothers weren't very good at cards. Together, he and Dickie holstered their guns, but continued their stare-down. As Lee and Dickie raked their remaining money into leather pouches, and the crowd dispersed, Chance wondered, not for the first time, if he was looking into the cool blue eyes of a murderer.

There could be no mistakes, not this time.

This time he had to be sure.

The marshal cleared the saloon, and by eleven o'clock that night the Royal Flush was closed.

"Don't seem fittin', seein' as it's Saturday night and all." Lily pressed her lips into a pout.

"Get your feathered behind upstairs and go to

bed." Delilah shooed her up the staircase, then followed with the rest of the girls.

A few minutes earlier, under the marshal's watchful eyes, the Hargus boys had packed their bags and gone. Dora had a bad feeling they'd be back.

"Come back to town with me. Now, Dora." John was insistent.

Chance was more than insistent, he was unbending. His resolve both thrilled and frightened her. She'd never seen him like this. "No," he said. "She stays here."

"With you?"

Chance locked gazes with the banker, and the fierce determination shining in his eyes convinced her he'd never let her leave tonight, even if she wanted to go, which she didn't.

"I'm not an idiot." John took a step toward Chance. "I've seen the way you look at her when you think no one's watching."

Chance didn't respond. She could tell from his tight expression he was considering John's accusation, as if until this moment he'd not been aware of his own behavior—or at least that anyone had noticed it.

"Only an idiot would take her back to town tonight," he said. "They're out there. Hell, Gardner, you're not even armed."

They referred to Lee and Dickie Hargus. Dora was still unclear as to why the notion of her father passing counterfeit currency to customers had triggered so emotional a response from the two brothers. To her knowledge, they'd never set foot in the Royal Flush before.

Why would two Southern gamblers care about the alleged crimes of a dead man? She knew they weren't lawmen. The idea was too far-fetched. Besides, despite the appearance of a few manufactured bank notes, she refused to believe her father was a counterfeiter.

I heard the real money was stashed somewhere here.

And what was this nonsense about a silent partner? No one here at the saloon knew anything about it. Neither did John. She supposed someone could be lying, but to what purpose? If her father had had a business partner, why hadn't the man stepped forward and declared himself?

Marry me, Dora.

John's proposal echoed in her mind, haunting her.

He took another step toward Chance, jarring her from her thoughts. ''I don't want her staying here with you another night.''

Dora moved between them, seeing the banker in a new light. ''John, I know you mean well, but this is my home, at least for now. I'm perfectly safe here, from everything and everyone.'' She gave Chance a hard look.

''Dora.'' John took her arm.

Chance went for him.

''Stop it! Both of you.'' She untangled herself from the two of them and moved behind the bar, out of reach. Jim ran out from the kitchen when he heard the ruckus. Chance backed off.

Dora addressed all of them. ''I'm staying here tonight and every other night, until I find a buyer for the saloon and the ranch.'' Her mind was racing with new thoughts, terrible thoughts, and the rivalry between John and Chance only served to distract her. ''Please, John, I wish you'd go.''

The banker looked at her, stunned. Unlike Chance, John Gardner was a man who wore his emotions on his sleeve for all to see. The hurt in his eyes was so genuine, she nearly called him back when he grabbed his hat and overcoat off a chair and stormed out.

"Good riddance," Chance said.

She asked Jim to give them a minute, and the bartender slipped back to the kitchen.

"I want answers." She came around the bar and faced Chance. "Now."

"You'll get them, but not tonight."

"The money's real, isn't it? At first I didn't think it was, then I did, but for the past few days I wasn't sure, anymore. It's here somewhere, isn't it?"

He didn't answer. He didn't have to. She knew from the look on his face that he believed it one hundred percent.

"Did my father really swindle his customers, like Lee Hargus said?"

Chance looked at her, his face tight with emotions she couldn't begin to fathom. "Yes."

"He was a counterfeiter?"

"I didn't say that."

"His...partner then. This silent business partner the congressman alluded to—he's the counterfeiter."

Chance said nothing.

And then it struck her.

"He didn't know, did he? Not until...recently." She fished her diary out of the pocket of her gown and paged through it, rereading some of her notes.

Chance remained silent.

"He fed my father counterfeit currency to use in the saloon. That explains the fake bank notes we found. In return he expected *real* currency. Only my father held some back, held a lot back, if you believe some of the rumors. His partner found out about it, didn't he? When my father refused to tell him where he'd hidden the real money, his business partner shot him."

She glanced at the spot behind the bar. "Right here in the saloon." She met Chance's steady gaze. "I'm right, aren't I? This partner, whoever he is, wants the money, and thinks he can find it."

Chance's eyes turned cool. He toyed with his watch fob, then began to twirl it, his gaze pinned on hers. For the second time that night, she was mesmerized by the pewter trinket. A moment before Dickie Hargus had drawn his gun, she'd made the connection. In the commotion, she'd forgotten—until now.

All the hairs on her nape prickled.

It was entirely possible she'd just made the biggest mistake of her life.

"John may not have been armed," she said, gathering her courage, "but I am."

She raised the hem of her gown, revealing her father's derringer, which she'd secreted in an ankle holster she'd found in his study earlier that evening. Just in case.

"You're full of surprises."

She feared he'd approach her, but he didn't.

Looking pointedly at his watch fob, she arched a brow at him. "So are you."

A few minutes later, locked in her cabin, a chair jammed up against the door and the derringer within easy reach, Dora slid the tintype out of her diary and studied every detail.

In the image her father was leaning against a battered, wooden table in a room she didn't recognize. It couldn't be here at the ranch. She'd been inside every room at one time or another, and in all the outbuildings. Never had she seen that particular table, nor the ornate birdcage sitting atop it.

He had a relaxed, faraway look on his face, the same expression Chance often lapsed into while engaged in one particular activity.

Dora stared hard at the smudge in the bottom left corner of the tintype, near her father's right hand, and knew for certain what she'd only guessed at in the saloon. It wasn't a smudge at all. The image was blurred due to an object in motion—a watch fob, the very same one that hung from Chance Wellesley's belt.

She smiled, noting her father twirled it in precisely the same manner as Chance. Or perhaps it was the other way around. She'd looked at the tintype dozens of times in the past three and a half weeks, and she'd simply never recognized what she was seeing.

What else had she missed?

She ripped open the desk drawer and retrieved her spectacles. She hadn't needed them much lately, now that her nights were occupied not with reading but with running a saloon. Popping them on, she placed the tintype on the desk and drew the lamp up close.

Despite the fact that her father had very likely been involved with a counterfeiter, he'd also been a clever man. Dora was now one hundred percent convinced that this was no ordinary tintype. It had been taken with a single purpose in mind—to provide her, and no one else, with clues that would lead her to the money he'd kept secret from his business partner and had hidden here at the ranch.

"Good Lord!"

She hunched over the desk, peering closely at the background captured in the tintype. The light-colored walls of the room in which her father stood were...swirled. No, not exactly swirled, but... Where had she seen walls like this before? They were almost like—

"Masonry!"

She jumped up from the table, upending the chair as she ripped off her spectacles, which clattered to the floor.

While it took her barely a minute to wrestle herself out of the gown she'd borrowed from Delilah and don her gray dress, she forced herself to wait. She extinguished her lamp and climbed into bed, not prepared to sleep but to think, for two more hours, until she could no longer hear any sounds coming from the house or any of the outbuildings.

Then, swiveling silently out of bed, Dora slid the tintype back into her diary beside her father's letter, and jammed it into the pocket of her dress along with a candle and two matchsticks.

Into her other pocket she slid the derringer. Ankle holsters were all well and good when one was dressed in an evening gown and had no other place to hide a gun. But she was no seasoned sleuth, she was a schoolteacher, and preferred to have the weapon close at hand.

After parting the draperies to peek outside, assuring herself no one was lying in wait, Dora removed the chair from beneath the knob and slowly opened the door. Nothing happened. So far so good.

It was a cool night, and the mountain air cleared her head. Glancing up, she noticed Chance's room was dark. That meant nothing, particularly now that he knew nearly everything she knew. Probably more. She'd have to be very careful.

There were no lights on in the house when she crept across the kitchen into the hallway. It was so dark, in fact, she nearly tripped on the carpet. The air was heavy with stale cigar smoke and the smell of Irish whiskey wafting from the blackness of the saloon.

Dora breathed shallowly, her heart in her throat, as she tiptoed down the hallway and, quiet as a church mouse, opened the secret door to the basement. Once she was safely down the stairs, she lit the candle.

The masonry *was* the same.

This was definitely where the tintype had been made. Dora held the candle high and searched the room, weaving carefully in and out between rows of boxes and old furniture, looking for the battered wooden table and the birdcage. They, too, might be clues.

After combing every inch of the storeroom, three times over, she gave up. Frustrated, she plopped onto an old, overstuffed chair. A cloud of dust exploded around her, and she let out a violent sneeze, promptly dropping the candle.

"Fiddlesticks!"

It took her several minutes to find it, scrambling around in the dark. She congratulated herself on having the foresight to have brought another matchstick. After relighting the wick, she righted an old mirror leaning up against the back wall of the storeroom.

"I look a fright." Her dress was covered with dust. She set the candle down on a box and prepared to clean herself up, but that was as far as she got.

"What on earth...?"

A shadow on the wall caught her attention. Pushing the chair aside to get closer, she studied it, realizing right away that it wasn't simply a flaw in the masonry. It was some kind of indentation.

She retrieved the candle and held it close, as she ran her fingers over the impression. It was carved... no, it was *molded*. It wasn't masonry at all, it was metal, painted over to look like masonry.

She made a fist and knocked on the wall. It resounded with a hollow echo.

"Good Lord!"

Knocking softly along the wall, using the echo to guide her, she discovered it wasn't a wall at all. It was a door! The edges had been painted over, and not long ago. The paint was definitely fresher here than on any other portion of the wall.

If this was a door, then...

"It's a lock!"

She held the candle up to the molded metal impression. It was definitely a lock, close to the edge of what she was certain now was a door. She set the candle down, and retrieved her diary. Again she cursed. No fountain pen!

There was a box of coal in the corner. She grabbed a small chunk, turned to a clean page and began to draw.

The shape of the lock seemed oddly familiar, yet, how could it be? She'd only been in the storeroom once before, and she'd never seen it. She wondered if Jim knew it was here. He'd have to know. How could he not?

As she put the finishing touches on her sketch of the door and oddly shaped lock, she heard the creak of floorboards in the hall above her. Dora went statue-still. Listening hard, she thought she heard soft footfalls. A man's? A woman's? She couldn't tell.

Stuffing her diary into her pocket, she grabbed the candle and tiptoed across the earthen floor toward the stairway. Someone was up there, waiting. Her hands were shaking now. Gathering her wits, she blew out the candle and exchanged it for the derringer.

She waited what seemed a lifetime before she dared move another inch. When all was still above her, she crept silently up the steps, cringing when a couple of them creaked. At the top she waited again, longer this time.

Then she tripped the cleverly devised latch from the inside, and cracked the secret panel leading back to the hall. Now that her eyes had adjusted to the blackness of the basement, it didn't seem nearly as dark in the hall as it had before.

She peeked out. All was clear. Quick as a fox, she stole back the way she'd come, toward the kitchen. At the end of the corridor someone struck a match.

Dora froze.

"You're up late again."

"Ch-Chance."

He lit the taper in the wall sconce behind him, then blew the match out, letting it drop to the carpet.

"I...couldn't sleep."

"Me, neither."

Her heart pounded in her chest. Her head throbbed with a riot of suspicion, conflicting information and fear. All of it vanished when she looked into his eyes.

Then he saw the gun in her hand.

"Dora?" He moved toward her.

She stepped back, raising the derringer, her whole

body shaking. She knew she wouldn't fire. He knew it, too, and kept coming. She was unsure of him and of John, of everyone who'd tried to help her. She'd gotten herself involved in something she hadn't been prepared for when she'd stepped off the stage in Last Call.

Chance stopped an arm's length from her. He could have grabbed the derringer out of her hand, but he didn't.

"I don't blame you," he said. "I deserve to be shot."

"Why do you say that?"

"You wouldn't understand."

"Make me understand."

She wanted to believe that her instincts about him were right, that he'd respected her father and had had nothing to do with his murder. She wanted to believe he wasn't William Fitzpatrick's silent partner, a counterfeiter, a killer.

It could be him, her brain told her. It could be, but—

Out of habit Chance reached for the watch fob hanging from the chain attached to his belt. She wondered if her father had given it to him, or if Chance had taken it after he'd died—or after he'd killed him.

Dora studied the pewter fob as Chance fingered it.

All at once her blood ran cold.

The shape of the fob was identical to the sketch she'd made in her diary. It was the key to the secret door! Behind that door in the basement was another room, and inside that room was the money.

Dora knew what she had to do in order to get it.

If you're willing to take a Chance...

Her father's words held new meaning. At last she'd deciphered the clues.

Looking into Chance's dark eyes, she slowly lowered the gun. A moment later he took it from her shaking hand and slipped it into his pocket.

"Take me upstairs," she said.

"To the parlor?"

She knew there'd be no going back once she started up that spiral staircase.

"No." She took his hand. "To your room."

Chapter Thirteen

Her purpose was singular, to get the key to the secret door from Chance's belt. In order to do that, she'd have to remove the belt from his trousers, and in order to do that, she'd have to remove the trousers.

"You shouldn't be here."

He lit a lamp whose soft light bathed the room in an amber glow. She studied their surroundings, paying attention to the precise scattering of objects on his bureau, the garish pictures on the walls, his clothes strewn a little too carelessly across a chair. His bedroom was like him, deliberately flashy on the surface, drawing one's eye away from its true character.

"I'm perfectly aware of that," she said, facing him.

Downstairs the thought had occurred to her that she simply could have waited until he was asleep, then crept inside his room and stolen the watch fob. Yet she hadn't. She'd come here with him of her own volition, and she knew her eyes revealed to him why. Perhaps her purpose wasn't so singular, after all.

"I'm not who you think I am."

"No?" She moved toward him, placed her hands

on his chest. "I disagree. I know exactly who you are."

He looked at her but didn't move, didn't risk touching her, for the same reason she went no farther than to rest her palm against his heart and feel the heat of his body through his clothes.

"You're a man my father trusted."

"You sure about that?"

She glanced at the watch fob hanging from his belt, and knew it couldn't be coincidence. "Yes."

His hands slid around her waist. "Sometimes trust is misplaced."

"Not this time." Looking into his eyes, she rose up on tiptoes and pressed her lips to his. It was the boldest thing she'd ever done in her life.

At first he didn't respond. The house around them was quiet, the wind in the trees outside the only sound. As she wrapped her arms around his neck, pressing herself against him, she heard his sigh.

"Dora," he said, then kissed her back.

Abandoning her good sense, she closed her eyes and let herself be swept away by her senses, expecting more of the same frenzied coupling they'd shared in the darkened hallway two long weeks ago.

His kiss was soft, achingly tender, and in that moment she knew her true purpose for being here had nothing to do with the watch fob at all.

She was in love with him.

Not the roguish gambler who tried too hard to convince her he was the kind of man who didn't deserve her respect. She was in love with the man who'd helped her father when other men hadn't, the man who'd followed her back and forth to town that first week to make sure she was safe, who'd advised foolish girls to get an education and unfortunate women to muster the courage to change their lives. She was in love with the man who, when her own life was threatened, had stepped in front of Dickie Hargus's gun.

"Stop me," Chance whispered against her lips.

She looked into his eyes and read a tangle of self-reproach and desire. His hands, twined around her waist, were quivering. "Why?"

"You know why."

Gently she brushed a hank of dark hair from off his face. She considered simply telling him, taking him back downstairs and showing him the secret door inside the basement storeroom, revealing his watch fob as the key.

"My father left me a gift," she began.

"No. What he left you was trouble. If he'd any damned idea what was to come, he'd never have done it." He kissed her again, softly, holding himself in check, just as she was.

"I don't mean the money. I mean you." She slid out of his embrace and retrieved her diary. Her father's last letter to her was tucked inside. She unfolded it on the bureau near the lamp.

"I've read it," he said.

"I know. I was there, remember?"

Recognition flashed in his eyes. "You wanted me to read it. Why?"

She turned purposely into his arms. "To see if you could make more of it than I had. After all, you knew him, I didn't."

"He was a good man. You would have liked him."

On impulse she stepped back and looked pointedly at the watch fob hanging from his belt. "This was his.'' She drew it toward her, gauged the weight of the cast pewter in her palm.

"You think I stole it, don't you?"

She knew her eyes held the question. She didn't have to ask it aloud.

"He gave it to me. Two days before he was shot." Her gaze followed his to the date on the letter. "The same day he wrote this."

"Why you?"

He didn't answer.

The room felt suddenly too warm, the air between them close. They stood inches apart, yet he was miles away, drifting somewhere in a troubled sea of memory that was reflected in his eyes.

"Tell me," she said.

Then he smiled, came back to the present, fixed his gaze on hers. "He said the damnedest thing when he gave it to me. 'Chance,' he said, 'this here's the key to the future.'"

"Your future?"

"No." He took her in his arms and pulled her close, tilted her chin so that his lips hovered over hers.

She dropped the watch fob.

"Yours," he said, and kissed her.

This time he used his tongue. This time she used hers.

The dream was different this time. Dora was there beside him, standing amidst the smoking ruins of the ranch house surrounded by slain cattle, looking with horror on the burned and twisted bodies of his mother and sister. His father hung from a tree near the barn, his body swaying hypnotically in the breeze.

Chance woke in a cold sweat, a silent scream rising up inside him.

"Dora?"

The lamp had gone out. The space beside him on the bed was still warm, but in the moonlight filtering through the lace draperies he saw she was gone.

"Damn it."

He moved to the edge of the bed and readjusted his clothes. His vest was undone, his shirt partially unbuttoned. Thank Christ he still had his trousers on. He sat there for a moment in the moonlight, thinking about her before he got up and lit the lamp.

His hands were shaking.

He looked at the rumpled bed and recalled the feel of her in his arms, the softness of her lips, her hair undone around her shoulders. He'd never in his life forget the passion in her eyes. as she'd pulled him down on top of her and said the words.

I love you.

Readjusting himself inside his trousers, he also suspected he'd never forget the moment he pushed himself away, stilled her protests with soft kisses, then held her close until they'd both drifted off.

He'd promised Bill Fitzpatrick he'd look after her, not use her then break her heart. Bill had been drinking the night he'd given him the watch fob. Chance hadn't really believed him when he'd said he had a daughter. He'd thought the old man was just rambling.

Out of habit he reached for the silver chain hanging from his belt. "What the—?"

The watch fob was gone.

He studied the chain and saw that the clasp had

come undone. He searched the bed first, then under it. It wasn't there. Hell, it had to be here somewhere.

As he went through the pile of wrinkled clothes draped over the chair, he recalled the fascination in Dora's eyes as she'd studied the watch fob. The last thing he remembered before falling asleep with her in his arms, was the way she'd run her finger along its edges, over and over, intrigued by its unusual shape.

Chance pulled on his boots.

The light in Dora's cabin was out. The half moon hanging in the sky over the bunkhouse told him it was after three. It didn't matter. He had to see her. It was time to tell her how things stood. He at least owed her that much.

Besides, he didn't trust those Hargus boys as far as he could throw them. They were out there somewhere, and until he was sure who they were and why they were here, he didn't want Dora sleeping alone out in that cabin. Chance grabbed his gun belt from the floor where he'd dropped it after he and Dora had moved to the bed.

Her father's trust in him *had* been misplaced, and make no mistake, the only thing Wild Bill had left his daughter was trouble.

His letter to Dora was still lying on top of the bureau. She'd forgotten to take it with her when she'd left. Chance picked it up and reread it. "You crazy old geezer. What the hell were you thinking dragging her into this?"

He turned to the last page and was surprised at what was sandwiched there between the sheets. It was a tintype of Wild Bill. Recent, by the look of it. Chance held it up to the light and studied the image. He wondered where Bill had had it made?

He recalled a photographer who'd passed through town a few months ago. The only reason he remembered him was because the man had lost most of his money at cards one night at the Flush. Lily had relieved him of the rest of it upstairs, as Chance remembered.

"Hmm." He stuffed the letter and the tintype into his pocket, blew out the lamp and left his room, locking the door behind him.

He didn't make it to Dora's cabin. He didn't even make it to the kitchen. The wall sconce was lit in the hallway, and the door to the basement storeroom stood wide. Who the devil was up this time of night?

At the bottom of the stairs he got his answer. Chance went stock-still. A single candle burned, providing just enough light to see by. Dora was pressed against the back wall of the storeroom, the watch fob in her hand. What she did next gave him the biggest surprise of his life.

He watched as she fit the pewter fob into a hollow in the wall. She turned it, and a moment later a narrow section of wall gave way.

Son of a—

"Dora, wait!"

Too late. She'd stepped into darkness.

Chance drew his gun, leaped over a stack of boxes and a dusty chair. A second later he was there. He grabbed the candle and stepped inside the tiny room.

Dora whirled on him, bumping against an old table positioned against the wall. "Chance!"

"Damn it!" It took him less than a second to realize they were alone and the secret room that she'd stumbled upon was empty, except for the ornate object sitting on the battered wooden table.

He holstered his gun and held the candle high.

"It's the birdcage!" she said.

The same one he'd seen in the tintype. The tiny room was damp, and smelled even mustier than the rest of the basement. Chance leaned against the table and let out a breath, ran a hand over his sweat-soaked brow.

"Don't you know you scared the hell out of me just now?"

It was the first time in the three weeks he'd known her that she looked sheepish. "I—I'm sorry. It's just that..." She shrugged.

He studied the secret door, impressed with the unusual lock. He'd never seen anything like it. He pulled the watch fob out of the indentation and looked at it with new understanding.

"It's the key." Dora looked him in the eyes. Even in the soft light he could see her cheeks were still flushed, irritated from his beard stubble, her lips still swollen from their kissing.

He felt a hollowness in his gut that burned almost as much as his feelings for her. "Why didn't you just tell me?"

She shrugged.

"What we did upstairs...you coming up there with me to begin with..." He paused, then shook his head, feeling like a damned fool. "You didn't have to pretend, Dora. Or lie. Not on my account. You could have just asked me for the watch fob. I would have given it to you. It was your father's."

He held it out to her, but she didn't take it.

"No. It's yours. He gave it to you, not me."

"Take it."

She wouldn't. "You think I don't trust you."

That's exactly what he thought, and while he'd told himself more than once it was a damned good thing she didn't trust him, it still hurt. And that's when he knew he was in way over his head.

He clipped the pewter fob to his belt, then from his pocket retrieved the tintype of Wild Bill along with the letter. "Here. You left these in my room."

She took them, then looked away, embarrassed.

There were two things, now, that he wanted most in the world, only he couldn't have them both.

One was to take her in his arms and convince her he was someone different, a man who had been there for his own father when Jack Wellesley had needed him most, a man who wanted her more than he wanted to punish himself, and more than the vengeance that both fed and ate away at him every day of his life.

The other thing he wanted so badly it burned inside him like white fire, was vengeance—a bloodlust so overpowering he could taste it in his mouth like the dead ash blanketing the earth where he'd buried his parents and sister.

"Go back to Colorado Springs, Dora. There's nothing here for you."

"Isn't there?"

He wanted to believe she hadn't been pretending upstairs, that when she'd whispered against his lips that she loved him, it hadn't been a lie.

He thought about the watch fob, the key, what she'd done to get it. He took one last look around the tiny room, laughing softly at the birdcage. "It's all a wild-goose chase. The letter, the tintype, this room."

"There is no money, is there?"

The moment of truth was here, but he couldn't

bring himself to come clean. If he told her, he'd have to tell her everything, and if he told her everything, she'd never go back to Colorado Springs. She'd stay here and try to help him. She'd try to fix him just like she tried to fix everything else broken in her path. The saloon, the town's finances, Susan's self-image and Tom's unrequited love. Hell, even Lily's bad attitude hadn't entirely escaped her good intentions.

But what was wrong with him wasn't fixable. Even if it was, he didn't want to be fixed. He didn't deserve to be. He didn't deserve her, either. Besides, if she did stay, he'd never be able to finish what he'd set out to do the day Wild Bill Fitzpatrick gave him his life back.

"No. There is no money." The words rolled off his lips as if he'd practiced them.

"You knew I was coming." She nodded at the pewter watch fob. "He told you. You knew."

He *had* known. And while he'd expected Wild Bill's daughter, never in a million years would he have expected *her,* a good woman with grit who reminded him every day of a decent world he no longer knew how to live in.

"Go home, Dora."

She took the candle from his hand, their gazes locking for an instant as their fingers brushed. He followed her out into the storeroom and closed the secret door. She stood on the bottom step leading upward to the hall and said one last thing to him before leaving him alone in the dark.

"I am home."

She hadn't been pretending, and it wasn't a lie.

Dora sat with her feet curled beneath her on the

narrow bed in her cabin and waited for dawn. She'd stoked the fire in the potbelly stove and tried to clear her mind by watching the flickering firelight dance on the rough-hewn beams. It did no good. She could no more stop her thoughts than she could her feelings.

In her diary she'd faithfully recounted the events of the past two days: the arrival of the Hargus brothers, the card game, the accusations regarding her father, the watch fob and secret room, John Gardner's renewed proposal and the precious hour she'd spent in Chance's arms.

She set the diary aside on the bed next to the tintype, her father's letter and the tortoiseshell comb wrapped in newsprint. Three clues that, so far, had led nowhere. A wild-goose chase, Chance had called it. Maybe, maybe not. Two things she knew for certain.

Chance Wellesley was a man in pain.

He was also lying.

More than anything in the world Dora wanted to know why. Until she did, the battle raging inside her between rational thought and raw feeling would never be resolved. She was in love with a man she didn't trust.

She picked up the tortoiseshell comb and studied it for what must have been the hundredth time. Chance had looked her in the eye when he'd said it.

There is no money.

And that had been his mistake. She knew him now. She knew when he was telling the truth and when he was lying—even when he didn't know it himself.

Upstairs on his bed when he'd stilled her roving hands, arrested her ardent kisses, he'd told another lie.

He'd said he wasn't made the same as she was, that he couldn't return her love, that he couldn't feel.

He was wrong.

She grasped the comb so tightly the tines dug into her palm. Chance was fighting his feelings for her, and the reason had something to do with his past, with her father and the money she was certain was here.

"It *is* here. Somewhere."

The comb was the final clue. It had to be. It was the one thing remaining her father had left her to which she'd been unable to make a connection.

What did it mean? What had he been trying to tell her.

"Delilah!"

Dora sprang from the bed and started to pace, her mind working.

Delilah had recognized the tortoiseshell comb at once, the night Dora had worn it to dinner with John Gardner. In the whirlwind of the past week, Dora had forgotten all about it. She knelt in front of the stove and held the pretty ornament to the firelight. It instantly came alive with color—whiskey-brown and deep russet, sun-gold and fiery red.

"Good Lord!"

It took her only seconds to rewrap the comb in the newsprint, grab her diary and pen and go. A minute later, the cabin locked behind her, she crept in the predawn fog across the yard toward the back door. The house was still and dark. Pausing behind the spiral staircase, she peered into the saloon.

The money had been here all along, right under her very nose.

She approached the bar, felt her way behind it and lit one of the elegant kerosene lamps flanking the cash register. "Oh!" Her own reflection in the mirror, distorted by rows of liquor bottles, spooked her.

After a calming breath, she emptied her pockets and set about documenting her theory before proceeding. She opened her diary to the entry she'd penned her very first night at the Royal Flush. Dora had always considered herself a fair artist, but as she studied the likeness she'd drafted that first night, she realized she'd missed the most important detail of all.

Unwrapping the tortoiseshell comb, she examined that detail now. Satisfied with her conclusion, she annotated the drawing in her diary, then in capital letters below it spelled out the precise location of her father's secret fortune.

There was only one thing left to do. Get it.

Dora capped her pen and closed the diary. She turned toward the cash register and nearly jumped out of her skin.

"Evenin'." Dickie Hargus's blue eyes sparkled in the lamplight. He stood at the end of the bar, blocking her retreat.

Her stomach clenched in fear.

"It's almost day, bro." Lee stepped out of the shadows. "You oughtta be wishing our little schoolteacher a good morning."

"Wh-what are you doing here? What do you want?"

Dickie inched closer.

Lee approached the bar, his gaze falling to her diary. "I would have thought that was obvious."

She grabbed the red leather-bound book and backed away, holding it protectively to her chest.

Dickie kept coming. Lee was already there. She had no way out.

"One of the girls told us you like to write things in that little red book of yours." Lee nodded at the diary. "That true?"

"One of the…girls?" Dora couldn't think straight. All she had to do was cry out and someone would come. One good scream would do it, but her throat constricted and her mouth went dry.

"You know where it is, don't you?" Lee smiled, sending a chill clear up her spine.

"Where wh-what is?"

Dickie backed her against the bar.

Lee leaned close enough to whisper. So close she could smell his whiskey-tainted breath. "The money."

"I—I don't know what you're talking about, I swear."

A floorboard creaked in the hallway. Lee and Dickie spun toward the sound.

"She doesn't know anything." Chance's voice was low and calm. He stood in the shadowed doorway, a Colt in each hand. "But I do."

Chapter Fourteen

A woman didn't have too many choices in this life, and Dora had always vowed to use hers wisely. But now, when she looked at Chance and saw a man she didn't know, what little wisdom she'd assembled over the years failed her.

"Let her pass." Chance eased toward the bar, both guns leveled on the Hargus boys.

Lee and Dickie put up their hands.

Hugging the diary, Dora slipped past them and ducked around to the other side.

"No need to get your bloomers in a twist, Wellesley. We were only talkin' to the little lady."

"About what?"

"The money, of course."

Dora stared at Chance, but he didn't see her. His gaze was riveted to Lee Hargus. "What do you know about it?"

"What everybody knows." He exchanged a glance with his brother. "Fitzpatrick was swindling his customers. The real money's here somewhere, and she knows where it is."

Their hands in the air, the brothers turned on her.

Dora backed away, smack into the cigar-store Indian at the end of the bar. She swallowed a high-pitched squeak.

"What's the money got to do with you two?" As Chance moved into the lamp light, a chilling ruthlessness she'd never seen before gleamed in his eyes.

"Nothing," Lee said. "Just thought we'd be neighborly and help Bill's daughter here return it to its rightful owners."

"At four o'clock in the morning." Chance didn't buy it, and neither did she.

Dickie made a move toward her.

"One more step and it'll be your last."

Lee grinned at his brother. "The man means business, bro. Back off."

No one moved.

"Th-there is no money," Dora said, and clutched the diary tighter.

Chance finally gave her his full attention. Remorse flashed briefly in his eyes. "Give me the diary, Dora."

For a moment she couldn't speak.

"Put it down, right there on the bar. Put it down and go."

"What?"

"You heard me."

She'd heard him, but his words hadn't registered. A sick feeling coiled inside her. "No."

"Do it."

Lee chuckled. "Well, well, well. Looks as if Wellesley's not your knight in shining armor after all."

Dora shook her head in disbelief as she eased

around the carved statue and backed slowly toward the door. "No. I—I won't."

Upstairs in his bedroom, when Chance had looked her in the eyes and told there was no money, she'd known then he was lying. She'd known it, and yet she'd been certain he had compelling reasons to do so. Honorable reasons which, once she discovered them, would explain his erratic behavior.

Now she didn't know what to think. "You've been lying to me all along."

"Yes."

She sucked in a breath, astounded by his candor. "About everything?"

"That's right."

You think I don't want you. You're wrong.

Her insides were twisted so tight she couldn't breathe. "Why?"

He grinned at her, and in that moment her whole world changed.

"Why do you think?" His voice was a whisper.

Everything she'd come to believe about his true character was once again in question. "The money?" She shook her head, unable to comprehend her own stupidity.

"Love hurts, don't it," Lee said, taking it all in.

"I'll ask you one more time." Chance's expression darkened. He took a step toward her, his guns still trained on the Hargus boys. "Put the diary down and go."

Lee grinned at him, then slowly lowered his hands. "How 'bout we split it?"

Dora's legs felt like stone. The air was suddenly too thick, the lingering stench of whiskey and cigar smoke permeating her senses. "How could you?"

Little more than an hour ago he'd held her in his arms, kissed her with an all-consuming passion she couldn't have been wrong about. Together they'd burned, and in a moment of clarity and trust she'd declared her feelings for him. Never in her life would she forget the look in his eyes when she'd said the words.

Never would she forget how he looked at her now, coldly, as if she meant nothing to him.

"The diary, Dora." Chance took another step.

There was no one, now, she could count on, no one to help. If she cried out, Jim would come to her aid, then Tom, Delilah and the girls. But that wasn't the kind of help she needed. It wasn't her safety she was concerned with, but her sanity. What she needed was to get away, to think, to tell someone who would listen and understand.

John.

"Just hand it to me." Lee nodded at the diary.

She stepped back, and he went for her.

Chance fired.

He'd never killed a man, and wouldn't have hesitated if he'd been sure he was aiming at the men who, eighteen months ago, had blazed a trail of deception, fraud and murder across three states.

As it was, the crystal chandelier exploded above Lee Hargus's head, along with a row of bottles behind Dickie's. A spray of shattered glass rained down on them. The cloying scent of peach brandy infused the air.

Dora was already out the door by the time Chance had Lee bent backward over the bar, a pistol jammed against his temple. He flashed his eyes at Dickie, who was about to go for his gun. "Don't even think about it."

"What in tarnation…?" Jim appeared in his union suit on the balcony above them, an old flintlock rifle in hand. Not fully awake, he blinked his eyes at them.

Delilah materialized next. She brandished a weapon Chance had more faith in, a nice little pepperbox revolver he knew Wild Bill had given her before he was killed.

The thundering herd was next to arrive: Columbine, Iris, Daisy and Rose. Tom and Susan brought up the rear. The instant the piano player saw the Hargus boys, he yanked Susan away from the balcony, shoved her into the upstairs parlor and locked her in. A moment later he trained his army revolver on Dickie Hargus's head.

"Want me to get the marshal?" Jim started down the spiral stairs, Tom and Delilah in his wake. The girls huddled together on the balcony, their eyes wide as saucers.

"No." Chance didn't want any interference from Max. He'd do this his way.

The Hargus boys exchanged a look, then Lee grinned. Chance thought it was a pretty gutsy thing to do, given the fact that one of his Colts was pressed firmly against Hargus's head.

Delilah lit a lamp, then the wall sconces flanking the bar. Something on the polished pine surface caught her attention, the comb Chance had seen Dora wearing the night she'd dined with John Gardner.

Chance peered at the wrinkled newsprint cradling the decoration. "Well, I'll be damned."

Delilah's voice brought him back to the moment. "Where's Dora?"

"Gone." Chance worked to keep his mind off her and the newsprint, and on the task at hand. Later, if there was a later, he'd remember the pain in Dora's eyes when he'd asked her to give him the diary.

At the time, he'd known it was the one thing that would drive her away from him to safety. What he hadn't counted on was that she'd defy him and take the diary with her. As long as she had it, she'd be a target for the Hargus boys, or anyone else who wanted to get their hands on Wild Bill's money and who thought his daughter knew where it was.

"Gone where?"

As if on cue, hoofbeats sounded outside. He could tell from their cadence the horse was Silas. Good. At least Dora would ride safely. For some damned reason the gelding liked her.

Delilah gasped as a shadowed shape rode past the window, then turned into the fog on the trail to town.

"Let her go," Chance said. "It's better she's not here for this."

"For…what exactly?" Delilah asked.

Jim approached Dickie, who hadn't moved a muscle since the first gunshot. "Damn, Chance. That was my best peach brandy." He surveyed the wreckage on the glass shelves above Dickie's head. "Why'd you have to go and do that?"

Chance shot him a look.

"Sorry," Jim said, then frowned at the mess. "It'll take me till opening to get the place cleaned up."

Tom edged closer, his army revolver aimed squarely at Dickie's head. "At least he didn't spoil Bill's painting. That's something, ain't it?"

Chance stared at the portrait above the bar. Dickie looked over his shoulder, following his gaze.

"Don't you move," Tom said to him.

"What exactly's goin' on?" Delilah moved toward Chance, eyeing Lee and Dickie with suspicion. "Why'd you boys come back?"

"And how'd they get in?" Jim frowned at the saloon's entrance. "I locked that front door myself."

"If you'd be so kind as to let me up," Lee said, "perhaps we could discuss this like gentlemen."

Chance thought about it, then stepped back, redoubling his grip on both guns. "All right, you two. Start talking."

Lee winced as he uncurled his back into an upright position. He spent a moment straightening his tie and smoothing his striped silk vest, as if he were getting ready to go out on the town. "I've already told you," he said.

"Yeah, the money. But what I want to know is how you knew about it."

"Just like everyone else, I suspect. Rumors fly fast around these parts."

"You knew before you got here, before you set foot out of Arkansas. Admit it."

Lee tossed him a look so innocent, Chance wanted to pull the trigger right then and there and get it over with.

"Wild Bill had a partner." Chance forced himself to calm down, to think with his head for a change and not his emotions. He had to be sure. He had to be dead sure. Once he was, he'd do the thing he'd burned to do from the second he cut his father's body down from that tree. "That partner was you."

For a moment no one breathed.

"You knew Bill was in debt. You set him up with

counterfeit currency, forced him into it, then reaped a profit off the top.''

Neither brother so much as blinked.

''Later you found out he was holding out on you, squirreling away real money you figured belonged to you.''

''You saying I killed him?''

''You or him.'' Chance gave Dickie a hard look.

Delilah sucked in a breath. Tom and Jim inched closer, their guns raised. The girls on the balcony began whispering. Chance was a heartbeat away from killing both of them.

''How?'' Jim said, breaking his concentration. ''How could they have killed Bill? They wasn't even here.''

''He's right,'' Tom said. ''We'd have known if these two was anywhere within fifty miles of the Flush. Don't get too many Southerners up here in the high country.''

Lee held Chance's gaze. ''You're wrong about us, Wellesley. But even if you weren't, what do you care? Who made you Fitzpatrick's almighty avenger?''

''Bill was a good man,'' Delilah said, then pocketed her pepperbox revolver.

''Or maybe this ain't about Fitzpatrick at all.'' Lee smiled at him. ''Maybe you got something else eatin' at you.''

It took every shred of control Chance could muster to stop himself from pistol-whipping Lee Hargus senseless.

''Put 'em away, Chance.'' Jim nodded at the twin Colts, then stood his flintlock up behind the bar.

"These two may not be innocents, but they can't have murdered Bill."

"Who did, then?" Tom still had his army revolver trained on Dickie.

"Maybe we'll never know." Delilah placed a hand on Chance's shoulder. It was then he realized his own hands were shaking. "What I do know is there's a girl out there ridin' your horse. You'd best go get her, Chance, and bring her home."

Slowly, not taking his eyes off the brothers, Chance holstered his guns.

"There now. Ain't that better?" Lee grabbed his hat off the floor where it had fallen when Chance overpowered him.

Chance stood for a moment, gazing at the portrait above the bar, considering his options.

"I've been thinkin'...."

He turned at the sound of Susan's voice. The doe-eyed girl moved down the staircase in her dressing gown. The other girls followed.

"How the devil did you get out?" Tom grabbed her at the bottom of the stairs and pulled her off to the side.

Susan produced a key. "Found it over the door-jamb. But as I was sayin', I've been thinkin' about this partner of Bill's, this counterfeiter. It would have to be someone with lots of money, right?"

"Not necessarily," Delilah said. "It could be anyone."

"So you believe the rumors." Chance studied her, and it was the first time since he'd known her that Delilah looked away.

"Makes sense, though," Lee said, "for it to be someone with access to money. Now, who do y'all know who's got piles and piles of it, right here in town in that fancy vault of his?''

"That banker," Tom said.

Jim's eyes bugged. "Chance, that's where Dora's likely gone!''

He forced himself to take a breath. He'd known when Dora rode off on Silas that's where she'd go for help. To Gardner. If he hadn't been so fixated on the Hargus brothers, he'd have stopped her. Now he didn't know what to do.

Access to money wasn't the issue. Access to counterfeit money was. In all his months in Last Call, Chance had never been able to tie John Gardner to any kind of counterfeiting scheme—and he'd tried, even harder since Dora had arrived at the Royal Flush and Gardner began courting her.

He stared into Dickie Hargus's eyes, then turned his attention back to Lee. The Southerner's smile dripped like honey on a hot day. Something was off about these two, and he meant to get to the bottom of it. All the same, Susan's innocent speculation ate away at him. First things first.

He plucked the tortoiseshell comb and the newsprint off the bar and stuffed them into his pocket, then grabbed one of Rowdy's oiled slickers off a hook beside the stairs.

"Goin' somewhere?" Lee said.

"Yeah. To saddle a horse." He shot Tom and Jim a look. "Keep an eye on these two while I'm gone."

The last thing he heard as he stepped into the fog was Lee Hargus's soft laughter floating from the saloon.

If it hadn't been for Silas's excellent sense of direction, she'd have gotten lost in the predawn mist blanketing the trail to town. The Platte River was high this time of year, glutted with spring runoff, and crossing it in the dark under cover of fog had been no picnic.

As the gelding turned onto Last Call's main street and broke into a lively trot, Dora offered up a silent prayer for her safe arrival. It appeared that no one had followed her, which she thought not only strange, but downright suspicious.

She tethered Silas to the hitching post in front of the bank. The fog was less dense here, away from the river. She peered up at the shrouded windows of the second floor where John Gardner lived and drew a calming breath.

She should have listened to him in the first place and moved to town. If she had, things would never have gone as far as they had with Chance. She wouldn't have lost her heart as well as her head.

Why hadn't he followed her?

If Chance was indeed after her father's money, surely he would have subdued the Hargus brothers, then followed her to town to get the diary. While Lee Hargus had just been guessing, Chance knew for a fact she'd recorded in the red leather-bound journal all her speculations and every shred of evidence regarding her father's money.

Why hadn't he come for the diary?

"Dora?"

The disembodied voice startled her. Silas snorted, then pounded the earth with a hoof, tossing his head high.

Squinting through the mist, she looked up and saw a friendly face. At least she thought it was a friendly face. The nightcap he wore completely covered his head.

"John?" She hadn't even heard him open the window.

"What are you doing here? What's happened?"

"I—"

"Wait. I'll be right down." He closed the window, and she breathed in relief.

John was a good man, she reminded herself, and he cared about her. He would take her in and help her think things through. Together they could sort through the facts in a rational manner. If her father had conspired with a counterfeiter, or at a minimum had been duped by one, John would know what to do. She was prepared to tell him everything.

She climbed onto the boardwalk in front of the bank and waited for him to open the door. Her diary was safe and sound in her pocket. In it was recorded the exact location of the money. She knew if her father had really dealt counterfeit bank notes to customers in exchange for real money, the fortune he'd amassed had never belonged to him and didn't belong to her.

A light went on inside the bank. A moment later Dora saw a shape approach the frosted glass panels of the front doors. She heard the brief clinking of a key, then John appeared.

"Come inside! You'll catch your death." He unlocked the double iron grating that during the bank's regular business hours was swung open out of the way. "Here. Take my hand."

"I'm fine. Really."

He drew her inside and locked both the iron grating and the double doors behind them.

"Come and sit down. In my office there's a sofa."

She remembered it from her first visit to the bank nearly four weeks ago. There was also a bottle of brandy on a silver tray on his desk that he kept for customers. She could use a little right now to stave off the chill that had followed her inside.

Together they sat on the sofa. He took her hand and pressed it gently between his. "Are you all right? Did Wellesley hurt you?"

"No. I—I'm fine. Truly."

"That's his horse outside, isn't it?" His eyes were sharp with concern.

The situation she now found herself in was far from amusing, yet she couldn't help the smile pulling at her mouth. She'd never seen the banker in quite this informal a state, and in the wee hours of the morning, too.

He was wearing a starched white nightshirt and matching cap, elegant mules on his long, pale feet. He'd tossed a light blanket over his shoulders, for modesty's sake she supposed. In his haste to get downstairs, he likely hadn't had time to retrieve a dressing gown.

"You're in shock. What has he done to you?"

She quickly recovered her composure. "Nothing. He's done nothing. It's just that—"

What could she tell him? That she'd fallen in love with a gambler, a rogue and a thief? That she'd lain with him on his bed and allowed him to kiss and fondle her? That she'd kissed and fondled him back? That if Chance hadn't stopped her, she'd have given herself to him?

Oh, yes, that would go over well with a man like John Gardner, wouldn't it?

"What is it, Dora?" he said, and continued to stroke her hand.

Should she tell him she'd found out the hard way she'd been a fool? That Chance didn't care for her at all, that what he wanted all along was her father's money? That he'd shielded her from the Hargus brothers not because he loved her, but because he wanted the money for himself?

Did she really believe that?

Despite all the evidence, in her heart she didn't believe it—which was more proof she was beyond reason. She could no longer trust herself to be objective, which was precisely why she was here.

"After you left," she said, "after we'd all gone to bed, the Hargus brothers returned to the ranch."

John's face paled. He inspected her for damage.

"No, I'm fine. Really. They didn't hurt me. Chance—"

"Chance what?"

"He…he stopped them."

John ground his teeth. "I guess I owe him an apology."

"I don't think that will be necessary." He'd agree with her once he knew the rest of what she had to tell him.

"Where are they?"

"The Hargus brothers? Back at the saloon with Chance." She drew a breath, then let the rest of it spill out. "They…he…wanted my diary." She fished it out of her pocket, then hesitated. If she were to ask John for help, she at least owed him the truth. About everything. She sucked in a breath, then looked him in the eyes. "I think I'd like a drink please."

"Water? I've got some right here."

"No. Brandy." Her gaze flew to the decanter on the oversize walnut desk.

"Oh." He looked surprised, but instantly catered to her request. "Here," he said after he'd poured it, and handed her the tiny glass.

It was little more than a thimbleful. Dora knocked it back the same way she'd seen Lily do a dozen times in the saloon.

"Better?" John said.

"Yes. Thank you."

"Go on."

She considered that he'd neither scolded nor reprimanded her for refusing his offer to put her up in town tonight. He was neither judgmental nor vindictive. John Gardner was simply a good man, and she no longer believed she deserved his good opinion. Another minute of explanations on her part, and she wouldn't have it.

"I…allowed myself to be taken in by his lies."

"Lee Hargus's lies? The ones about your father?"

"No. Chance's lies. What the Hargus brothers believed about my father, the rumors, it's all true. There is a secret fortune hidden at the ranch, and I know where it is."

From the look on John's face she could tell he was flabbergasted. Either that, or he thought her completely insane.

"Here," she said, opening her diary to the last entry. "It's all right here. Read it."

He took the diary from her and scanned the page. She elaborated as he studied the drawing of the tortoiseshell comb and the other clues. Finally, she flipped the pages backward to the beginning, and pointed to one of the earliest drawings she'd made after her arrival at the Royal Flush.

"I wondered all along why he left you the comb. I mean it's pretty, but—"

"All along?"

He blushed, redder than a hothouse rose in winter.

With a shock it dawned on her. "You knew what was in my father's safety deposit box before I opened it."

He bit his lip, but had the courage not to look away from her.

"You opened the box before I arrived."

He hesitated, then said, "I did. It was a horrible thing to do. I can't tell you how many nights I lay awake afterward, regretting I'd done it."

"That doesn't matter now. What does matter is that the money is real. My father had a silent partner, a counterfeiter who fed him fake currency. Who knows how much real money is hidden right here?" She tapped her fingernail on the drawing in her diary.

He closed the journal and handed it back to her. "I want to ask you a question, and I want you to think before you answer."

"All right."

"This silent partner of your father's…do you know who it is?" He stared into her eyes so intently it unnerved her.

"No." Which was the truth. Regardless of how Chance had used her, she'd never believe he was a counterfeiter and a murderer.

For a moment John said nothing. He stood up and began to pace the length of the rich carpet in front of the desk. "That money belongs to the government. You know that, don't you?"

"Yes. But how do I return it?"

"Leave all that to me. Wait here. I'm going upstairs to dress. I'll be right back."

She watched him as he took the steps leading up to the second floor two at a time, then listened as he thrashed around upstairs. Certain she'd done the right thing in telling him, she relaxed a bit. The rest of what she had to tell him, what she should tell him about her and Chance, could wait.

Besides, there were still some things she needed to get straight in her own mind, the most nagging of which was why Chance hadn't come after her to get the diary. On second thought, why hadn't he simply threatened her? He'd had two very big guns.

And if he hadn't wanted to do something that distasteful, he could have used his most effective weapon on her—he could have lied. If he'd continued to make her believe he cared about her, she would have just told him where the money was. Surely he must have known that.

So why did he demand the diary?

"Of course!" Dora spun toward the door. That was it all along. He knew she'd bolt. He knew it. He knew her. That's why he pretended to turn on her. To get her to leave. With the Hargus boys there, as long as she stayed, she'd be in danger. As long as she had the diary, she'd be...

"Good Lord." She stuffed the diary back in her pocket and made for the door. Locked!

John crashed down the stairs. In one hand he held his coat, in the other a rifle. "No!" he said. "You stay here. I'll deal with this."

"But you don't understand."

"I do understand. More than you know." He set

the rifle down and donned the coat, then pulled her back into his office. ''I know you cared for him. Wellesley wanted the money, didn't he?''

Embarrassment heated her face. Despite the fact that she'd kept her diary secret from everyone, John read her like an open book.

''You don't have to explain it to me. I know men like that draw women. And men like me, well…''

''Don't.'' She started to touch his cheek, then stopped herself. ''Besides, things aren't entirely what they seem on the surface.''

Perhaps Chance did care for her. She knew he was caught up in something serious that in some way was tied to her father. She just didn't know what it was. He was shielding her on purpose. Or maybe he was shielding himself.

''I want you to promise me you'll stay put while I'm gone.''

''What?'' Her mind had drifted from the task at hand. ''No! I want to go back to the saloon with you.''

''Absolutely not.'' He grabbed his rifle off the bank's counter, then jumped over it and made for the door.

Dora followed.

''One last thing.'' John turned and swept her against him. Before she could stop him, he kissed her.

She tried to like it, but didn't. John Gardner was everything a decent woman could want in a suitor, but he simply wasn't the man for her. He simply wasn't her Chance.

After it was over, he left her standing there in the bank in mild shock. His keys jingled in the locks, then he was outside. She bolted after him, but too late. He shut her in, locking both the double doors and the iron grate behind him.

"Fiddlesticks!" She beat against the doors until she thought the glass would shatter, but it did no good. He was already gone, down the street toward the livery where he kept his buggy and horse. Like lightning, she shot around the counter and burst into the office, heading for the high window behind John's desk.

She had to get back to the saloon! She had to talk to Chance. She had to know, once and for all, how he felt about her, and what it was that consumed him, that drove him to push her away.

The window was too high, and incredibly small. Like the insets in the front doors, it was fashioned of frosted glass. Likely it had bars on the outside, but she wouldn't know that until she got up there. What could she use to stand on?

The desk was too heavy to move, and John's chair was the spinning kind, made of soft leather. She'd lose her footing for sure. No, what she needed was something solid, like—

"A box!"

She spied a large wooden box under John's desk. A few seconds later she'd dragged it out and positioned it under the window. When she tried to step up the lid moved. She lifted it off, thinking to reposition it, and froze.

"Good Lord."

The box was full of money. Bank notes! Why wasn't it downstairs in the vault? Bankers didn't keep money in big boxes under their desks. She set the lid aside and palmed a handful of the bills. Holding one up to the light, she inspected it, then another, and another, using the tricks Chance had taught her and one or two she'd read about in the handbills posted outside the bank.

A sick feeling curled inside her.

She dumped the box on its side and grabbed more notes, checking them at random, then letting them fall to the floor. Each one she studied was the same. The money in the box was all counterfeit.

Chapter Fifteen

If Dora had learned anything in the past three weeks it was that things aren't always what they seem to be, and that people aren't always who they say they are— Chance Wellesley and John Gardner included.

The trouble was that she could no more believe John was a counterfeiter and a killer than she could Chance, despite the evidence beneath her feet. The box of counterfeit money she'd found in John's office would seem to implicate him, but she'd read too many good mystery novels where the person everyone suspected was the murderer really wasn't.

Like a sensible sleuth, she'd reserve her judgment for now and use the box the way she'd originally intended. It made the perfect platform from which to reach the high, small window above her head.

A few minutes of rifling through John's desk drawers resulted in her finding the key to the iron grate barring her escape. Unfortunately the key didn't work on any of the other, more accessible grates. That would have been too easy.

She'd already broken the frosted glass window and, using a letter opener, had smoothed away the remaining sharp edges around the sill. The key fit, and as she swung the grate out of the way it clanged dully against the brick exterior of the building.

The only question remaining in her mind was could she fit through the small opening without getting stuck. She had to try. If she did get stuck, she could always call for help. Surely someone would hear her.

Dora stood on tiptoes and peered out into the mist. The drop to the ground on the other side was a long one. This was the back of the bank and there was no boardwalk. She prayed she wouldn't twist an ankle or break a leg on the fall. If only there was something on the other side of the window to stand on. Something tall and sturdy and—

"What an excellent idea!" She wet her lips and tried to whistle. The sound was barely audible. Hmm. That wasn't going to work. "Silas!" she called. She tried whistling again, this time with better results. "Silas! Here boy!"

She'd tethered the horse to the hitching post outside the bank, but very loosely—and he was a very canny horse, a master escape artist, Gus called him. On several occasions she'd seen Silas come when Chance called him. Perhaps it would work for her. "Silas!"

In response she heard a faint whinny.

"Good boy! Here boy! Come to me! Here, Silas!"

A few moments later she heard the gelding's snorts and soft footfalls as he trotted around the building and materialized below her in the mist.

"What a smart horse you are!" If only she'd had half his sense.

Back at the saloon she should have listened to her heart and not her head. She should have known

Chance was trying to protect her by demanding the diary. She should have known.

Silas neighed and shook his head, then pounded the earth with a hoof, as if telling her to hurry up. She took the hint. Grabbing on to the window ledge with one hand and a sturdy-looking wall sconce with the other, Dora hoisted herself up and managed to get a foot hooked through the window.

Her skirts bunched up around her middle as she pulled herself higher. One good grunt and she found herself straddling the opening. "There! That wasn't so hard. Don't move, Silas, I'm coming down."

She maneuvered her other leg through the window, and took the rest on faith. Blindly, she slid out of the opening, hanging on to the top of the window frame for dear life. Her hips barely cleared.

"Silas!" Her skirts were pushed up around her face, still caught in the opening. Her bloomer-clad legs flailed in midair. "Where are you?"

"I'm right here."

The familiar voice registered in her mind at the same moment his hands slid around her thighs and pulled her from the window. She let go. A heart-stopping moment later she found herself coiled around him like a snake, her legs twined around his hips, his hands cupping her bottom.

"Chance!"

She expected him to set her down, but he didn't. "You okay?"

"I—I think so." The fog enveloped them like a shroud, the gray light of dawn barely penetrating the ghostly ether. "Where's Silas?"

Chance whistled, and the horse stepped into view.

He set her lightly on her feet next to the gelding, then drew his gun. "Where's Gardner?"

"You didn't see him?"

"No." He glanced up at the broken window. "He's not here?"

"He's gone to the ranch, to the saloon. Surely you must have passed him on the trail."

"No." He holstered the Colt. "It's pea soup out there. And maybe he didn't stick to the trail. Why did he go to the ranch?" Again he glanced at the window. "And what the hell were you doing up there, breaking in?"

"Breaking out."

"Son of a—" Chance grabbed her hand and pulled her toward the street. Silas followed. "Did he hurt you?"

"Of course not. He locked me in so I wouldn't follow him. At first I thought he'd done it to protect me, but now—"

"What happened here? What did you tell him? Are you sure he headed for the ranch?" He lifted her onto the boardwalk, leaped up beside her, then took her firmly by the shoulders. "Tell me everything."

She'd waited for this moment, had planned it in her mind. She just hadn't expected it to happen here, and so soon. *You first* was what she'd planned to say to him, and when he didn't answer she'd say, *You lied to me.*

Looking into his eyes, feeling the tension in his grip, the slight trembling of his hands, she realized none of that mattered now. What mattered was that she trusted him. What mattered was that she loved him.

Reaching into her pocket she produced her diary.

"Here," she said and offered it to him. "Isn't this what you want? Isn't this what you came for?"

He was silent for a moment. Dora didn't dare breathe. In his eyes she recognized the same longing she'd seen before, once as they'd looked out over the range together at what remained of her father's cattle, and again when he'd stood a hairsbreadth from her in her father's study and told her she was right not to trust him.

"No," he said quietly. "I came to make sure you were all right."

She drew the chill morning air into her lungs and felt suddenly renewed. "John's gone for the money. I told him where it's hidden. The tortoiseshell comb my father left me…it's a clue. It's the same comb that—"

"I know."

"The money's hidden inside—" She stared at him, stunned. "What?"

"I know where the money is. I've always known."

"But…"

"Why didn't I just take it?"

She nodded.

"I have my reasons."

Her head was spinning, trying to make sense of what he was telling her, to somehow put it in context along with the other clues, the evidence.

"Why didn't you tell me?"

He said nothing to that.

"This counterfeiter, this man who killed my father… You've been trying to…draw him out?"

"Yes."

She took a breath, then asked him the same question she'd asked him twice before. She'd done what her father had wanted her to do. She'd taken a chance. She'd trusted the man standing here before her in the fog, and now she hoped he would trust her. "Who are you?"

He stood there for a moment longer, looking at her, studying her features as if it was the final time he'd lay eyes on her. Then he reached into the pocket of his vest and retrieved the last thing she expected.

A silver star.

"Charles Wellesley, United States Secret Service." He handed her the badge.

A dozen seemingly unrelated enigmas suddenly made perfect sense to her. She turned it over in her hands, running her thumb along the engraved lettering. His eyes registered surprise when she pinned it on him. "There," she said. "That's better."

"I couldn't tell you, for a lot of reasons."

There was more he couldn't tell her, or wouldn't. Much more. She could see it in his eyes and feel it in the way he softly grazed her cheek with the back of his hand.

Barely an hour ago she'd watched him with the Hargus brothers as he'd changed before her very eyes into a man with deadly intent, a man with more than justice on his mind. He wasn't simply another lawman tracking a counterfeiter.

Something else was at work here. Something evil and dark.

"I found a box," she said. "In the bank under John's desk, after he'd gone."

"Go on."

"It was full of counterfeit bank notes."

She watched him as his mind worked. "Is John the man you're hunting?" she asked.

Chance whistled for Silas. "I don't know, but I'd best get out there."

She didn't bother asking if she could go along. She knew his answer would be no. "Be careful," she said instead.

He smiled at that. "Go to the hotel and stay there until I come back for you."

"You *will* come back, won't you?"

His face tightened. He mounted Silas, then touched her on the cheek one last time. The fog swallowed him up as he spurred the gelding down the street.

Dora ran after him. "What I said to you in your room…"

Silas's hoofbeats stalled.

Chance's hat was pulled low over his eyes, his oiled slicker wet. The silver Secret Service badge she'd pinned on his chest was already damp with dew. He looked like a ghost in the mist. A goose walked over her grave when she met his gaze.

"I meant it," she said. "I meant it, Chance."

"I know."

With the dawn came a still, gray silence that spread out over the range like a cold fever. Chance knew the moment he rode up over the last hillock and spied Gardner's horse but no one else's tied to the hitching post in front of the saloon, that the day of reckoning he'd lived for, had burned for the past eighteen months was finally here.

He dismounted, then turned Silas loose in the tall grass under the oak tree beside the well. The dissipating mist curled like smoke around his withers.

Chance drew his guns, then climbed the steps to the porch. The outer doors to the saloon stood wide.

Inside the shallow vestibule the swinging doors creaked softly in the breeze blowing south off the Platte.

It was time.

He entered the saloon and trained both guns on the man who was scrambling onto a chair he'd dragged behind the bar. A late-model rifle rested on the polished pine surface, just out of reach.

The Hargus brothers stirred when he came in, but Chance paid them no mind. They were bound and gagged, and tethered to the elaborate ironwork of the spiral staircase. The room was a wreck. Tables were overturned, and the piano was riddled with bullet holes. Chance was impressed.

Delilah's pepperbox revolver lay on the floor beside the wooden Indian, but Delilah was nowhere in sight. Neither were the girls, or anyone else for that matter.

A faint sound echoed from the hallway, disrupting his concentration. It was a dull pounding, first rhythmic, then random, as if someone was beating on a door—or a wall. In his mind he pictured the secret entrance to the basement.

The man on the chair stiffened, finally aware of his presence. Chance had to give him credit. It wasn't every day a lone man could waltz into a saloon and subdue not only the entire staff, but men as ruthless as the Hargus boys.

"Go on," Chance said, as he paused. "Don't let me stop you."

John Gardner turned. His gaze narrowed on the silver badge pinned to Chance's overcoat.

"Take it down."

"W-what?" Gardner slowly raised his hands.

"That's what you came for, isn't it?"

The banker's face was a mask of disbelief.

Lee Hargus grinned behind his gag, a dirty bar towel. Dickie's eyes were sharp and cool. Chance thought it peculiar the brothers didn't even struggle against their bonds.

"You." Gardner raised his hands higher as Chance approached. His blue eyes bulged. His face, which was already three shades of pale, went stark white. "You're a...a..."

"Looks can be deceiving, can't they?"

"...an agent of the Secret Service?"

He stopped in front of the bar and nudged Gardner's rifle out of the way with one of his Colts. "I'm your worst goddamned nightmare is what I am."

"But..." Gardner began to shake.

Chance's gut twisted so tight he could hardly breathe. His fingers massaged the Colts' triggers as he aimed directly at Gardner's face. "Take it down," he repeated.

"W-what?"

"The painting." He glanced at the nude portrait hanging above the bar.

The Hargus boys watched them, silent, riveted to Gardner's every move.

Shaking, Gardner removed the painting from the wall, grunting under its weight. For a second Chance thought he might drop it. "That's right. Set it right there, facedown."

Gardner set the portrait on the bar.

"Got a knife?"

"N-no."

"Jim keeps one next to the cash register. Get it."

Gardner did as he was told.

The Hargus boys exchanged a look as Chance continued with his instructions. In the background the pounding grew louder. They could hear Delilah's muffled shouts and Jim's swearing.

"Do it," he said, turning his attention back to Gardner. "You know you want to."

With a shaking hand, Gardner slit the heavy brown burlap backing the canvas. "How could you do it?" he said.

"I haven't done it yet. You'll know it when I kill you. Believe me, you'll know it."

Gardner looked up, his tawny brows creased not in surprise but confusion. "I meant Dora. How could you trick her this way, make her love you then break her heart?"

Chance stopped breathing. He stared into Gardner's eyes and what he read there didn't make any sense. He shook off the odd feeling and went on with the questioning he'd lived out in his mind a thousand times over the past year and a half.

"How did it feel when you hung my father, when you raped my sister and slit her throat?"

Gardner choked, then froze, staring at Chance as if he were a madman.

"How did it feel when you made my mother beg for her life before putting a bullet in her head?"

"W-what are you talking about?" Gardner shook his head, then dropped the knife and again raised his hands in the air.

"He wouldn't do it, would he? My father was a good man. He was a judge, goddamn it. He wouldn't take your dirty money, your counterfeit notes, and cheat the people who depended on him. Would he?"

Gardner's mouth dropped open. He continued to shake his head.

"The ranch wasn't enough. You had to kill them." Chance motioned to the slit burlap with one of his guns. "Go on. Take it out. Look at it. I want you to see it before I kill you."

"I think there's been some—"

"Do it!"

Gardner tore at the burlap. With shaking hands he reached inside and pulled a banded stack of bank notes from the space behind the canvas. Real bank notes Bill Fitzpatrick had squirreled away from his dealings with the counterfeiter. Real bank notes that had cost him his life.

Gardner hadn't been here the night Wild Bill was murdered, but that didn't mean anything. He could have paid to have it done. There were plenty of men in the West who made a living off killing for others.

As he stared into Gardner's terrified eyes, it occurred to Chance that the banker didn't have it in him to commit the kinds of atrocities that had been perpetrated against Chance's family. Had Gardner hired that done, too?

"D-did you hurt her?"

"What?" Chance's brow was cold with sweat, his trigger fingers quivering.

"D-Dora. You made her tell you where it was." Gardner nodded at the money. "Tell me you didn't…force her."

Chance ground his teeth. Gardner's reactions made no sense. Moreover, he knew what Dora had told him about the box of counterfeit money in Gardner's office meant nothing. All bankers collected counterfeit notes. They saved them up and returned them to men like him, agents of the U.S. Secret Service who were charged with seeing them destroyed.

Desperate to release the volatile fusion of pent-up rage, confusion, and a nightmarish feeling he'd made a mistake, Chance fired into the air.

Gardner jumped. The Hargus boys watched them, rapt. The pounding in the hallway stopped, and for a long moment the only sounds they heard were the wind outside and the tinkling of the crystal chandelier above their heads.

Then the pounding resumed in earnest. Chance expected Gus and Rowdy to show up any moment, rousted out of their beds in the bunkhouse by the gunshot.

"I already knew where the money was." Chance had to work fast. He stared hard at Gardner. "I've always known."

"What?" The banker's eyes bulged. "How?"

"Bill told me. Two days before he died."

Gardner stared back at him in what Chance believed was genuine confusion. "That doesn't make sense. I thought *you* were his silent partner, that he was hiding the money from you, that you killed him in order to get it." Gardner's gaze slid to the silver star on Chance's chest. "But that badge…"

Now both of them were confused.

"Those things that were done to your family." Gardner again shook his head. "You've got the wrong man, I swear it."

Then Chance did something out of character, something he wasn't used to doing but that he'd begun to do more and more of ever since he met Dora. He set aside his emotions and considered all the facts. Gardner was lying. He had to be. Why else would he have come out here alone.

"You didn't wake Max. Why?"

Gardner looked baffled.

"The marshal. When Dora told you where the money was, you came out here alone to get it. Only one man would have done that. The man who killed Wild Bill. The man who ruined my father's cattle business, then murdered my family in cold blood."

"No!" Gardner stepped toward him, and Chance raised his guns.

"Why didn't you wake the marshal, let him and his boys come out here to get the painting?"

Gardner said nothing.

Chance leaned over the bar, slid one of his Colts against the banker's forehead. "Why didn't you?"

Gardner stopped breathing. His face flushed red as an autumn apple as he stared into Chance's eyes. "I—I did it for her."

Nothing he could have said would have done more to diffuse Chance's muddled rage. "What do you mean?"

"For Dora. I…wanted her to think I was…" Gardner glanced at the Hargus boys, whom he'd apparently managed to somehow get the best of. "Brave," he whispered. "A man. A man like you. Like she thinks you are, or thought you were, or… Hell, I don't know anymore."

Chance stared at him, noted the embarrassment in his eyes, the hands that were still shaking, Gardner's apparent disinterest in the thousands of dollars that were wedged between the back of the portrait and its heavy burlap backing.

A moment later he holstered his guns.

A heartbeat after that, both he and John Gardner got the shock of their lives.

"Nice work, Chance."

They turned at the sound of her voice. It was different somehow. The cadence, the accent…

Lily stood with her feet planted in the doorway leading to the hall. She had a shotgun pointed directly at them.

"Miss Sugrah!" Gardner said. "W-what are you doing?"

Lee Hargus smiled behind his gag. Dickie's eyes gleamed.

Chance started for his guns, but Lily's face hardened to Spanish steel. "I wouldn't, Chance. I'd hate to have to kill you. It makes such a mess."

As she moved into line with the bound men, Chance saw what a man in his position never should have missed.

The resemblance.

"Sugrah," he said in disbelief. "Hargus."

Chapter Sixteen

"She's their sister?" Gardner slid a sideways glance at Chance.

"Looks that way."

Lily cut her brothers' bonds, her shotgun still trained on Chance. Lee Hargus made a show of dusting himself off before drawing his gun. Dickie's six-shooter was in his hand an instant after he was freed. The brothers approached. Chance considered his options. There were damned few, and none that he liked.

"Delilah always did like to change the names of her girls." Lily smirked at them. "What she didn't know was I'd already changed mine. Sugrah was my brother's idea."

"Which one?" Chance asked, buying time.

"Which one do you think?" Lee grinned at him. "Dickie here's not much on alphabet puzzles. He's more the musical type. I, on the other hand, take pleasure in the written word. I guess that makes me a lot like that schoolteacher ya'll seem to think so much of."

"Leave her out of this." Chance's blood began to

heat all over again. "It was you all along, wasn't it?" he said to Lee. "You murdered my family."

"Well, technically that ain't true. Dickie here did the killin', but I did all the upfront work. Always do. Find the marks, make the deals…" He flashed his eyes at his sister. "Lily here does the collectin'. She does a mighty fine job of it, too. Usually."

Lily and Lee exchanged looks of mock disdain.

Chance saw red. It took every shred of control he could muster to stop himself from drawing his guns. It would only get Gardner killed right along with him, and he couldn't be sure if he'd even get one shot off before he went down. No. He wanted all of them, Lee and Dickie especially, but all of them would pay.

"Y-you were the one who set Dora's father up." Gardner's voice was a raspy croak. It occurred to Chance that he owed the innocent banker an apology. If he got out of this alive, he'd deliver it. "Y-you were his silent partner."

"That's right." Lee smiled.

"*You* murdered Wild Bill," Chance said to Lily. "You were here that night. It was you."

Lily sighed dramatically. "Hated doin' it. Bill was a nice old geezer."

"My sister here jumped the gun," Lee said. "Thought she knew where the old man had hidden the money. Our money."

"We got it now," Lily said. "That's what counts." The three of them turned their gazes on the portrait. The burlap backing was stripped away, revealing bundles and bundles of cash. "How much is there, do you reckon?"

"Don't rightly know," Lee said.

"Fifty thousand, give or take." Chance knew that bit of information would raise a brow or two.

It had the desired effect. The siblings' attention was momentarily fixed on the money. Chance noticed that the pounding in the hallway had stopped. Looking past the Harguses, he recognized the business end of Tom's army revolver slide around the doorway behind the spiral stairs. Gardner noticed it, too.

At the far end of the saloon, Jim stepped silently from the opposite end of the hallway into the room, his old flintlock rifle trained on the Harguses.

Chance shot Gardner a look. The banker's rifle was still on the bar, an arm's length away from him. Gardner surreptitiously nodded back. It was now or never.

Chance went for his guns.

Lucky for him, Lily's aim was as bad as her judgment. She jumped back as she fired, slamming into Lee, whose shot went wide. Chance felt the burn in his left shoulder as he drew his Colts. Gardner, to the surprise of everyone, didn't go for his rifle, but plowed headlong into Dickie.

The room exploded in gunfire.

All of them went down in a pile. A moment later, amidst a chorus of feminine shrieks, Delilah and the girls burst from the hallway on Tom's heels and inserted themselves into the confusion.

At one point Chance was wedged between Columbine and Rose, who were both struggling to rip the shotgun from Lily's hands. Lee was on top of him, Dickie and Gardner beneath him. More shots were fired and more screams rent the air. Pain exploded in his shoulder as Lee grabbed him. The last thing he remembered before blacking out was the smell of blood.

His own.

* * *

"W-what happened?" Chance sprang up and instinctively reached for his guns. They were gone.

"Whoa! Hold up there, Chance. You been shot." Jim tried to push him back down onto the Persian carpet where they'd evidently moved him.

Chance wouldn't let him. Seeing friendly faces around him, all save one, he struggled to his feet. His shoulder burned like a son of a bitch. "Christ." He looked around. "Where are they?"

"Gone," Tom said. "Got away."

Chance swore.

"Rowdy went after 'em. Gus got hisself shot. Susan's tending to him upstairs. We sent Daisy and Iris for the doctor."

"How long have I been out?"

Tom shrugged. "Not long. Ten minutes. Maybe a little longer."

"Damn it!" He scanned the room for his guns. They were lying on a nearby card table. He quickly checked the ammunition in his coat pockets.

"We got *her,* though. That's something." Jim nodded at Lily, who was tied to a sturdy chair. Delilah and Rose were putting the finishing touches on the knots.

"And we saved the money." Columbine smiled brightly, as if she were talking about the proceeds from a church bake sale. "Well, most of it, anyway." She removed the rest of the bundled bank notes from between the portrait's canvas and backing and stacked them on the bar.

"Where's Gardner?"

"Here." The banker poked his head up. "Just gathering up the rest of the cash."

"You okay?"

"Miraculously, yes. Not a scratch on me. Don't know how I managed it."

"What about them? They wounded?"

"The Hargus brothers? I don't rightly know. But there's a lot of blood on the floor. Can't all be yours."

"Yeah, it could." Delilah approached him. "You'd best sit down, Chance."

"There's no time." He reloaded his Colts, holstered them, then tightened his gun belt across his hips.

"Wait for the doc," Delilah said. "And the marshal. Why didn't you bring him back with you to begin with?"

Gardner looked at him. He already knew why. This wasn't about justice or the law. It was about vengeance.

"Are you really a federal agent?" Rose's gaze fixed on the silver star Dora had pinned to his coat.

"Can't say it surprises me." Delilah arched a fiery red brow at him as she pressed a clean bar towel into his shoulder. "I always knew there was more to you than meets the eye."

Lily spit at him. Her green eyes blazed.

Never in his life had Chance ever struck a woman. He wanted to now. Badly. "Where'd they go?"

She tipped her chin at him and smirked. "What makes you think I'd tell you?"

"Why, you little—" He had to physically stop himself from picking her up, chair and all, and shaking her.

"Chance, wait." Delilah produced a slip of paper.

"I found this in Lee's pocket. He got away, but his jacket didn't." She nodded at the torn suit coat on the floor next to the wooden statue of the Indian, which had toppled over and split clean in two.

"Let me see that." Chance took the note from her.

"Looks to me like the name of a ranch. Could be their local hideout. Know the place?"

He ground his teeth together so he wouldn't curse. "Yeah. I do." He pocketed the slip of paper, then looked around for his hat.

Columbine finished with the portrait, and with Tom's help, turned it face-up on the bar. For a moment they looked at the nude who, in the portrait, lounged on a velvet chaise, her back turned.

"Wild Bill's favorite whore." Tom let out a low whistle. "No wonder the danged thing was so heavy." He shot Jim an amused look. "And all this time I thought it was just the frame, ordered special all the way from Kansas City."

"It was special, all right." Jim examined the portrait. "It was right under our noses all the time. You were waitin', weren't you?" he said to Chance. "Using the money to draw 'em out."

"That was the general idea."

"It was you who kept bringing the picture up from the basement and hanging it up again each time Tom and me took it down." Jim grinned from ear to ear. "Who would have thought, eh, Tom?"

Chance didn't have time for explanations. He would make time, however, to speak with Gardner. "Got a minute?" he asked.

The banker came around the bar. "I don't mind saying now that it's all over, I sure was worried, Mr. Wellesley, er…Chance. I didn't think you were going to believe me, that I wasn't the man—or men, as it turns out—you were after.''

He took Gardner aside, out of earshot of the others. ''I'm sorry. Truly. I…wasn't thinking clearly, but I am now.''

''I owe you an apology, too. I had no idea you worked for the Secret Service. No wonder Miss Dora thinks so highly of you. I don't know what to say.''

He locked gazes with Gardner. ''She didn't know till an hour ago, but that doesn't matter. You're the one she needs now, not me.'' He fished the newsprint and the tortoiseshell comb out of his pocket and handed them to the banker. ''Give these to her. Tell her her father did leave her something, that her future's secure after all.''

Gardner frowned at the comb, then looked at the newsprint.

''See that she reads it. She'll know what it means.'' He unclipped Wild Bill's watch fob from the chain hanging from his belt and placed it into Gardner's hands. ''Give her this, too.''

''You're not coming back, are you?''

Forgetting his shoulder, Chance ran a hand through his hair. He winced in pain.

''Don't do it,'' Gardner said. ''Wait for the doctor and the marshal.''

He held the banker's steady gaze. ''I…can't.''

''You'll bleed to death if you ride out now.''

''I expect I can hang on till I find them.'' He nodded at Lily. ''When Max gets here, tell him what happened. He'll know what to do with her. And put the money in your vault. Max'll deal with that, too.''

''You mean to kill them, don't you? The Hargus

brothers. You're going to hunt them down and kill them.''

Chance didn't answer. He yanked the silver star from his chest and tossed it on the bar. He turned toward the door then paused, looking back at Gardner. ''You'll take care of Dora, see she gets this place sold and gets that school in town she wants so bad.'' It wasn't a question, it was a demand.

Gardner looked at him for a long moment, then nodded.

''Chance?'' Delilah called after him as he strode toward the door.

Jim followed. ''Where you goin'?''

He hit the swinging doors at a solid clip and stepped into the cold spring morning. The mist had cleared. Silas stood saddled and ready where he'd left him, grazing under the oak by the well.

Chance mounted up, pulled the brim of his hat down low over his eyes, then rode east into the sun toward Denver.

''It was you?'' Dora stood at the bar, her fists balled at her sides, as the marshal motioned for his deputies to take Lily Hargus away.

Lily took one last, bitter look at the stacks of money on the bar—more money than Dora had ever seen in her life—then shrugged. ''It wasn't his, it was ours. Your daddy had no business hiding it from us.'' Her Southern accent was milder than her brothers', but unmistakable now that she wasn't hiding it. How had they ever missed the connection?

''So you killed him,'' Dora said.

Lily gave her a cool look. ''What did it matter? He was old. Would have died sooner or later.''

Dora went for her.

John grabbed her around the waist and held her back as the deputies dragged Lily outside.

"Good riddance," Delilah said.

Columbine chimed in with an unflattering remark that Dora thought quite fitting under the circumstances.

"Go on," Delilah said to her and the rest of the girls. "Get back to work." She handed Rose a broom. "Customers'll be arrivin' soon."

"You okay?" John led Dora to one of the card tables and pulled out a chair. "Why don't you sit."

"No, I'm fine. I—" She drew a deep breath, tried to gather her thoughts, then she looked at him. "I owe you an apology, John."

"You're the second person who's said that to me this morning."

She knew who the first person was. Chance.

"Did he say anything before he left?" Her gaze drifted to the Persian carpet, focused on the dark blood.

"He'll be all right." John reached into his coat pocket and produced a small bundle. It was the tortoiseshell comb wrapped in newsprint. "Here." He placed it into her hands. "He said to give you this. That you should read that newspaper article, that you'd know what it meant."

"Oh." She remembered she'd left the comb on the bar when she'd fled the saloon.

"There," Tom said. "Good as new." The piano player had cut away the rest of the burlap backing the canvas. He and Jim righted the portrait, then leaned it up against the only intact row of glass shelving behind the bar.

"She sure is pretty," Jim said, admiring the nude.

Delilah smiled, ran a lacquered nail across the fine brushstrokes detailing the woman's fiery red hair.

"She certainly was," Dora said, approaching her. "But she's even more beautiful now if you ask me." She unwrapped the tortoiseshell comb and offered it to Delilah. "This is yours, I think."

Jim and Tom looked at them, stunned. Along with John, they studied the painting, then stared at Delilah as if seeing her for the first time. The evidence had been under their very noses all along. Only the marshal seemed unsurprised. He grabbed a cup of coffee from behind the bar and watched them, amused.

Jim was the first to speak. "*You* were Wild Bill's favorite...er, well you know." He flushed all the way up to his bald pate.

A half smile graced Delilah's painted lips. "I was once, but that was years ago." She turned to Dora and said, "You knew."

"I suspected from the beginning that you and my father were somehow linked. He left me the comb so I'd find you."

"There's things you don't know," Delilah said, and cautiously met her gaze. "Things your pa should have told you, but didn't."

"You tell me, then, but later. After all this is over."

Delilah's smile warmed. "I'd like that."

They stood there for a moment looking at each other, then John cleared his throat, uncomfortable with the turn in their conversation. "But the comb led you to the money." He nodded at the marshal who was stuffing the stacks of bank notes into one of Jim's old carpet bags.

"That, too." Dora approached the painting. "Look

at the hair. See this?'' She ran her finger over brush-strokes that, to an unschooled eye, looked like auburn highlights.

Tom looked closely at the painting, then shifted his gaze to the tortoiseshell comb Delilah had placed in her hair. ''It's the comb!''

''Well, I'll be.'' Jim studied the fine oil detailing. ''He's right.''

Delilah laughed softly.

''I discovered it last night,'' Dora said. ''But then the Hargus boys returned, and...well, you know the rest. I'd thought the comb might be more than just a connection to Delilah. I thought it might be a clue.''

''Clue?'' The marshal looked at her strangely.

''I guess I should explain.'' She withdrew her diary from her pocket, slid her father's letter from between the pages, opened it and began to read.

''...*Rest assured, your financial future is secure. I've left you something at the ranch. Something only you, seeing as how smart you are, will recognize.*''

''The comb!'' Tom said. ''Bill wanted you to find the money.''

''I don't think that was his intent. My father knew the money wasn't his and would have to be returned to the government.''

''But you made the connection to the portrait all the same,'' John said, ''and the money was, indeed, there.''

''That's right.'' She reflected on the fact that Chance had known its location all along.

''I'll wire the Secret Service in Denver first thing tomorrow,'' Max said as he struggled to close the carpet bag.

"But if the money's not what Bill left you…" Jim scratched his bald head. "What is?"

Dora glanced at the newsprint she'd left, forgotten, on the bar and which all this time she'd used merely as wrapping paper for the comb. Picking it up, she turned it over. Her heart stopped. "Good Lord!"

John read over her shoulder. "I don't understand."

She spread the newspaper article out on the bar. They all crowded around her to read it. Even the marshal was intrigued. The girls stopped their clearing up and joined them.

Dora read the headline. "Rare Chinese Artifact Lost in Poker Game."

"That ain't a Colorado paper, is it?" Jim scrunched up his face.

"No," Dora said. "It's from San Francisco." She pointed to the top. "The *News Call Bulletin,* July 8th, 1881." The article, which her father had used to line his safety deposit box, was nearly three years old.

John read the first paragraph to them aloud, then together they peered at the tiny drawing at the bottom. Dora's breath caught.

"What is it?" Tom said.

"Looks like a birdcage." Jim's face scrunched even more. "Seems to me I remember an old birdcage Bill brought home from one of his trips. Was painted red, I believe. Thought it was just junk. You don't think…?"

"Says here it's made of gold." Delilah narrowed her gaze on the words. "From the Fourth…"

"Dynasty," John said. "It's worth… Great balls of fire, it's a fortune!"

"Where is it?"

Jim scratched his head. "Don't know. Haven't seen the danged thing in years."

"I know where it is."

That got their attention.

"In the secret room. The one in the basement."

"Secret room?" Delilah and the others exchanged befuddled looks.

"Yes. My father's watch fob...the one he gave to Chance before he was—" The pain was still too raw. His murder hadn't seemed real to her until she'd looked into Lily Hargus's glittering eyes.

"You mean this?" To Dora's astonishment, John pulled the watch fob out of his vest pocket.

"Where did you get that?"

"Chance gave it to me to give to you."

"He did?" She weighed the pewter fob in her palm, wondering why Chance hadn't waited and returned it himself. An uneasy feeling gripped her.

"What's that old trinket got to do with the birdcage?" Jim's question brought her back to the task at hand.

"I'll show you."

A few minutes later they all crowded into the secret room Dora had discovered in the basement. Tom held up a lantern, illuminating the birdcage, while Jim used his pocketknife to scrape away the red paint.

"It *is* gold," Delilah said. "And there's jewels, too. Look!"

Dora fingered the watch fob that her father had deliberately given not to her, but to Chance. He'd called it the key to her future. She knew by heart the rest of his letter. One line stood out above all others. *It's the Chance of a lifetime, Dora. Take it.*

The word *Chance* had been purposely capitalized.

"How long until Agent Wellesley returns?" she asked the marshal.

"Depends on how long it takes him to catch up with the Hargus boys and bring 'em in."

"You knew who he was all this time, didn't you?"

Max shrugged. "It's my job to know."

John fidgeted on his feet and lowered his eyes. His discomfort was so apparent Dora couldn't help but notice it. "There's, uh, something I think you should know."

"What?" Her uneasy feeling returned.

"You'd best come upstairs."

She followed him up to the saloon along with the marshal, but the others remained in the secret room, captivated by the golden birdcage.

"What is it?" she said to John. "Tell me."

He appeared uncomfortable with Max's presence, but the marshal's pointed interest in what he had to say made it clear he wasn't going to give them any privacy.

John forged ahead. "I know you're in love with him, with Chance."

She didn't deny it, and knew her face told all. Despite a successful history of controlling her emotions, Dora was an open book where her feelings for Chance Wellesley were concerned.

"He's a good man, Dora. He deserves your love, and you deserve to be happy. All the same, he, um…asked me to take care of you."

She gripped the pewter watch fob so tightly it dug into her palm. "What?"

"Doesn't surprise me none," Max said.

She looked from John's somber expression to the marshal's and knew right away they knew something she didn't. They knew the one dark thing Chance had kept from her.

"Go on," she said to Max.

"Them Hargus boys been at this counterfeiting scheme for a spell. Got involved with Chance's pa about two years ago. Chance never knew."

"Oh, God."

"Jack Wellesley had a cattle ranch near Denver. He was also the local judge. He and Chance had some kind of falling out, so the story goes. That winter Chance went west. Stayed away a year. By the time he got back, his pa had already had a couple of run-ins with the Harguses. He never told Chance who they were, just that they were swindlers of some sort. One day Chance came home and…" Max looked away, ran a hand over his face.

"And?" Dora's heart was in her throat.

"Dickie had burned the ranch," John said. "Hung his father. Murdered his mother and sister, too."

Dora closed her eyes.

Max continued. "Chance went kinda crazy after that. Dropped outta sight for a while, so they say. I met him about six months ago, when he showed up here in town decked out like a riverboat gambler. I knew what he was right away. He asked me to keep it quiet, so I did."

"He joined the Secret Service so he could hunt them down." Dora drew a couple of deep breaths, trying to get a hold of her racing thoughts and unstable emotions.

"Seems he already knew your pa. Don't know how. Took up residence here at the Flush and…well, you know the rest."

"I'm sorry," John said.

She felt as if the world as she knew it was slipping out from under her. "Sorry?"

"He, uh, said I should look after you."

Dora shook her head. "No, he's coming back. He said he would. He promised."

But he hadn't. He'd said nothing in response to her plea. Worse, she'd recognized the look in his eyes when he'd mounted Silas and disappeared into the fog. She'd seen that look before, in men who'd come back from war and were never the same.

"He...took this off and set it on the bar before he left." John produced the silver star she'd pinned on Chance's coat in the street barely an hour ago.

Too clearly she recalled the hard set of his jaw, his lackluster eyes when he rode off. It was the look of a man with a death wish.

Chapter Seventeen

After two days of pleading, Delilah finally told her where to find him. Dora revealed to only one other person she was leaving. John Gardner. She knew he'd try to talk her out of it. She'd have thought less of him if he hadn't. It was a dangerous action for her to take, a desperate one, too, but she had to try.

After missing the morning stage out of Last Call, she rode all the way to Garo to catch it. The next day in Colorado Springs she checked with local physicians to see if any of them had treated a man who'd been shot in the shoulder. None of them had. But by the time she reached Denver, she'd spoken to half a dozen people who'd seen the Hargus brothers, who remembered Lee's smile and Dickie's cool blue eyes.

"Just another couple of miles," she said to the horse she'd hired in the small town east of Denver where Chance's father had once been a circuit court judge. "I think."

It turned out to be farther. It was dark by the time Dora turned onto the weedy, rutted lane marked by a broken gate sporting a brand confirming she'd arrived at her destination. *JW*. "Jack Wellesley. This is it."

She dismounted, tethered the horse to a fence post just inside the property, and made her way on foot toward what remained of the house. There wasn't much. A burned-out shell and a pile of toppled brick from where the fireplace once stood. The barn was still intact, but its roof was caved in. Several other outbuildings were in disrepair.

There were no other horses in sight, no signs of life at all, except for the chirping of crickets and the sounds of rodents scurrying among last year's rotting apples, which had fallen from the tree in what had once been a fine front yard. The smell of burned timber lingered, turning Dora's stomach as she thought about what had transpired here eighteen months ago.

With a sigh, she realized her journey had been for nothing. Chance wasn't here.

Delilah had shared with her the information written on the scrap of paper she'd recovered from Lee Hargus's jacket, the same information she'd shared with Chance just moments before he'd left the Royal Flush in search of the two brothers.

Earlier that day, Dora confirmed in Denver that the title to the Wellesley ranch had passed by way of a lien against the property to one Lily Sugrah, also known as Mary Hargus, after Jack Wellesley was found murdered. Chance thought the Hargus brothers would come here, and Dora herself had discovered the two men had actually lived here early on, in the months after Chance had left.

There was a lot one could learn in a small town while hiring a horse.

She took one last look at the eerie scene, gone silver under a moonlit sky, and was glad she hadn't arrived any sooner. She didn't think she could take seeing the place in the light of day. What had happened to Jack Wellesley and his family was too terrible to contemplate. What details John and Max had refused to part with, she'd learned on her own a few hours ago at the local livery.

"May God have mercy on their souls," she whispered, "and on yours, Chance Wellesley, wherever you are."

"I'm right here."

Another second in the open and they'd both be dead.

Chance didn't care what happened to him as long as he was able to finish what he'd come out here to do, but he did care what happened to Dora.

He grabbed her hand and jerked her behind a blackened pile of bricks a heartbeat before a gunshot whizzed past their heads.

Dora screamed.

"Son of a—" He pulled her down beside him and checked her for injury.

"I'm fine, but—" She gasped when she noticed the sling around his left arm and the blood soaking through the bandaged wound on his shoulder. "They told me you'd been shot, but never let on how bad it was. Chance, you've got to see a doctor."

"Saw one yesterday. In the town you must have come through to get here."

"But, Chance…"

"What are you doing here, Dora? Are you crazy?" He peered out into the night, straining to see the road where she'd come in. "Who's with you?"

"No one."

"You came all the way here alone?"

Her eyes widened in the moonlight. He had to fight himself from drawing her close, from wrapping his arms around her and burying his face in her hair.

"Yes. No one knows I'm here. Well, except Delilah and John."

"I told him to take care of you, to—"

She stilled his lips with her hand. Her fingers were trembling. "I've come here to give you something. Two things, really."

Another shot rang out, this one closer. The bricks above their heads exploded. Jagged chips of rock and mortar rained down on them.

Chance swore. He shielded her with his body. When the dust cleared he got to his knees and peeked around the side of the toppled fireplace, his gun aimed directly at where he'd last seen Dickie Hargus's hat.

"Here," Dora said. "Take it. Take it back." She had something in her hand.

He tensed as pale moonlight glinted off the silver star.

"You have to take it."

"No." He'd made his mind up long ago, long before he'd met her.

"You never meant to bring them in. All along you meant to kill them. At whatever cost, even your own life."

He didn't want her mixed up in this. Why the hell had she come?

"I know what happened here. I know what you lost."

"No, you don't."

"I do. I know what you feel when you look into Dickie Hargus's eyes. I felt the same thing when I stared into Lily's." She pushed the badge at him.

"Take it. You're not a killer. You're a man of the law, like your father."

He looked into her eyes, remembering the morning they'd stood together in the pasture, the air infused with the heady scents of sage and her lilac perfume. If he looked away from her now, he feared he'd lose the memory altogether. Like the rest of his life it would vanish, crushed by the stench of death that he carried with him always, but was strongest here in the place he'd once called home.

"He was a good man," Chance said.

"*You're* a good man."

"I wasn't there for him. I should have been." That's why he was here. Not for vengeance so much as penance. He'd known all along he wouldn't survive this kind of gunfight, but not because he wasn't a good shot. He was. He wouldn't survive it because deep down he didn't want to.

Looking into Dora's shimmering eyes, he realized she knew it. She knew *him*. That's why she'd come.

"Maybe," she said. "Maybe not. I don't know what went on between you, but I do know this…" She pinned the silver star to his chest, just as she had three days ago in the street in the fog. "The man I fell in love with is neither a killer nor a martyr. Yes, he's been wronged, and maybe he's wronged others, and he's eaten up with pain. But he's also his father's son, just as I'm my father's daughter."

She paused and looked at him, biting her lip. Never had she looked more beautiful.

"Wild Bill should have seen you all grown-up. I owe him my life, you know."

Her pale brows met in a frown.

"Remind me to tell you the story sometime."

She smiled at that, her eyes lighting with hope. He wished he hadn't said it. Damned if knew why he had.

The dull thud of footfalls in the dirt to their right brought him back to the moment. He spun toward the sound, raised his gun over the pile of burned brick. "Stay down!" he whispered, and felt Dora tense beside him.

More footfalls sounded to their left.

Chance swore.

He'd arrived late last night, after tracking the Hargus boys north out of Last Call, then east to Denver. He'd lost them in the city, but knew they'd show up here at the ranch eventually. He'd staked out a position in the barn, and they'd appeared just like clockwork, just a few minutes before Dora had come traipsing up the road. He had to get her out of here. Now.

"See that big oak behind us?"

Dora scrambled to her knees. "Yes."

"I'll cover you. I want you to run for it. Get behind that tree and stay put."

"But—"

"Don't argue. And once the shooting starts, I want you to make your way through that brush back to the road. You have a horse?"

"Yes. I left her near the gate."

"Good." He shoved his pistol into his sling, then fished its twin out of its holster. "Here. Take this. I can't use it with only one arm."

"I—I've got one." She reached into the pocket of her cloak and produced the little derringer that had been her father's.

"Take mine anyway. You might need it."

She pocketed the derringer, pressing her lips together in a hard line. He knew what was coming next. "No," she said. "I'm not leaving you."

"The hell you aren't." He shoved the Colt into her hand.

Hoof beats sounded on the road, more than one set. He pulled her down with him into the dirt. "I thought you said you were alone."

"I am. I mean, I thought I was."

Any minute they'd be surrounded.

"Chance, you have to listen to me."

"Not now. I—"

"Chance!" She squeezed his bad arm, and he saw stars. "I said I had two things for you. This is the other." She fished the pewter watch fob out of her pocket and tried to make him take it. "The key to the future, my father told you. *My* future. But he gave the key to you."

"It doesn't matter now."

"It does! He knew, Chance. He knew who you were when he gave it to you. He knew you were Secret Service. He knew about your family. He knew everything."

Her words hit him like a punch.

The hoof beats grew closer. Lee Hargus called to his brother to fall back.

"H-how do you know this?"

"Max told me. My father wanted us to meet, don't you see? He knew you'd help me find my life, and he knew I'd help you remember yours. You were a rancher once. You could be one again."

His head throbbed almost as much as his shoulder. "I don't know."

"You have a job to do first. To bring these murderers to justice. Justice, Chance, not whatever it is you've been planning. I didn't know your father, but he couldn't have wanted this for you. This... obsession that's likely to end with another of his children in the grave.''

"Wellesley! You out here?" The hoof beats stalled. Just off the road a trio of riders came into view.

The Hargus boys opened fire.

Chance pushed Dora into the dirt and fired back.

"U.S. Secret Service!" the voice called out.

Damn it! Chance watched as the three men abandoned their mounts and took to the brush behind them.

"Who are you, Chance?" Dora pulled herself up beside him. "It's time to show your true colors." She gazed at the silver star, then at him.

He'd never loved a woman before. He guessed this was how it felt. He hadn't expected it would hurt so bad.

"The first night I met you, you said, 'Can't always judge a book by its cover.' It's the last chapter, Chance. How's it going to end?"

Ten days later

Dora toyed with the pewter watch fob as she stared blankly out the window of the upstairs parlor at the Royal Flush.

Susan sat beside her with last week's *Rocky Mountain News* across her lap. "Shall I go on?"

"Why don't we read from the *New England Primer* today. I don't think you're ready for newspapers."

The truth was, *she* wasn't ready for what nearly

every Colorado paper had splashed across its front page the morning after Chance's shoot-out with the Hargus boys.

"But this is so much more exciting."

That wasn't the word she'd have chosen to describe the events that had taken place at the Wellesley ranch. But she'd suffered through the telling a dozen times over. She guessed she could hear it again. "Go on."

Susan began to read where she'd left off. "The gunfight broke out after local agents of the…"

"United States Secret Service." Dora had committed the article to memory.

"Thank you, Miss Dora." The girl continued. "Su-sur-rounded the ranch."

"Very good."

Susan looked at her with wide eyes. "Did Chance really take them both single-handed?"

"I don't know. When the shooting started more lawmen arrived, including the local marshal and a couple of his deputies. Chance made one of them take me away."

And she'd neither seen nor heard from him since. Gazing at the pewter watch fob, she recalled the look on his face when he'd refused to take it back.

"Federal agent Marvin—"

Dora couldn't stand it. She grabbed the newspaper. "Yes. It says that the Hargus brothers shot and killed two federal agents and the town marshal before they were subdued."

"Sub…dued. That means caught, right? By Chance?"

She rose abruptly from the chaise, marched to the fireplace and tossed the newspaper onto the dancing flames. Turning to Susan she said, "Yes. It says he brought them in wounded, but alive."

"That's somethin', ain't it?"

It *was* something. She couldn't imagine what it had cost him to have done it.

"But they was killed anyway, wasn't they?"

"Yes." The newspapers reported that at the town jail Lee Hargus managed to free his hands and grab a rifle. Chance shot him dead. Dickie died later of his injuries.

"Good," Susan said. "They were bad men."

Yes, she thought. They were. And somewhere out there was a good man, a man she loved more than anyone or anything on God's green earth.

"Miss Dora, you okay?"

She smiled, pushing her feelings aside. There'd be plenty of time for her to reflect on all that had happened here later. "Are you and Tom packed?"

Susan's face lit up. "Nearly. The preacher in town's gonna marry us tomorrow. Tom already bought our tickets for the stage. He wired the orphanage two days ago. They're expectin' us."

At least there'd be other happy endings. "You'll have your son back. Tom will be a wonderful father and a good husband. You deserve that, Susan."

The girl hugged her. "Thank you, Miss Dora."

Together they walked out to the balcony overlooking the empty saloon. Dora had closed the Royal Flush a few days earlier. John had helped her arrange for the sale of the valuable Chinese birdcage back to its original owner in San Francisco. The man was wealthy and had paid a small fortune to get it back.

Rumor had it that the railroad was considering a new line that would pass through Last Call. The railroad meant new business, that Last Call would thrive on its own, without the Royal Flush. All the same, Dora intended to invest some of her money in local enterprise, just to help get things started. And the town still needed a school. There was a lot to do.

Jim and the rest of the girls were already looking for new jobs. Dora didn't think they'd have any trouble. It looked as if Gus was going to recover just fine from his gunshot wound. He and Rowdy would stay on, of course, until she decided what to do with the ranch. It seemed silly to keep it. What would she do with six thousand acres and a big rambling house on her own?

Susan returned to her room to finish packing. Dora was headed downstairs when she noticed the door to her father's bedroom was cracked open. That was strange. No one went in there except her. No one else had a key. Well, no one else except…

"Delilah?" she said, pushing the door open. "Are you all right?"

The older woman sat on the bed with the toy rabbit that had once been Dora's in her lap. Dora entered the room, a knot of tenderness twisting inside her.

Delilah gave her a half smile. "I'm fine. Just reminiscing a bit."

"You're still determined to leave?"

"Oh, I think it's high time I skedaddle. My sister lives back East, you know. I wrote her yesterday. She'll be expectin' me before the month's out." Delilah patted the bed. "Come here. Sit a spell. I've got a story to tell you, if you're ready to hear it."

"About you and my father?" Dora sat beside her.

"First you need to know about *you* and your pa, about your ma, too."

"Go on." This was why she'd come to Last Call in the first place. To learn about her father and her mother, what had happened between them, and what it meant.

"She was in love, your ma was."

"With my father."

Delilah paused and looked at her. "Yes. They were engaged. His name was Frank O'Donnell. He was Wild Bill's best friend."

"What?" She stared at Delilah openmouthed. "Y-you mean…"

"That's right."

Dora had to take a minute to let it all sink in. "William Fitzpatrick wasn't my father?"

"Not blood relations. But he was in his heart."

"Keep going," Dora said. Her stomach felt as if it had done a somersault inside her.

"See, Bill was always gettin' him and Frank mixed up in all kinds of crazy business deals. Risky ventures. Some of 'em dangerous. Your ma didn't like it none."

She thought briefly of her father's dealings with the Harguses. It had been smart on Delilah's part to make her sit. She didn't think, at this point, her legs would have held her up.

"G-go on."

"Bill was young and passionate, and had a way with words. He talked Frank, your pa, into some kind of cattle deal. The whole thing went south, and in the end Frank got himself killed."

Dora's breath caught in her throat.

"Your ma was already pregnant with you."

"Good Lord!" She could guess the rest. "He…Bill… He married her."

"That he did. Your ma didn't have no choice about it. She needed a name for that baby. Bill never forgave himself for what happened to Frank. He married her the same month."

"But he loved *you*." The tragedy of it was almost too much to bear, on top of everything else that had happened.

"We knew it was the right thing. Bill couldn't have done otherwise, and even if he could, I wouldn't have let him."

She looked at Delilah with new appreciation.

"But your ma, she never got over it, and she never forgave him."

"*She* made him leave, didn't she?"

Delilah nodded.

"All this time I thought he was the one who'd left us."

"He wouldn't have done that, not in a million years. He loved you like his own blood kin. It was your ma's way of punishing him, making him promise to not see you."

"But he did see me, he watched over me, from afar."

"And he sent money every month, along with those letters."

She hadn't known that. She'd always wondered how her mother had made ends meet. She hadn't even known about the letters until recently.

"Here," Delilah said, and handed her the toy rabbit. "He'd want you to keep this."

Dora looked at the faded and battered stuffed animal. "I'll always keep it, to remember him by. To remember his love."

"He'd like knowin' that." Delilah sighed and got to her feet.

"What about you? How did you bear it all these years?"

Delilah's smile was bittersweet. "Oh, child. True love endures. Through thick and thin, hellfire and brimstone, it finds a way."

"I wish that were true." She stared off into space, only half aware she'd spoken.

A knock sounded on the open door. They both looked up to see Jim standing in the corridor. "Someone here to see you, Miss Dora."

"Oh." She shook off the muddle of emotions churning inside her and stood. She placed the toy rabbit on top of her father's bureau and gave it a little pat. "Who is it, Jim?"

"A cattleman. Says he wants to buy the ranch."

She exchanged a look with Delilah.

"Really?"

"Yes, ma'am. He stopped in town first. John Gardner sent the paperwork along with him."

John had been a good friend to her through all of this. She'd always be grateful to him.

"Says he would have come sooner, but it took him a while to get his financial affairs sorted out. Seems he's gettin' some kind of restitution from the government."

"Oh. Well, I'd be happy to see him. Please tell him I'll be right down."

Jim grinned from ear to ear, then winked at Delilah. He pulled her out into the corridor and whispered something in her ear.

"What are you two up to now?" Dora followed

them out. She peered over the balcony into the saloon below.

Her heart stopped.

Chance stood at the bar with a sheaf of papers in hand. He looked up as she floated down the spiral staircase, her knees shaking.

"You're the cattleman," was all she could think of to say. She stopped an arm's length from him, drinking him in.

His shoulder was still bandaged, but he looked well, rested. The wild look she remembered the last night she'd seen him, as they'd huddled together behind the pile of toppled bricks, was gone. He'd come to terms with what had happened. She felt it as surely as she felt her love for him surge anew.

"I hear you have a ranch for sale." His voice was like the slow burn of a good cognac. His gaze was just as hot.

"Six thousand acres," she said. "And a few head of cattle to go with it."

"Awfully big place for a single man." He took a step toward her, and her mouth went dry.

"You…mean to live here alone, then."

"Hadn't planned on it."

The breath rushed from her lungs. A second later she was in his arms. "Chance!"

He crushed her to him and released a storm of kisses upon her face, in her hair, lifting her off her feet as he spun her around. "I love you, Dora."

"You do?"

Laughing, he spun her again.

"Since when?"

He glanced up at the portrait of a much younger Delilah hanging above the bar, and laughed so hard his eyes watered. The tastefully draped silk scarf covering the subject's bare bottom was a nice touch, Dora thought.

"Since the moment you first saw that picture and you fainted dead away."

"I seem to recall that *you* were the last thing I saw before becoming overwhelmed by my, um, surroundings."

He made a lusty sound in the back of his throat and shot her a roguish look not unlike those he'd bestowed upon her while in gambler's guise. "We could try that again. This time I promise to keep you conscious."

It was her turn to laugh. ·

He kissed her, and she let go of all her fears. When the time was right, she'd share with him all that she'd learned about her family and all she'd come to discover about herself. When she looked into his eyes she saw that he was ready to share with her, too.

He set her on her feet and held her face between his hands. "I love you, Eudora Elizabeth Fitzpatrick. Will you marry me?"

She made a mental note to herself to document every word in her diary, every look, the light in his eyes and the tenderness of his touch, though she knew this moment would burn forever in her heart, a memory she'd never forget.

"Yes," she said. "I will."

Epilogue

Six months later

"**I** look so stern." Dora studied the recently completed portrait of her that Chance had commissioned as a wedding gift.

"Well, you are a schoolmarm, aren't you?"

She thumped him playfully on the arm. "School-*teacher*."

He grinned and pulled her into a bear hug. "And a fine one at that."

A month after they'd married, Dora opened a school in Last Call in the small, whitewashed church at the end of Main Street. Construction had already begun on a new schoolhouse, along with several other new businesses, in anticipation of the long-awaited railroad. For the first time in its history, Last Call was booming without the trade the Royal Flush saloon had once brought in.

Dora couldn't have been more thrilled. "I like this room much better as a parlor, don't you?"

Together they studied the fruits of their recent labor, the transformation of the saloon back into a proper ranch house. While Chance had converted the stage into a nice living area, they'd decided to keep the red velvet décor, the rich pine bar with its brass fittings and even the cash register, as a tribute to Wild Bill Fitzpatrick, the man whose ultimate gift to them both was love.

"Oh, I don't know. You were a damned good saloonkeeper, too." He pecked her on the cheek, and she thumped him again.

"Don't you have some cattle to brand or fences to mend or whatever it is you cowboys do all day?"

"Cattlemen, though I prefer the term cattle baron. Next spring we'll have better than a thousand head of red Herefords."

She watched his mind working. "You love it, don't you?"

"I love *you.*" He kissed her again. "Which is why I'd best get this portrait hung and get back to work." He released her and turned the oil painting over on the bar to secure its backing.

The portrait of Delilah had once again been moved, this time permanently, downstairs to the secret room, which Chance had turned into a wine cellar. As always, he wore the key, her father's pewter watch fob, on a chain attached to his belt. As a wedding gift, Dora had given him a pocket watch to go with it.

"Silas will be happy when his portrait is finished." Dora peered outside to the front yard where the same artist who'd painted her was putting the finishing touches on an oil of the black-and-white paint gelding. Silas stood statue-still under the oak tree, looking bored.

"I don't know," Chance said. "I believe he likes the attention."

"Speaking of attention…" Dora sorted through the stack of incoming mail sitting on the bar. "It seems that Columbine and Rose and the rest of the girls have garnered a bit of their own."

"News from Denver?"

She put on her spectacles and opened the letter from Susan she'd begun reading earlier that day. "Good news from the sound of it. It seems that Jim has purchased a theater."

"No kidding?"

"Tom's been writing musicals that the girls perform in. Evidently they're quite good. Delilah's coming out next month from Kansas City to sing in their new production. And Susan and Tom bought a house. Her son's thriving and… Oh! They've got another baby on the way."

Chance looked up from his work and shot her a devilish grin.

Dora placed a hand on her growing belly. "Three more months," she said, "and we'll have some news of our own to write back."

Love shone in his eyes.

Dora retrieved her old, red leather-bound journal from the pocket of her dress.

"There," Chance said. "It's done." All that remained was to seal the lower edge of the backing to the picture frame.

On impulse, Dora pushed the diary toward him. "Here. You always did want to read this. Now's your chance."

He hesitated, then reached for the journal. To her surprise he didn't give it a glance. Instead he closed it, then placed it behind the canvas and sealed the backing to the frame. For the rest of their lives it hung there on the wall over the bar for future generations to find.

* * * * *

TAKE A TRIP TO THE OLD WEST WITH FOUR HANDSOME HEROES FROM HARLEQUIN HISTORICALS

On sale March 2004

ROCKY MOUNTAIN MARRIAGE
by Debra Lee Brown

Chance Wellesley
Rogue and gambler

MAGGIE AND THE LAW
by Judith Stacy

Spence Harding
Town sheriff

On sale April 2004

THE MARRIAGE AGREEMENT
by Carolyn Davidson

Gage Morgan
Undercover government agent

BELOVED ENEMY
by Mary Schaller

Major Robert Montgomery
U.S. Army major, spy

Visit us at www.eHarlequin.com

HARLEQUIN HISTORICALS®

HHWEST30

New York Times bestselling author

STELLA CAMERON

Married to a scoundrel, Hattie Leggit is desperate to earn enough money to pay off her parents' debt and leave her husband, Bernard, for good. But someone else has plans for revenge against Bernard—plans that involve Hattie.

John Elliott, the dashing Marquis of Granville, blames Bernard for the death of his brother and plots to bring about his ruin by seducing his wife. Little does he know that Hattie might be a willing participant—and that Bernard may be more dangerous than he ever expected.

✍ A ✍ USEFUL AFFAIR

"…[a] well-written, funny, sensual love story."
—*Romantic Times*
on *About Adam*

*Available the first
week of March 2004
wherever paperbacks are sold.*

Visit us at www.mirabooks.com   MSC2020

LUNA

In Camelot's Shadow

An Arthurian tale comes to life....

Author of a *New York Times* Notable Book...

SARAH ZETTEL

An Arthurian tale comes to life...

In Camelot's Shadow

From the wilds of Moreland to the court of Camelot, a woman searches for her true powers....

Risa of the Morelands refuses to be a sacrifice. Promised to the evil Euberacon, the infamous sorcerer, Risa flees armed only with her strong will and bow. When Risa stumbles upon Sir Gawain returning to Camelot, she believes she has discovered the perfect refuge: Camelot, noble Arthur's court. The sorcerer would never dare to come after her while she was under the protection of the Knights of the Round Table! Clearly, Risa has underestimated Euberacon's desire to have her as his wife.

On sale February 24. Visit your local bookseller.

www.Luna-Books.com

LSZ204

eHARLEQUIN.com

For great romance books at great prices,
shop www.eHarlequin.com today!

GREAT BOOKS:
- **Extensive selection** of today's hottest
  books, including **current** releases,
  backlist titles and new **upcoming** books.
- **Favorite authors:** Nora Roberts,
  Debbie Macomber and more!

GREAT DEALS:
- **Save every day:** enjoy great savings
  and special online promotions.
- *Exclusive* **online offers:** FREE books,
  bargain outlet savings, special deals.

EASY SHOPPING:
- Easy, secure, **24-hour shopping** from the
  comfort of your own home.
- **Excerpts, reader recommendations**
  and our **Romance Legend** will help
  you choose!
- **Convenient shipping and
  payment methods.**

Shop online
at www.eHarlequin.com today!

INTBB2